G. W. Kent's books have been published in more than twenty different countries. He has written fourteen novels, a number of critically acclaimed non-fiction books and several prize-winning television and stage plays. He has written and produced hundreds of radio plays and features for broadcasting organizations all over the world. As a freelance journalist he has written for many national newspapers and magazines. For eight years he ran an educational broadcasting service in the Solomon Islands. He lives in Lincolnshire.

D0180448

KILLMAN

A Sister Conchita and
Sergeant Kella Mystery

G. W. Kent

Constable & Robinson Ltd
55–56 Russell Square
London WC1B 4HP
www.constablerobinson.com

First published in the UK by C&R Crime,
an imprint of Constable & Robinson Ltd, 2013

A copy of the British Library Cataloguing in
Publication data is available from the British Library

ISBN: 978-1-84901-342-0 (paperback)
ISBN: 978-1-47210-476-2 (ebook)

Printed and bound in the UK

Typeset by TW Typesetting, Plymouth, Devon

1 3 5 7 9 10 8 6 4 2

ACKNOWLEDGEMENTS

I am grateful to Markson Koroa for his help on my trip to Tikopia, and to Jimmy Kenekene and his family for their hospitality during my stays on the island of Savo. As always I am deeply indebted to my dedicated agent Isabel White for her unswerving understanding and enthusiasm. The charming and gifted editorial team at Constable & Robinson of Krystyna Green, Nicky Jeanes and Jane Selley has again contributed considerably. I am also conscious of how much I owe to Emily Burns and the sales, marketing and publicity departments for all their efforts on my behalf. My American publishers Soho Crime continue to be a source of much-appreciated enormous support and expertise.

1

JAPANI HA HA!

The twenty naked young virgins undulated slowly in front of Sister Conchita and the morose visiting female academic on the plateau next to the waterfall above the saltwater village. Beneath the enervating afternoon sun they were dancing the *tue tue*, the traditional Lau fishing song. Their fluttering hands raised above their heads depicted the graceful movement of frigate birds soaring over the canoes. Their sinuous, kicking legs represented the movement of fish leaping from the water to snap at bait dangling on hooks from kites attached to the imaginary gently rocking craft.

Sister Conchita wondered how the American researcher was reacting to the titillating entertainment on offer. At first glance she had seemed a little on the prissy side. From where she was sitting, Sister Conchita could no longer see the woman. Earlier she had caught a brief glimpse through the crowd of visitors of a thin white girl of about thirty in a nondescript blue dress. She had a pinched, discontented face and seemed uncertain of herself and uncomfortable in her exotic surroundings.

The pan-pipe music ended and the virgins stopped dancing with a flurry of smooth bare brown arms and legs. They stood giggling and revelling in their voluptuous nudity before their guests from all parts of the island. The entertainment was not yet over. Papa Noah, the custodian of the ark, clapped his hands. He was a fragile, grey-haired,

1

almost fey man in his sixties, light on his capering feet and wearing a much-washed calico lap-lap extending from his waist to his knees.

A drum formed from a tree trunk with a hole gouged in the side started beating on the sidelines. The girls stopped undulating and stood to attention, composing themselves. In true, clear voices they began singing in pidgin, the lingua franca of the Solomons:

Me fulae olobauti, longo isti, longo westi.
Me sendere olo rouni keepim Solomoni
Me worka luka luka longo landi long sea
Ha ha! Ha ha! Japani ha ha!

Papa Noah clapped his hands again gleefully as he stood up. 'No more tra-la-la! Time for our feast,' he announced.

The virgins, glistening with perspiration in the hostile sun, broke ranks and ran back skittishly down the slope to the women's house in the village below to dress. The hundred or so islanders who had been watching the dancing at the side of the waterfall scrambled to their feet and waited respectfully for the food to be carried across the clearing and placed on pandanus leaves on the ground. Some of them had walked for several days to attend the ceremony and were hungry. They showed no impatience; to do so would be regarded as impolite.

A raucous group of a dozen larger, lighter-skinned men sat a little to the left of the main gathering of guests, keeping a well-judged distance from them. Sister Conchita was sure that they came from the remote outlying Polynesian island of Tikopia. They had probably been working on one of the local plantations and were now waiting for a boat to take them home. They were ignoring the Melanesians at the ceremony but were chattering happily enough among themselves. There was a carelessly swaggering air to their posture. To fit the occasion they were determined to be happy, but they carried menace like a club and were capable of changing in an instant to something more dangerous but for them equally enjoyable.

It had been raining monotonously for several weeks, but there was a temporary lull in the downpour. The sun had eased through the clouds, causing a haze of steam to rise in tired exhalations from the wet grass. It was apparent that despite the threatening weather, the meal was going to be a sumptuous one. It was being prepared on the treeless plateau next to the waterfall, halfway down its leaping descent before the frothing, roaring water plummeted further down the rocks to the river a hundred feet below. At the far end of the plateau, trees and undergrowth grew thickly in almost impenetrable plenitude. This was where the jungle began. A steep, winding path led to the village below, built on the banks of the river where it ran out into the calm blue waters of the Lau Lagoon.

A dozen pigs had been slaughtered and quartered in advance. The grease-laden quarters were now being roasted over log fires on spits before being immersed in a sauce of grated coconut and milk. Chickens smothered in grated manioc were cooking in ovens scooped with clamshells out of the earth and covered with red-hot stones. A savoury vegetable broth was simmering in an iron cooking pot. There were piles of yams, taro and sweet potatoes, baskets of shellfish and bunches of bananas. As it was the pineapple season, pyramids of the fruit were scattered about.

Brother John, the gigantic Melanesian Mission travelling preacher, bullocked out of the trees and approached Sister Conchita, muttering an apology to Papa Noah for his tardiness as he passed him.

'Did I miss anything?' he asked the nun in low tones, surveying the scene before him. He was about thirty, six and a half feet tall and wide in proportion. His skin was a deep brown in colour. His face was broad and friendly, giving him the appearance of an affable bear, but one capable of being roused to rib-breaking retaliation by injustice or too much unnecessary torment. He wore the distinctive costume of his order, a black shirt and lap-lap and a broad black and white belt. The Melanesian Brotherhood was an Anglican sect, formed before the war by Ini Kopuria, a former policeman, who had adapted the then current police uniform for his evangelical order. Only Melanesians were permitted to join. Each volunteer brother spent a few years dedicated to poverty, celibacy and obedience, sometimes touring the islands, preaching and living off the land. The calm and imperturbable Brother John, Conchita knew, had been proselytizing in the Lau area of Malaita for almost two years, and should be coming towards the end of his tour of duty.

'Just a couple of dances and a pidgin song,' Sister Conchita told him, falling into step with Brother John as they walked towards the heaps of food.

'I bet the song was the *tue tue*, the maidens' fishing song,' chuckled the big missionary. 'It gives the girls a chance to get their kit off, and they like that, though not half as much as the boys do, of course. I've seen it performed all over Malaita.' He paused. 'Except on Sikaiana,' he added.

'Why not there?' asked Sister Conchita. As soon as the words passed her lips she regretted them. She had given Brother John an opening, and she knew from experience that the big, rough-hewn man delighted in teasing young and inexperienced nuns from other orders, especially Roman Catholic ones.

'They can never round up enough virgins on that island,' said the Anglican pastor with a guffaw.

Sister Conchita resisted the temptation to laugh out loud. She struggled to maintain her habitual reserved expression. In the eleven months she had been at her mission station in the Solomon Islands, she had learned that if she could not seem old and wise, she could at least try to appear serene and above the fray, even if her current fate seemed to be acting as a straight woman to an overexuberant comic.

'Which song did they sing?' asked Brother John.

'It was called "Japani Ha Ha!". What's it all about?'

'It was a pidgin song of defiance that the Solomon scouts used to sing in the war when they were ambushing the Japanese troops in the bush,' explained the huge Melanesian missionary in his deep operatic bass as the nun hurried to keep up with his raking strides. 'It means *I keep watch everywhere, to the east and west, all over the Solomons. My duty is to guard the land and the sea against the invaders. I am not afraid. I laugh in scorn at the Japanese.*'

'Japani ha ha!' nodded the nun. 'But why sing that particular song here today? The war's been over for fifteen years. There aren't any Japanese left in the islands now, except for a few tourists now and again.'

'I don't know,' said Brother John. 'But I'm sure we're going to find out. Just as I expect we'll discover why Papa Noah has invited that American woman here with her recording device. The old man doesn't do anything without a reason.' He glanced at the dark clouds assembling threateningly over the sacred hill called Matakwalao. 'Even if it means organizing a feast in the middle of the rainy season.'

Before Conchita could reply, she heard the scrawny woman's voice complaining in petulant disappointment. She seemed to be arguing with Papa Noah on the far side of the clearing. Sensing trouble, Sister Conchita hurried over to try to defuse the situation. There was never any telling how easily an obtuse or arrogant visiting expatriate scholar might unwittingly offend against local protocol and upset the host tribe.

The white woman was plainly upset about something. The nun arrived in time to hear the tail end of her breathless protest, delivered in a New York whine. Sister Conchita noticed that the other woman was carrying a portable battery-operated Uher recording machine.

'You promised me that there would be more songs,' the thin woman was complaining. 'That's the only reason I agreed to come here today.'

'I'm sorry, but there has been a change of plan,' said Papa Noah placidly. 'I know that you are particularly interested in pidgin songs of this island. Indeed, I particularly chose the one you have just heard to represent the unity showed by Solomon Islanders and your fellow countrymen from the USA when we fought the Japanese together here fifteen years ago. But I'm afraid there is no time for more music. We have a crowded timetable this afternoon.'

The woman turned away in obvious disappointment but said nothing else. She was not a fighter, decided the nun. Sister Conchita did not know what was going on, but she would have thought more highly of the other woman if she had stood her ground. She moved forward.

'Papa Noah has a point,' said the nun smilingly. 'We're here this afternoon to celebrate the success of his church, not to pursue individual agendas, however important they may seem to us.' She extended a hand. 'By the way, I'm Sister Conchita, from Ruvabi Mission on the coast.'

She did not ask the other woman her name. It would have been a breach of Lau etiquette to do so. A third person would have to introduce two strangers.

'Sister Conchita, this is Professor Florence Maddy,' beamed Papa Noah. 'She is here to study the music of the Solomon Islands. Sister Conchita works at the Catholic mission station a few miles away. There are those who say that she runs it, now that Father Pierre is no longer a young man. But then neither am I, and the gods have seen fit to keep me in good health, despite the threats issued daily against me. Don't worry, Professor Maddy. Later there will be another visitor you might be interested in meeting, someone who may be able to help you with your doubtless fascinating research. I shall have something of a surprise for you all afterwards. But let us go and eat first, before I make my announcement.'

'Which university are you from?' asked Sister Conchita, in an effort at small talk as they walked towards the feast.

'Juneau,' muttered the other woman, not looking at her. 'You won't have heard of it.'

The reassuring form of Brother John appeared, as it did so often at awkward moments. Smilingly the Melanesian put a protective tree trunk of an arm around the small woman's shoulders and guided her shrinking, reluctant form towards the waiting food, talking reassuringly in undertones as they went.

'Come, Praying Mary,' said Father Noah to Sister Conchita, giggling and performing a sprightly but incongruous little jig in a grotesque parody of the *tue tue*. He seemed to appreciate the fact that the nun had not been fazed by the blatant nudity of the village girls. 'Let us break bread together.'

2

TABU

A discreet cough of thunder reverberated over the central mountain range. As if on cue, a man clad in a loincloth loped out of the trees of the tangled bush area skirting the plateau. He differed greatly in appearance from the squat, dark Melanesian islanders on the plateau. He was about thirty, six feet tall, and broad-shouldered. He was not heavily muscled, but his smooth arms and legs were thick with power. His skin was a light tan in colour. He had high cheekbones and a straight nose. He moved clumsily, like an affable puppy capable of causing considerable upheaval without really meaning to. This was a cheerful man, thought Sister Conchita, and probably a good and caring one as well. He would be a Polynesian from one of the outlying islands, probably from Tikopia like the others in the separate group.

He was carrying a large wooden cage. Father Noah raised an eyebrow in an exaggerated blend of surprise and censure at the sight of its contents.

'Shem, my dear son!' he said in a carefully guarded neutral tone. 'What have you brought this time?'

'A pair of bird-wings,' said the other islander happily, speaking English in deference to the expatriate sister's presence. 'Assuredly they were on the way to the ark by themselves, but the noise of the singing bothered them and made them stop on a nearby bush, so I put them in the cage for the last part of their journey and brought them here for you.'

Papa Noah frowned. 'But you had to carry them,' he pointed out disapprovingly. 'You know that I only take animals that make their own way to my ark. They must come of their own free will.'

'These two had almost finished their journey,' argued the islander called Shem. 'I just helped the poor tired creatures at the end of their flight. Look, aren't they beautiful?' He turned appealingly to Sister Conchita, lifting the cage so that she could see its contents. The nun could not help smiling in response to the man's ingenuous enthusiasm. Inside, behind the slatted rails, were two enormous butterflies. The bigger of the pair had a cream-coloured body and brown wings with white markings. As Sister Conchita watched, the glorious insect spread its wings. They must have been twelve inches in diameter. The other butterfly, cowering on the same perch, presumably its mate, was smaller, with blue and green markings.

Papa Noah shook his head stubbornly. 'The Bible has told us,' he said. '*And there went in unto Noah, into the ark, two and two of all flesh, wherein is the breath of life*. It does not say that they were carried into the ark in boxes. No, Shem, I am sorry, but I cannot take your bird-wings.'

'We're never going to fill the ark,' said Shem, sadly, but still smiling hopefully. 'Every time I bring you a fresh pair of animals, you tell me that they must come of their own free will! At this rate we won't be ready to sail away when the flood comes.'

'Oh yes we will,' said the old Malaitan confidently. 'I have had another of my visions. Someone is coming from far away to help us. I shall tell everyone about it after we have eaten.'

'Surely we don't need any more help,' said Shem, looking alarmed. 'You and I are together in this, Papa Noah. You told me that the gods had given the two of us the task of filling the ark and sailing away when it is full. That's why I joined you and became your son.'

Papa Noah did not speak. The younger man hesitated, and then shrugged and opened the front of the cage with a gentle twist of his powerful wrists. The two magnificent butterflies vibrated their wings expectantly and then flapped regally back towards the trees, climbing steadily. Shem watched them go, and then moved on towards the waterfall, muttering disconsolately to himself like a good-tempered but disappointed child.

The centrepiece of the Lau Church of the Blessed Ark lay ahead of him on the edge of the cliff. This was the vessel still being assembled lovingly, section by section, by Papa Noah. To an outsider it might appear to be a crudely constructed assemblage of brushwood, tree trunks and aggressively bristling thatch hammered and slotted together into a listing caricature of an ark, but to the hundreds of adherents of the cult it represented nirvana. It was thirty feet long and half as wide, constructed roughly in the shape of a cutter boat and rising to twice the height of the average islander. A deck constructed of weather-beaten planks of various shapes salvaged from the lagoon and the ocean beyond covered a hull extending the length and breadth of the landlocked craft. A spindly tree trunk formed a rough approximation of a mast rising from the centre of the deck. Piles of creepers had been thrust into gaps in the sides. Two doors, one at each end of the static vessel, had been roughly hewn and fitted into the hull. About fifty yards away from the ark was a scattered deposit of mildewed planks, spars, salvaged rusted nails and indefinable hunks of metal, all ready to be pressed into service for the next stage of the building process.

'Please take your places,' cried Papa Noah to the crowd back at the feast, gesturing expansively towards the food.

The islanders surged forward eagerly. Within minutes, most of the men, women and children were eating without inhibition. Papa Noah sat on the mat at the head of the feast, beaming in an avuncular fashion on his guests. At his invitation Sister Conchita sat on his right. Brother John occupied the mat next to the patriarch on his other side. Florence Maddy sat farther down, next to the large Melanesian missionary, still simmering mutinously and only picking sulkily at her food.

As she ate, her eyes cast down modestly, Sister Conchita observed the situation around her without seeming to do so. She had consulted Father Pierre, the elderly priest in charge of her mission at Ruvabi, at some length before deciding to accept the invitation from the Church of the Blessed Ark.

'It's a breakaway cult, there's no doubt about that,' the old man had said. 'However, it claims to be at least semi-Christian. We don't want to close the doors on it too quickly. Go along and see what you can find out.' Then Father Pierre had smiled, an increasingly uncommon event these days. 'With your genius for investigation and getting to the heart of matters, that should be an easy task for you.'

Almost certainly the priest had overestimated her capabilities on this occasion, and probably on many others, thought the nun. So far she had discovered relatively little. She would have been better employed back at the mission. It needed a thorough spring-clean. She had heard several rumours over the past few weeks that Ruvabi was due for a visit from the bishop's inspector, an ominous augury.

There seemed to be nothing here worthy of report to Father Pierre. Papa Noah appeared to be an innocuous, almost saintly man, concerned only with the stocking of his embryonic ark in an appropriate fashion. His followers were all ordinary Melanesians and Polynesians, with no obvious extremists among them. The Tikopian called Shem had seemed mildly resentful when Noah had ordered him to free the butterflies, but he had done as he had been told.

The only real problem lay in the looming presence of Brother John. Why had he bothered to attend the ceremony? Sister Conchita was there because her mission was situated in the area and her superiors needed to study and analyse the newly founded Church of the Blessed Ark in case it might impinge upon the work and numbers of the established church. But Brother John was an itinerant preacher, covering the whole northern section of Malaita, from coast to coast.

What interest could such a shrewd, busy and knowledgeable man have in an insignificant splinter group like Papa Noah's?

Conchita developed the line of thought in her mind. Not only had Brother John attended the feast; the normally taciturn missionary was actually at this moment attempting to initiate a conversation, a rare occurrence in her experience. He leant forward, almost anxiously, and addressed the still beaming Papa Noah.

'You said that someone was coming from a distance to help you with your duties,' said the big man. 'I wonder who that might be.'

'Can't you guess?' asked Papa Noah playfully, obviously enjoying the moment. 'I thought you might be able to work it out from the subject of the entertainment just provided.'

'Which part?' asked Sister Conchita caustically, unable to restrain herself. 'The naked girls or the war chant?'

Papa Noah laughed. He was teasing whitey and getting away with it, an event that would have been unheard of among the islands of his youth fifty years ago. 'A little of both, Praying Mary,' he chuckled, 'a little of both.'

'This visitor,' persisted Brother John. 'Who is it to be?'

'A surprise,' said Noah archly. 'You must be patient, Brother John, like Job in the Bible. Soon we will be rich.'

The long-threatened storm arrived like a flustered overdue guest. Warm drops of rain the size of leaves began to fall. In a moment clouds screened the sky, sucking all the light from it. It grew steadily darker on the plateau. In the background, thunder roared sonorously, calling the always alert evil spirits of the area out of their hiding places behind the rocks and at the bottoms of the streams. Lightning crackled and sparked spasmodically over the trees and waterfall. As if to make up for lost time, the rain began to fall seriously and steadily. It came down first in jerking spasms and then in solid, stinging rods, and finally as an inescapable seamless, soaking sheet. A snarling wind toyed with the trees at the edge of the clearing. The food on the ground was scattered, hurtling across the plateau. The guests screamed in alarm at the unexpected velocity of the attack. Only Papa Noah was not cowed. It was almost as if he had been expecting such a hurricane. The old man staggered joyously to his feet, his frail body tottering a few paces forward at an angle into the wind. He raised his stems of arms.

'*Ala tagalangaini dafa fasui fasui fulas!*' he cried to his adherents.

'The old fool's telling them that it's all over,' Brother John shouted to Conchita. 'He's saying that the great flood is coming and they are all doomed! He even seems happy about it! Look at him!'

Sister Conchita was already contemplating the old islander with concern. Papa Noah's eyes were closed in concentration. He was dancing again, like a poorly carved marionette. His thin legs whirled maladroitly through the air as he performed a series of pirouettes. He looked like a man vindicated in a course of action he had followed for too long. He performed one particularly towering final leap and fell to the ground in a clumsy concatenation of flurrying limbs. He lay still for a moment and then scrambled to his feet and scampered off into the driving rain as if late for an appointment.

By now most of the guests at the feast were on their feet and running screaming in terror down the slope towards the shelter of the village below. The rain clouds had obscured the sun and it was difficult to see what was happening in the sudden incongruous mid-afternoon gloom. Sister Conchita, standing up, was aware of the emaciated shape of Papa Noah disappearing in the distance, cantering awkwardly in the direction of his ark. She started to hurry after the old islander. Brother John loomed out of the darkness, seized her by the shoulder and shook his head.

'*Tabu!*' he shouted. 'Women aren't allowed in the ark.'

Obstinately Sister Conchita squirmed out of the big missionary's grip and ran towards the vague distant outline of the simulated vessel. Soon Brother John was lost to sight in the rain-thrashed quarter-light behind her. She would have been unable to tell anyone why she was searching so determinedly for the patriarch of the Church of the

Blessed Ark. She only felt that she had to find the old man before something dreadful happened to him.

On her concentrated self-imposed odyssey across the assaulted clearing she was vaguely aware of the outlines of dozens of milling, panic-stricken figures, bent double against the force of the tempest. Sheer resolve allowed her to continue to grope her way against the general tide of terrified humanity in the direction of the ark. Through the driving rain it almost seemed as if the twisted, tortured planks of the vessel were causing the shrine to move, grunting sluggishly, across the plateau.

In the general confusion she lost sight of Papa Noah. Several times she veered in the wrong direction and had to retrace her steps, feeling her way back towards the ark, avoiding the water-filled potholes in the ground. More than once she stopped to assist terrified disorientated women and children to their feet and send them on their way to safety. By the time she reached the vessel, Conchita was exhausted. She leant against the wooden side of the shattered edifice and gulped for air. There seemed to be fewer people in the clearing now. Presumably they were huddling for shelter in the village and in the caves at the base of the waterfall, a few hundred yards inland from the beach below. The nun forced herself to stand upright. Tentatively she began to fumble her way along the side of the ark, feeling for one of the doors. It was as dark as ever, and still the storm showed no sign of abating.

It took her five minutes, leaning into the wind with the rain whipping viciously into her face, to find an opening in the wall of the ark. Someone had preceded her, because the door was banging arthritically on its hinges. She forced her way into the structure and stood inside the open doorway, clutching a swinging beam descending crazily from the roof, trying to accustom her eyes to the change in the light.

It was even darker inside than it had been out on the rain-swept plateau. Slowly her eyes adjusted to the darkness. In the gloom she could just make out a few cages containing small animals of indeterminate types. Their stench was devastating. Frightened by the storm, their howls and screeches merged into a discordant barking cacophony of terror.

Abruptly Sister Conchita felt that she was not alone in the ark. Take it easy, she told herself; this would not be a good time to disintegrate. A rod of lightning illuminated the far side of the interior. For a brief moment she was sure that she could see a tall, light-skinned islander, almost certainly a Tikopian, wearing only a loincloth. Clasped in his hand was a large knife. Then the lightning faded and the ark was in darkness again. She heard a door at the far end of the vessel open and slam shut. She peered through the gloom, but it was too dark to see.

She stood still. Once or twice already in her life Sister Conchita had been aware that she had been in the presence of God. Today she knew with sickening finality that in this dreadful, musty, warped facsimile of a Christian site of pilgrimage she was surrounded by an evil tangible enough to be touched. Her instincts told her to flee, that even the worst atrocities being wreaked outside by the storm on the clearing and trees would be preferable to this overwhelming claustrophobic malevolence. Whether he knew it or not, when Papa Noah had nailed the cursed warped slats and planks into place, somehow he had trapped within the ark the worst excesses of the anguished demons and devil-devils existing in the wood, determined to continue their fight against the one-God religion brought to the bush by the white visitors, and struggling precariously to continue its existence among the customs of the ancient time before.

She could feel her heart pounding. Sister Conchita had no doubt that such spirits, good and bad, existed in the island, intertwined with some of the teachings of her own faith, which had been implanted so far only in shallow soil. Father Pierre himself, after a lifetime on Malaita, was convinced of their presence and had even once sent her to encounter them so that she would be aware of their power. Her friend Sergeant Kella, sneered at as a witch doctor by some expatriates, was the only man she knew who walked in both worlds, somehow a rugged, untouched high priest of pantheism.

She reached out and touched one of the walls. It moved beneath her fingers, cold to the touch like the clammy skin and flesh of a living entity, then began to writhe sluggishly. Sister Conchita was reminded of the faint pulse of a patient struggling for life. She could tolerate the fetid atmosphere no longer. Almost with relief she turned back towards the open door and plunged out into the storm.

The rain was still hurtling down, making it difficult to see anything. Doggedly the nun groped her way forward. What had the man been doing inside the ark? Had it been the Tikopian called Shem? She could not be sure.

She had hardly gone a few yards when she stumbled over something soft and yielding on the ground. Almost physically sick with apprehension, she bent over and scrabbled with her hands. At first she thought that she was patting a wet sack. There was a staccato drumbeat of thunder, and then another searing shimmer of white light illuminated the plateau, and the nun saw that she was standing over the inert body of Papa Noah.

Conchita dropped to her knees and clutched the islander by his shoulders. The old man's face was immersed in one of the now flooded rock pools scattered about the plateau. She seized his wrist and tried to feel a pulse, but there was no response. Gently she lifted the old man's lolling head. Something dark and sticky stained her fingers. She could feel a large contusion at the back of Papa Noah's skull. She blew air into the old man's lips and started pounding at his chest with her small fists. The patriarch was soaking wet, to a far greater extent than could be explained even by his exposure to this hurricane. It was almost, she thought wildly, as if the islander's whole body had been immersed in water.

A decade ago, long before she had contemplated taking holy orders, Sister Conchita had been a good enough college swimmer to secure a vacation post as a lifeguard at Boston's Veterans Memorial Pool on the Charles River. On one occasion, still impressed irrevocably on her mind, she had helped secure the body of a youth who had got into difficulties in the water. She remembered the symptoms as the lifeguards had toiled to revive the boy: the blue cyanosis-induced lips, the complete lack of pulse and heartbeat. Another dart of lightning confirmed that these were all the signs that the old Solomon Islander beneath her was also exhibiting as the nun knelt over him, trying to force life back into his unresponsive, water-sodden torso.

After a few frantic, doubt-racked minutes, she recognized the futility of her endeavours and despairingly stopped attempting to revive the man. There was no doubt about it, she decided with increasing horror and incredulity.

Noah had drowned.

3

ARTIFICIAL ISLANDS

Sergeant Ben Kella of the British Solomon Islands Protectorate Police Force paddled his dugout canoe through the night past the artificial islands of the Lau Lagoon. He was puzzled. He had only returned to the islands from Hong Kong a few days ago, but already he had heard several rumours of the abduction of a white woman in his home area. The first had come from a *wantok*, a member of his extended family who was a customs official at Honiara airport, when Kella had descended from the inter-island plane from Port Moresby in Papua New Guinea. Two days later, when he disembarked from a Chinese trading vessel at Auki, the government administrative centre on the island of Malaita, on the final stage of his journey home, he had heard the same disquieting information from an elderly Lau fisherman bringing his catch to the weekly market.

Neither of his informants had been specific. Even to have attempted to adopt such an unambiguous approach would have been impolite, spurning the customary oblique story-telling technique of Malaita, in which a few salient facts were enclosed as carefully in a web of tangents and embellishments as a succulent bonito fish in a palm leaf. Nevertheless, Kella had emerged from both encounters with sufficient knowledge to worry him, both as a policeman and as the island's *aofia*. If he had understood his informants, both trustworthy men who owed him a duty of truth and were not given to gossip, a white woman had been abducted in the Lau Lagoon and was being held a prisoner on the tiny artificial island of Baratonga.

Kella found it difficult to believe what he had heard. As a rule, foreigners, especially white ones, were sacrosanct in the Solomons, unless they deliberately transgressed against island customs. To make matters worse, the Lau area was his own home. Who would dare lay a hand upon a *neena*, one of the unprotected, among the artificial islands, unless it was as a direct and deliberate challenge to his authority? Who would want to do that? Kella did not often get angry, but tonight he was simmering dangerously. This was what happened when he was sent overseas on useless courses! His authority on Malaita went to hell in a handcart! He increased the rate of his paddling as he headed for the strangers' island at the northern edge of the large seawater lake protected from the ocean by a reef of coral.

All around him, lanterns swaying on poles illuminated the outlines of many of the fifty or so islands in the lagoon. It was late, so he could no longer hear the cries of playing children; these had been replaced with the whoops of young bucks as they prepared to paddle far out to sea on night fishing forays in their canoes or to try their luck with unmarried girls on other islands.

The reef water was high. The entire twenty-six-mile length of the lagoon, several miles wide, was constantly refreshed by more than a dozen rivers pouring down from the mountains of the main island and by the tides seeping through the protecting reef from the open sea. Over a period of a hundred years, the tiny islands had been built, stone by stone, by men and women from the mainland seeking to avoid the malarial mosquitoes and the constant warfare between the saltwater dwellers and the bushmen of the interior. The closely knit Lau men and women, the *too i asi*, or people of the sea, spent much of their lives on these stone fortresses, going ashore only to hunt and tend their gardens.

Although he could hardly make out the details of any of the artificial islands in the gloom, Kella could recite the location and provenance of each one as its outline loomed before him. He was passing his own island of Sulufou, the largest of them all, eighty yards long and fifty yards wide, with fifty thatched huts and his own special *beu*, the traditional sacred home of the peacemaking *aofia*. According to custom, the island had been constructed in the nineteenth century, when the legendary chief Leo had paid labourers one porpoise tooth a day to ferry the foundation rocks out from the shore. He noticed that there seemed to be more canoes than usual moored at the long stone jetty. Perhaps some travellers from other islands outside the reef, fearing a storm, had claimed a night's lodging at the custom sanctuary stone placed in front of the church.

On the other side, closer to the shore, was Funaofou, sheltered behind tall wooden palisades to guard the inhabitants from raids by their traditional enemies from the coastal village of Alite. Further out towards the reef was Liulana asi, which had been built in the time before close to the tideway by a man from Saua in memory of a beloved son taken at sea by a shark. Looming through the night was Ferasuba, once the home of the great warrior Marukua from the Morado clan on the mainland.

Kella stopped paddling and rested, taking stock of the situation. Floating ahead of him he noticed in the moonlight a coconut with a piece of flint embedded in its side. The sergeant clicked his tongue in annoyance. It looked as if another internecine blood feud had got under way in the lagoon his absence. Someone had coaxed a charmed piece of flint from a minor shark priest, hammered it into the side of the coconut and cast it into the water in the presence of his rival in love or a land dispute. His adversary was bound by custom to seek out the coconut at sea the next day, lean from his canoe and attempt to lift it from the water. If the second man's *mana* should prove weaker than that of the islander with whom he was in dispute, then a shark would appear from nowhere to tear the trailing arm from his shoulder. If, however the second man stood higher in regard with the sharks, then nothing untoward would happen to him and it would be his turn to seek out his foe and issue a similar challenge.

Kella resolved to investigate the causes of the incipient feud the following day. He considered his immediate course of action as his dugout rested easily on the calm, moon-burnished surface. His destination was only a hundred yards ahead of him. Baratonga was one of the smallest of the artificial islands, its solitary one-roomed hut raised on stilts like the others in the lagoon to keep out the spring high tides. On its surface of compacted rock and soil, there was further room only for a palm tree and several banana bushes snuggled next to one another to provide a modicum of shade in the daytime. A galvanized-iron trough next to the hut was used to catch and store rainwater running down from the thatched roof of the dwelling. It rained often in the lagoon, and the trough was usually full, although the water had a bitter taste after coursing over the thatch.

Normally this did not matter, as Baratonga was uninhabited. It had once been used to keep pigs belonging to a neighbouring island, but now was occasionally hired out to overseas visitors, usually foreign academics carrying out research in the Lau area. They did not come often, and when they did, neither did they stay long. The inhospitable climate, bare terrain, underfoot pig droppings, poor water and basic standard of living usually restricted their sojourns to a week or so at the most before they scurried back to the tenured comfort of such establishments as the Australian National University, the University of Auckland and the University of Hawaii.

Kella had not even been aware that there was a *neena* in the lagoon at the moment. She must have arrived unannounced during his six-week absence in Hong Kong and secured the necessary permission to live on Baratonga from one of the lesser clan chiefs in need of a few quick Australian dollars. He wished that he knew more, but he had not yet landed on Sulufou to seek news and get up to date. By this time in the evening most of the elders whom he could trust would be asleep. He could not wake any of them up in his quest for information. By Lau tradition the soul left the body when a person slept at night. Should the sleeper be awakened roughly, there was a chance that this wandering *nunu* would not return and would be cast adrift eternally. This evening Kella would have to find out for himself what had been going on during his absence. In the meantime he sought protection from the spirits for what might lie waiting for him in the dark by muttering the common mantra of ancestor worship to his dead forebears: 'Take care of your canoes and mine!'

The sergeant stood up, stripped off his uniform shirt, sandals and red beret, placed his paddle on the floor of the canoe and lowered himself over the side into the lagoon. The gently lapping water was warm, and he cut through it powerfully and quietly, using the universal island form of the crawl stroke that had been introduced by Alec Wickham from the Roviana Lagoon to Australia in 1898. Within ten minutes he was approaching the shore of Baratonga. He clutched at the lower reaches of the small stone jetty as he trod water and surveyed the strangers' island. There were no signs of lights or life on the small man-made hump. Cautiously he pulled himself up on to the surface and tiptoed towards the hut, the water dripping from his muscular, scarred body. No guards had been posted outside the simple structure, which seemed strange under the circumstances.

Kella was mystified. His information had seemed genuine enough at the time, but there was absolutely no sign of anyone being kept under duress on the tiny stone outcrop. Neither could he sense any aura of distress. The police sergeant padded round the hut towards the water trough.

He was greeted with a shrill scream. Standing in front of the basin was a slender white woman of about thirty. Presumably this was the overseas academic who had taken up residence on the island. Identification was difficult, because at the moment she was stark naked. She was holding a plastic bucket in her hand. Her dark hair was plastered close to her head where she had been emptying the contents over herself.

The woman shrieked again, threw the bucket viciously at Kella and turned and ran into her hut, slamming the door after her. The sergeant was conscious only of a fleeting pleasing glimpse of the pale bikini outline of her scrawny naked buttocks before she disappeared. He heard the sound of a heavy table being dragged across the floor of the hut and placed against the reinforced door.

'It's all right!' he shouted, annoyed with himself for his clumsiness. 'I mean you no harm! I'm a police officer.'

'Oh yes?' came a quavering American voice from behind the closed door. 'Prove it!'

Kella became aware that he was wearing only his soaked khaki uniform shorts.

'What would you like me to do?' he asked. 'Sing you a chorus of "The Bold Gendarmes"?'

There was a pause. 'Stay there and don't move,' came the woman's voice. 'I'm coming out. I warn you, I'm armed!'

The table was pulled back, scudding across the earthen floor of the hut, and the door opened. The woman came out into the moonlight. She was wearing only a faded cotton skirt and was staring defiantly at Kella. Her small bare breasts were trembling. In her hand she was carrying a heavy kitchen knife. She waved it in uncertain arcs before her.

'I'll use this if I have to,' she threatened.

She meant it too, thought Kella. The edgy woman might have too many barely concealed nerve-endings as well as currently too much exposed flesh for her own good, but there was no doubting her valour.

'I'm sorry I frightened you,' he said. 'I'll come back and explain when I've got more time. Right now I've got something else to attend to that won't wait.'

'Don't bother!' said the young woman vehemently. 'Just stay away from me!'

'I still owe you an explanation,' persisted Kella, backing away. 'I'll come back. My name is Kella. Sergeant Kella.'

'Kella?' the girl said, her attitude changing reluctantly. 'I've heard that name. Aren't you the *aofia*, the law bringer?'

Another whitey who had heard too much local gossip and did not understand any of it, thought Kella. Aloud he said: 'I'm Sergeant Kella, the local police officer. I'll come back and apologize properly as soon as I can. Believe me, you're perfectly safe here.'

He turned and dived back into the water. Within minutes he had located his gently drifting canoe and was paddling it urgently towards Sulufou. He was burning with fury. Kella did not like being tricked, and he was sure that he had just been made the victim of a hoax. Almost certainly it was time for payback.

4

KIBUNG

He tethered the dugout to the long, carefully maintained Sulufou jetty, shrugged into his shirt and sandals and started running past the huts towards the men's longhouse at the far end of the village. There were four islanders on guard at the door, each carrying a club. Recognizing the unarmed scowling police sergeant and sensing his mood, they stood aside hastily to allow him to enter.

The interior was crammed with old men basking circumspectly under a transparent cloud of cigarette and tobacco pipe smoke. There were at least forty gaunt, gnarled veterans, clad in their workaday lap-laps, squatting in rows on the floor of the low-roofed building. Without appearing to look, Kella saw that every one of them was a custom chief and that, unusually in such a fiercely divided area, they came from all over the northern and central part of the island and even farther away. Such a multi-clan assembly among the island leaders was almost unheard of. There were shark-worshippers from his own coastal district of Lau, ancestor-venerating mountain-dwellers from the inaccessible flesh-eating region of Kwaio, custom priests of the Fataleka lowlands, where the gigantic knee-high orchids grew as profusely as grass, and other chiefs from the distant Christian areas of Mbaengguu, Doro and even Kwara'ae and Isabel.

These were all genuine chieftains, noted Kella as he hurried through their ranks to the front of the *heu*, not government-appointed but ultimately powerless headmen who flattered expatriate government officials and impressed them with their mission-school-accumulated knowledge of English. The men assembled silently and coldly before him would never deign to address or even appear before a visiting white man, should one venture into their districts. These were influential warriors who controlled wide swathes of land and could, if the need arose, raise whole armies. Some he knew personally, others by reputation. There was the one-eyed and vicious Volomo, who as a young man in 1927 had taken part in the murder of District Officer Bell at Sinaranggo over a head-tax dispute and had survived the consequent bombardment of the coastal villages by an Australian gunship and the desecration of his tribal shrines by Christian native police patrols sent by the authorities from northern Malaita. Further down the hut squatted Dauara and Nakongo, as usual sullenly watchful. After the Second World War, each had served four years' imprisonment at hard labour for their part in the abortive independence uprising known as Marching Rule. Sitting on his own was the remote and supercilious Basiana, the chieftain of Aiseni, who had the gift of being able to build and consecrate according to ancient rituals the holy dwelling known as a *beu aabu* on his own in a single day. He guarded his precious reputation so jealously that he seldom spoke to mere mortals, even others of chiefly rank.

Uneasily Kella realized that he had never before seen so many influential headmen gathered together in one spot. There were blood feuds represented in this *beu* that probably went back decades. One hasty word might bring a long-dormant vendetta back to life in an instant in the shape of a sudden fatal knife thrust between the ribs. Only an event of monumental importance could have persuaded the leaders of so many warring factions to declare a truce and assemble, no matter how warily, in this fashion. This truly was a *kibung*, a meeting of the mighty. The thought tempered the sergeant's approach to the elderly clan commanders as he began to address them in an improvised amalgam of pidgin and dialect.

'Mighty *fisi kwau*,' he said reproachfully. 'You did not have to trick me into meeting you here by pretending that the white woman had been taken.'

'How else were we to be sure to get you back to Lau?' gruffly demanded a clan leader from the Doro district. 'These days you are spending all your time with the white men. How many times have you left Malaita already this year? On the other hand, how often have you visited our villages to make sure that there is peace among them?'

There was a general murmur of agreement from the wizened old men in the room. They had a point, thought Kella, although he was not about to admit it publicly. As usual, he had a balancing act to fulfil. Aloud he said mildly: 'The government sends me abroad to learn more, so that I might become a better policeman.'

'We are not interested in whitey's law,' said a chieftain from Kwara'ae. 'You are the *aofia*, our peacemaker. The priests anointed you when you were small, and it is your job to make sure that no blood is spilt on Mala.'

'These days you spend too much time as a black white man,' said one of the four clan leaders of Sulufou witheringly. 'You live in their houses and eat their *kai kai*. They say you even fornicate with their women, although I hope you have better taste than to do that. Tonight we thought that the only way to get you here to attend to our problems was by sending word that a white woman was in trouble. We could not be sure that you would return just for our humble and unimportant concerns here on Big Mala.'

The old men in the audience drummed their heels in agreement on the earthen floor of the men's house. Matters were even worse than he had feared, decided Kella. He was being accused of disrespect.

'How may I help, my chiefs?' he asked humbly. There must be a series of particularly complex boundary disputes that he was going to be called upon to adjudicate, he assumed. Either that, or some bored and mischievous young bushmen had destroyed the canoes of a saltwater village once too often after the dugouts had been drawn up overnight above the high-water mark on an isolated shoreline.

He was not expecting the reply that came from the body of the room. With some difficulty, two younger islanders supported an elderly and emaciated chieftain to his feet. When he spoke, the shrivelled man's voice was surprisingly firm.

'There is a killman at work on Mala,' declared the venerable chieftain briefly. 'He is murdering our people!'

5

VAUTUUTUNI OKA

It was as if a dam had been breached. Suddenly a dozen of the leaders were talking at once, arguing with one another and demanding the right to be heard. Some of them started pushing their neighbours in their eagerness to speak. A stunned Kella tried to think on his feet. This was the last thing he had expected. Killman was the pidgin name for the old-style professional killer whose kind had once flourished on Malaita. The last time the sergeant had heard of such a hired warrior being in action had been in the 1920s, long before his birth. Surely some terrifying, ill-founded rumour must have got out of hand.

'Has anyone seen this killman?' he asked, trying to keep the note of scepticism out of his voice.

'I have seen the results of his actions,' said Nakongo, the Marching Rule veteran, rising. His teeth were stained red from constant use of the narcotic betel nut. 'One of my young men foolishly went hunting for wild boar on his own. We found his dead body by the side of the track.'

'An Aiseni man was slain while he was clearing a space for a new garden,' growled Basiana. 'What killman would dare enter my territory?'

'I expect he knew that you were busy building another holy dwelling at the time,' sneered a chieftain from a bush village.

29

The chieftains were now in full spate. The incensed district leaders were on their feet, howling at Kella from all over the hut, demanding retribution before the assassin struck in their areas, spitting deadly insults at one another. As the row reverberated around him, the sergeant tried to work out the essence of what they were saying. As far as he could judge, two men, each from a different district in the north and central regions of Malaita, had been murdered recently while they had been on their own, occupied on mundane tasks, in unfrequented parts of the island. Both deaths had occurred along the coastal, saltwater strip of the district. The two killings had been many miles apart. The men and women of the vast area were now panic-stricken and demanding that their chieftains put a stop to the apparently random slaughter before the killman struck again, hence this hastily constructed meeting. It also appeared as if both the deadly assaults had taken place over the last six weeks, while Kella had been on secondment to Hong Kong.

'Has anyone seen this killman?' he asked desperately. He did not expect anyone to answer. To his surprise, Chief Basiana stood up, brandishing above his head something wrapped in pandanus leaves and secured with bush twine. 'One of my men found this beside the body of the dead man in his garden,' he said. 'The killman must have dropped it.'

The chieftain passed the package to Kella at the front of the *beu*. Kella undid the wrapping and took out a rusty blade about twenty inches long. He recognized the type of weapon immediately. He had seen a number of them when he had been working as a twelve-year-old scout with a coast-watchers' raiding party against the Japanese in the Roviana Lagoon in 1942, eighteen years earlier. It was a Japanese Type 30 bayonet for a Meiji 38 rifle. The blade was straight, and it had a quillon cross-piece hand-guard that also made it suitable for stabbing purposes.

'*Bilong Japani*,' grunted a chieftain in the front row.

'The Japanese left hundreds of these behind after the war,' Kella told him. 'Anyone could have found such a blade and used it to kill an innocent man, or even two of them.'

The room was suddenly silent with the unvoiced scepticism of the elderly islanders present. Kella wondered what he could have said to affect the tough old chiefs so palpably. The oldest man in the room indicated that he wished to be helped to his feet again. As he stood tottering between two younger leaders, his quavering voice could be heard clearly.

'Neither man was killed with a knife,' he said briefly, hawking up a globule of phlegm.

'How did they die, then?' Kella asked.

'They both drowned,' said the old man. He paused and took a deep breath. The veteran of a dozen battles was actually trembling with apprehension. 'And there was no water near either of them. Take my word for it, the evil spirits are playing jokes on us through this killman!'

His words were a signal for a precipitous jostling exodus on the part of the assembled chiefs as they made their way out of the meeting hut back to their waiting canoes. They had presented the *aofia* with their problem. How he dealt with it was now up to him. Kella decided that he would start his journey to the sites of the two reported killings at first light in the morning.

One of the older chieftains paused in front of the sergeant on his way out. Covering his face and upper body were the tribal markings of a leader from Santa Isabel.

'There is another thing,' he said. 'The two men who were killed both belonged to the Church of the Blessed Ark.' He looked at the police sergeant almost with pity. When he spoke again, it was in the local Bugotu dialect.

'*Vautuutuni oka!*' he muttered.

Of all the words that Kella had heard that evening, these were the ones that struck the greatest chill into his heart and over the next few weeks were to prove the most unwelcomingly prophetic.

6

TIME LONG SUN

Sister Conchita approached the ark slowly. Several days had passed since the death of Papa Noah. She had not wanted to come back, but something had told her that amid all the disorder after the events of the big feast there would be one task remaining, and that she must accomplish it. She had come back from Ruvabi Mission in her lunch hour to take care of the matter.

As she walked across the plateau through the spray of the waterfall, the scene looked calm and almost pastoral. It was daylight, 'time long sun' in pidgin, and there were no obvious reminders of the dreadful events of a few days ago. The trees whispered softly, seeming to call all the creatures of the bush to their shelter. Papa Noah's body had been removed for burial and there were no signs of any police investigation. Presumably Ben Kella had not yet had time to visit the scene of the crime. Not that there would have been much to see. The rain from the storm had churned up the ground and then washed it clean. Soon the sun would compact it into new shapes.

Sister Conchita could hear the despairing cries of the animals imprisoned within the ark. She increased her pace. As she had feared, these were not the protests of birds and beasts merely denied natural light and fresh air. She was hearing the frantic protests of neglected animals that had not been fed or watered for days.

She opened the door of the ark and went in. The stench from the cages in the darkened building was almost indescribable. No one could have been near the imprisoned creatures since the death of Papa Noah. Shem and the other members of the Church of the Blessed Ark must have been too busy or too frightened to think about the care of the poor beasts in their charge.

Sister Conchita knew that she had no right to do what she was about to attempt. At the very least she should have asked the permission of the local headman. However, on her way through the village below the plateau, she had not seen a single human being. She had no idea how long it would be before people started returning to their homes. In the meantime, Papa Noah's carefully selected retinue of beasts was suffering.

The nun started walking up and down the main row housing the cages. One by one she opened them. As she did so, the incarcerated birds and beasts tumbled awkwardly out of their stinking enclosures and stumbled and fluttered in a confused mass to the open door of the ark. Their cries of relief reverberated from wall to wall. Within a couple of minutes the deck was almost empty. Sister Conchita could hear the running feet and beating wings of the released animals as they struggled to the welcoming pools and sustaining fruit and nut trees of the jungle.

Only one cage had not yet disgorged its occupants. Sister Conchita walked up to the far end of the deck towards it. Snuffling disconsolately behind the wire mesh were two small wild bush pigs. They squealed ferociously as the nun approached. She tried to lift the cumbersome wooden bar that kept the door closed. It was too heavy for her and remained obdurately in its socket. Calling upon all her strength, she tried again. Still it would not shift. Sister Conchita took a backwards pace, wondering what she could do next. Even if she could lift the bar, and after her earlier failures that seemed a most unlikely outcome, the small but heavy pigs would probably bowl her over and perhaps savage her in their hunger pangs.

Nevertheless, she approached the cage again. As she did so, a large brown hand clasped her shoulder gently from behind. Sister Conchita screamed convulsively and pivoted round. A tan-skinned islander had entered the ark and walked along the deck without her hearing his approach. Sister Conchita cringed away for a moment. Then she recovered her equilibrium and surged forward again, determined to sell her life as dearly as someone of her diminutive stature and generally pacific views could hope to do. The big man half-smiled in approval and placed a finger to his lips to indicate silence. Then he squeezed past the nun and clasped the large bar on the door of the cage. He lifted the wooden plank effortlessly and opened the door. The pigs stood in stupefied silence, and then raced along the deck, disappearing through the door of the ark.

Sister Conchita gazed at the empty cage. 'Thank you,' she said. 'I don't know . . .'

She saw that she was talking to herself. The man had followed the pigs out of the ark at a pace resembling their own, leaving her alone in the gloom. Sister Conchita walked to the door and stared out of the ark. As she had expected, the man was no longer in sight. She stepped out into the warm sunlight, wondering what she had just witnessed. Of one thing she was certain. The large light-brown islander was the same man she had seen in the ark on the day of Papa Noah's death.

7

PROFESSIONAL DEVELOPMENT

'One more question, Sergeant Kella,' said the overweight middle-aged white woman from the Ministry of Overseas Development. 'In what ways do you think this proposed secondment will add to your professional development?'

It won't! Kella wanted to scream. It will be a complete waste of time! I'll be sent to a country that has nothing in common with the Solomons to spend another three mind-rotting, boring months watching other people do their jobs while I should be back on Malaita trying to do mine.

'I suppose it will provide me with more experience,' he said.

Surreptitiously he scanned the faces of his three interlocutors, hoping that in some way by sheer force of personality he had managed to antagonize them to such an extent that they would dismiss him ignominiously from the conference room in the Secretariat building. To his dismay, he saw that they were all nodding benign approval. As so often before on these dreary occasions, he had been served a lob and had returned it innocuously to the baseline in the approved manner. It was becoming a frightening habit. If he was not careful, it might develop into a skill.

'Quite so,' said Chief Superintendent Grice, the Deputy Commissioner of Police, attempting without success to contain his satisfaction. 'We shall of course be sorry to see you off on your travels again so soon after your recent return from Hong Kong, but it is essential at this stage in your career that you get as broad and objective an overview of policing in general as possible.'

And the more often I'm kicked into touch somewhere thousands of miles away, the less chance I'll have of getting up your nose here in the Solomons, thought Kella. He and Grice were old adversaries, but these days his colonial superior officer was beginning to defeat him with monotonous regularity by the simple dint of approving the frequent courses on which the Foreign and Commonwealth Office mandarins in London were so keen to send Kella and other educated islanders in the long run-up to independence for the Protectorate. This time Kella had been tempted to ignore the invitation to visit Honiara, the capital, but at the same time he had received an urgent but ambivalent invitation for the *aofia* to look in at the fishing village just outside the town that afternoon to discuss a possible exorcism, so the interview could serve as an excuse for his journey across from Malaita.

'Any more questions?' asked Welchman Buna, the appointed member of the Legislative Council for the Roviana Lagoon, who was chairing the meeting. He was a tall, greying, dignified man from the western Solomons who, not long before, had saved Kella's life when three rogue FBI agents had menaced the sergeant and Sister Conchita on the island of Olasana, where a young John F. Kennedy and the fugitive survivors of the crew of PT-109 had once taken refuge. Buna was one of the quietest but most influential of the local politicians and widely tipped to become the first indigenous prime minister of the Solomon Islands when the British could finally be persuaded to hand over the reins.

'There is one more thing,' said the woman from London. 'It has to do with this peacemaker business.'

There was an explosion of silence in the room. Even the insensitive and suddenly panic-stricken Chief Superintendent Grice knew that expatriates never discussed the spiritual beliefs of Malaitans in public.

'I hardly think——' began Buna, but the plump woman interrupted him.

'I know that I've only been in the Solomon Islands for a few days,' she ploughed on, leaning forward eagerly. 'But I've already heard a great deal about you, Sergeant Kella. I understand that you are some sort of spiritual leader of your people. Do tell me about it.'

Kella wanted to inform her to mind her own business, but restrained himself. Aloud he said quietly: 'The *aofia* is the hereditary law-enforcer of the Lau Lagoon area and of most of the rest of Malaita. The tradition goes back hundreds of years. When I was a boy, the custom priests of the island selected me for the position. They anointed me, took me from my home for some years, brought me up and trained me in the old traditional ways.'

'And then you came back to civilization and became a policeman,' marvelled the woman. 'Fascinating!' She consulted a typed sheet of paper on the table before her. 'You even went on to take degrees from the London School of Economics and Sydney University. Tell me, how do you become involved in these peacemaking activities on Malaita?'

'If the chieftains on the islands decide that my services are needed, they send for me,' Kella said. And a lot of good it does them sometimes, he thought, remembering the recent disastrous *kibung* of the high chiefs at Sulufou that he had only just survived.

'When you have the time,' said Chief Superintendent Grice nastily. 'Sergeant Kella's more mundane official position, madam, is as a police officer in charge of the sub-station at Auki on Malaita. That's what he's paid for.'

'The day job, as it were,' beamed the woman, apparently oblivious to the note of censure in the senior police officer's tone. 'I see! So you can combine both functions?'

'Kella thinks he can,' growled Grice.

There was another pause. Kella and Grice glowered at one another.

'If there are no more questions, it's almost lunchtime, so I think we can bring the meeting to a close,' said Welchman Buna hastily. 'Thank you for attending, Sergeant Kella. We shall contact you with our decision as soon as possible.'

'But I don't think you need have any concerns,' beamed the woman from London, rising in creaking sections. 'It has been fascinating meeting you, Sergeant Kella. Such a reminder of the continuing strength of links with the primitive past in this remote part of the world.'

She allowed herself to be swept away by the attentive chief superintendent to lunch at the capital's Guadalcanal Club. When the chattering pair had left the room, Buna shrugged apologetically. 'Sorry about that,' the council member said. 'Her ministry controls the purse strings back in Britain. We have to keep in with her and a few other glorified tourists, just as long as they're signing the cheques.'

'I need another overseas course like I need a hole in the head,' Kella told the politician.

'Of course you do,' said Buna. 'I know that. All the same, you'll take what you're given and like it.' He expanded on the subject. 'For a hundred years we've been one of the most neglected colonies in the world. A succession of expatriate high commissioners sent to govern us regarded this Protectorate as the arse-end of the world. Now that they're beginning to think about independence for us, the whiteys are realizing that we occupy a position of strategic importance in the Pacific, and one that will be infiltrated by the Japanese if they don't watch out. That means that for the first time, the Brits, Yanks and Aussies are starting to pump money into the islands. It's part of my job to hold one hand out in supplication and touch my forelock with the other. In short, I'm here to keep our benefactors sweet. And if that involves ordering an ungrateful *kanaka* like you to have his suitcase permanently packed, so be it.'

'There's no answer to that,' said Kella. 'But Alaska! What the hell will I do there?'

Buna shrugged. 'Shiver?' he suggested. 'Take up harpoon lessons? Watch reruns of *Nanook of the North*? How the hell should I know? I've got a country to run, if possible without letting the white African retreads clinging on to their positions here like frightened crayfish on a slippery rock know that I'm doing it.' He regarded the sergeant suspiciously. 'You're putting up even more of a stubborn fight to stay at home than usual. Why? Have you got another of your private *aofia* projects tucked away that you're not telling anyone about? I looked up your file at police headquarters, and you seem to have Malaita nicely in hand as always. You're not sitting on top of another smoking volcano over there that you're not telling us about, are you?'

'No, of course not,' lied Kella. He liked Buna but did not trust him. The Western District man was a politician. In the last analysis he would sacrifice anything in what he regarded as the best interests of his political prospects, especially with rumours circulating that the first national elections for the Legislative Council would be held any day soon. Buna hoped to be returned unopposed to his western islands constituency. Kella started to edge, he hoped unobtrusively, towards the door.

'Am I keeping you from something important?' asked Buna, not looking up.

'No, of course not,' said Kella guiltily, stopping. 'I've arranged to meet some *wantoks* before I go back to Malaita, that's all.'

'Your *wantoks* will be the death of you one day, perhaps literally' said Buna. 'Everybody who speaks your Lau dialect thinks he is entitled to favours from you.'

'This will be just a social gathering,' said Kella hastily if inaccurately.

'I'm glad to hear it,' said Buna, moving towards the door in his turn. 'You're a first-rate policeman, Ben, but you've got too much of a varied agenda for my liking. Are you going to help us drag the Solomons into the twentieth century, or are you going to live on some rock in your forsaken lagoon, chanting magic incantations? One day you're going to have to make up your tiny mind which you'd rather do, otherwise we may have to make it up for you.'

The threat could hardly have been more explicit, but Kella did not bother to respond. In his time he had been menaced and even cursed by far more potent magic men than the civilized Buna. He allowed the politician to get clear of the administrative Secretariat building and then followed him out into the noon sunlight of Honiara, the small capital town on the island of Guadalcanal.

Mendana Avenue, the town's single main street, named after the Spanish discoverer of the islands, was lined with flowering flame trees and frangipani. About three thousand people lived in the town, a constantly changing kaleidoscope of itinerant British, Australians, New Zealanders, Americans Chinese, Fijians and Solomon Islanders. On both sides of the street were shops and government offices. Many of the shops and the Point Cruz cinema were housed in old Quonset huts left behind by the Americans after the war. The office buildings, the two banks and the courthouse were of more recent stone construction. Inland, overlooking the town, lay a series of ridges containing the pleasant residences of government officers and their families. On the other side of the main road, behind the line of buildings, were the placid bay and the harbour. A few cars chugged along the dusty thoroughfare.

Kella's mind was on other things. Before leaving Auki for his interview, he had gone through the files awaiting his attention on his desk. As usual, he had been left with the cases that no one else wanted to handle. An expatriate trader on Small Mala had made two claims over the last three years for vessels he insisted had been lost in bad seas. The Australian insurance company involved, too mean to send out a claims adjuster to such a remote and inhospitable area, wanted the local police to investigate the matter. Some Lau labourers at a logging camp were suspected of stealing dynamite from their employers to sell on for the purpose of stunning large quantities of fish in rivers. A bushman from Areare had thrown a spear at two saltwater fishermen from Alite in a dispute involving exchanging fish for taro at a neutral venue at the foot of Mount Tolon. One of the fishermen had been slightly wounded in the shoulder, while his friend had broken the spear into pieces in retaliation. There were threats of an inter-tribal vendetta.

Kella was passing the front of the Mendana Hotel when he heard his name being called. A bespectacled middle-aged Japanese in a smart safari suit hurried out of the foyer.

'Excuse me,' said the Japanese. 'The waiter tells me that you are Sergeant Kella of the local police force. My name is Mayotishi. I wonder if I might have a word with you. It's rather important.'

'I'm sorry,' said Kella, looking at his watch. 'I have another appointment. I'm late already.'

'It won't take long,' said Mayotishi.

'I'm sorry,' reiterated Kella, beginning to move off. 'I really must go.'

'Is it because I'm Japanese?' asked Mayotishi. 'I appreciate that you fought against my people during the war. Perhaps you still have feelings of animosity because of this.'

'The war ended in the Solomons in 1943,' said Kella. 'It has nothing to do with that at all. If you want to get in touch with me, try the police headquarters building at Auki on Malaita. They usually know where I will be. Now you will have to excuse me. Good day, sir.'

'Three deaths on Malaita, Sergeant Kella,' the Japanese called after him. 'You're going to need all the help you can get to solve them! I can provide that assistance!'

Mayotishi was still standing outside the hotel as Kella continued his walk.

It had been a mistake to annoy the tourist. He recalled the basic rule of thumb inculcated into him on his attachment to a savage police force in the north of England. *Never mess with the middle classes*, he had been told. The same applied in spades to all overseas citizens in the Solomons, as far as indigenous officers were concerned.

He wondered if Mayotishi had been right in his accusation of prejudice. Was Kella biased against the Japanese? He did not think so, but after all, they had killed many of his friends, and had had a good go at killing him.

The policeman tried to concentrate his mind on his impending problem at the fishing village. At the same time, he could not help worrying how Mayotishi could possibly have heard about the murders on Malaita, when Kella had told no one in Honiara about them. And what had the Japanese meant by *three* deaths? So far, Kella had heard of only two.

8

INCANTATIONS

It took Kella half an hour to walk through the town and over Matanikau Bridge to the Malaitan fishing village on the beach opposite the labour lines. As he passed the road leading down to the stores of Chinatown, two drunken middle-aged expatriates reeled out of one of the all-day bars and staggered convivially arm-in-arm in the direction of the Mendana hotel. Kella stood aside to let them pass. He recognized them both. One was Maywood, a forty-five-year-old New Zealander who owned a small business collecting and preparing the sea slugs known as *bech-de-mer* and selling them on to the Chinese to be turned into soup essence and herbs.

The other man was ten years older and English. He was a broad-shouldered, pot-bellied, dishevelled former government officer called Ebury. Before the war he had served as an administrator in the districts and the government offices at Tulagi. He had stayed on during the fighting and served with some distinction as a coast-watcher on Vella Lavella in the western islands, where he was rumoured to have conducted a brave solitary vigil. Always a drinker, in the later years of his career, with the return of peace, he had taken to the bottle with so much enthusiasm that even the other expatriates had noticed. Five years earlier, after a number of public indiscretions, his contract had not been renewed. Having nowhere better to go, he had stayed on aimlessly in the islands, buying a shack on the beach near Visale ten miles outside the capital, where he existed in a state of semi-exile, shunned by his previous colleagues, ignored by the islanders and forced to seek the undiscriminating company of fellow topers like Maywood.

The Englishman glanced up as the two revellers passed Kella, but showed no signs of recognition. The sergeant continued on his way. A section of the main road to Henderson Field airport lay between the lines of dormitories housing government manual workers from various islands on one side of the road, and the collection of thatched huts on the shore. The village comprised emigrants from the Lau area who now earned their living by supplying fish to the market in Honiara. Kella had lived there with his *wantoks* for six months at the beginning of the year when he had been confined to a desk job in the capital after narrowly surviving a court of enquiry into his alleged misconduct concerning the murder of a missionary by the bushmen led by the old chief Pazabozi.

Most of the male adults of the village were already lined up apprehensively to greet him in the *sara*, the village square. The headman came forward to shake Kella's hand. He was a worried-looking middle-aged man wearing a pair of old blue shorts. Kella knew that the man was a conscientious, fair-minded leader who took his duties seriously but could be easily overwhelmed by unexpected occurrences. From behind the closed doors of the huts emerged the constant monotonous shrieks of the unseen women and girls of the village. They would continue to keen in this fashion until all the mourners from afar had arrived to pay their respects to an old woman who had died a few days ago.

'*Aofia*,' said the headman respectfully, using the Lau dialect. 'We want to thank you for coming back to help us. We need you to say the sacred words taught to you by the custom priests to clear us of this dreadful visitation.'

'Show me where you said your first prayers for the old woman's soul,' said Kella.

Obediently the other man conducted the sergeant through the huts to the shore, where the waves lapped indulgently against the pebbles. The other islanders followed them at a careful distance and formed a nervous semicircle on the beach as they regarded the uniformed police sergeant with awe and trepidation.

'You'd better me all about it,' said Kella.

The headman took a deep breath and embarked upon his story. As he spoke, the other men gathered ever closer around them. The tale took some time in the recounting because the leader took care to include the customary Melanesian ramblings, digressions and tenuous links with Lau legends and custom law. He also stopped every so often to argue with and then threaten some of the other men, who were inching forward with the intention of turning his monologue into the general village discussion with which they were all more familiar and comfortable. By dint of much concentration Kella emerged from the process with a headache and some sort of grasp of an outline of what had been happening among the exiles around him.

An old woman of the village, without any family remaining, had died. Everything that needed to be done had been carried out meticulously, according to custom. The body of the septuagenarian had been laid out in the women's *beu* and after a few days would have been transported inland, to be buried secretly in the hills beyond the residential ridges. A shark priest had been called over from Malaita at considerable expense in cherished shell money to conduct the official farewell ceremony at the stone shrine, close to them now on the shore, known as the *bae'ana hackwa*, where sharks were known to bask, even among the busy shipping lanes off the shore of Honiara. The priest had come highly recommended and had presented an impressive appearance, with his hair falling down to his waist as, by virtue of his high office, no mortal was allowed to touch his head or cut his tresses.

After the priest had roasted a pig and buried it, he had said the usual dignified prayers of the *lau agalo* for the dead before departing. That should have been an end to the subject. Soon afterwards, however, matters started to go wrong in the fishing village. Before the body could be smuggled out by night for its surreptitious inland burial on someone else's land, various villagers had started meeting the ghost of the old woman around the village. She had been seen walking silently along the shore and coming out of her hut, among other places. Finally she seemed to have settled her domicile on a pile of torn and discarded fishing nets on a patch of sand several hundred yards from where they were now standing. Apart from a slight ethereal haziness around the edges of her body and an obdurate refusal to answer any greetings or even look up when addressed, she had appeared remarkably lifelike, perhaps even more so than during the closing years of her existence on earth.

Greatly daring, the headman and some of the elders had broken tribal law and peered into the women's *beu* to see if, by some miraculous happenstance, the corpse had either recovered consciousness or come to life and departed. Unfortunately for their peace of mind, the old woman's body had still been resting there on a pile of pandanus leaves. So, as a last resort, the village had sent for the *aofia*.

'Do you want to see where the ghost walks?' asked the headman when he had finished.

Kella shook his head. To have asked for proof in this matter would have been discourteous, implying that he had doubts about the veracity and judgement of his hosts. 'Show me her body,' he asked instead.

They walked back through the village to the long, low thatched hut that had been erected according to tradition for the domicile of women during their menstrual periods or before giving birth. As a priest of the highest rank, Kella alone among the men present had the undisputed right to enter this *beu*.

While the others waited outside, he bent over the body of the old woman. She was now lying on a bed of sago palm leaves replacing the old sun-bleached pandanus fronds, and was wearing a faded blue dress. Her face was calm and peaceful, the lines of seven decades almost entirely smoothed out in easeful death. Carefully the sergeant turned her over. In the Lau culture corpses were neither sacred nor *tabu*, so he was able to examine the woman closely without offending her gods or village decorum. He pulled down the back of her dress gently at the neck to reveal a whorl of ancient tattoos on her wrinkled flesh. They would have been incised with a bamboo splinter dipped in coconut juice and lime when she was very young and unlikely to feel the pain so much. There were circles representing the sun, chevrons indicating the tracks of the crab and many other time-encrypted impressions, all running into one another.

It took him some time to find what he had been looking for. The mark had almost been obscured by age and a pattern of a large star with a circle of rays emanating from it on the old woman's skin. It was almost as if the constellation had been deliberately superimposed over a small inverted *w* shape. Kella grunted in triumph at the sight and knelt to examine the ancient scratch more closely. Then, satisfied, he pulled up the back of the dress and turned the old woman's body back respectfully.

'All right, Mother,' he said gently. 'I tell you, you will soon be free to leave us and travel to the island of Momolu, where the spirits of the dead assemble, to live happily among good gardens and be sheltered for ever in cool shade from the heat of the sun. I, Kella, the *aofia*, promise you this.'

The headman and the other men were waiting for him outside the *beu*. Kella nodded. 'Let us release her spirit and send it on its journey,' he said.

There was a murmur of relief and appreciation from the group. The headman turned to lead the way to the shark altar on the shore, but Kella restrained him. 'Not by the sea,' he said. 'That's where you made your mistake.'

He led the men inland a few yards until they were among the palm trees sheltering the village from the constant traffic on the main road.

'I'm going to say the *manatai burina* here,' he announced briefly.

A puzzled hum spread through the group of islanders, like a riff being played lightly on a guitar. The *manatai burina* was a general prayer of apology offered to the gods when they had been wronged or slighted. It was performed rarely, and then only by the most learned among the priests. Only a few of the oldest men present had even heard of it. Kella ignored them and threw back his head so that he was facing the white clouds scudding across the sky. He called upon all the gods of ancient Malaita to hear him. He begged them to accept the spirit of the old woman on Momolu. He chanted the *lau agalo*, asking the gods to forgive the people of the village for their earlier mistake, which had been made out of ignorance, not spite. He promised to slaughter another pig when he returned to the Lau Lagoon, one he had first blessed, making it special, and then offer it to all the gods in their retreats, as an appeasing *faamola* to make things right again. Finally he picked up a handful of sand and threw it into the air. It was all accomplished in a few minutes, a sign that the gods were listening on the wind.

'What do we do now?' asked the headman.

'Nothing; it is all done,' Kella said. 'You can send someone to the fishing nets if you like. They will find that the ghost has left the village.'

Two young men broke away from the throng, running hard.

'Why did you say the *manatai burina*?' asked one of the islanders. 'Why did we have to apologize to the gods? How had we offended them?'

'What do you know about the old woman?' asked Kella in return.

'Nothing,' said an ancient man. 'She was very old. It seemed as if she had always been here.'

'Not always,' said Kella. 'She was not even a Lau woman.' He paused to let the information sink in. When he saw that he had their complete attention, he went on: 'It was an understandable mistake. After you told me that the gods had rejected her, so that her spirit couldn't leave your village, the most likely reason seemed to be that you had made her farewell ceremony to the wrong gods.'

'We always perform the *alu* to our shark gods,' protested the headman.

'Exactly,' said Kella. 'And naturally they never reject the ghost of a Lau man or woman. If they would not accept the spirit of the old woman, perhaps secretly she did not worship them. When I looked at her body, I found the tattoo of her original clan on her back. It was small and had faded over the years, and was almost hidden by other tattoos she had had engraved over it, but her original clan totem was still there, obscure as it was, for those with eyes to see.'

'What was it?' asked the headman.

'The wings of a bird in a small *w* formation,' Kella said. 'Your old woman worshipped the eagle gods. Originally she must have come from the Tolo clan in the bush hills. That is their sign. Many years ago she must have married a Lau man, moved down to one of the saltwater villages and had his children. By the time of her death here everyone who had known her had passed away, so it was assumed that she was a shark worshipper like the rest of us.'

'But why did she keep it a secret that she came from Tolo?' asked one of the islanders.

'Wouldn't you?' asked Kella as his listeners nodded. 'The Tolo people are supposed to be foolish and primitive. She had married into the Lau clan and so had taken a step up in the world. She and her husband kept quiet about her shameful background, but secretly all these years she still sacrificed to the eagles.'

'And now that you have said the *lau agalo*, the eagle gods have sorted matters out and taken her ghost over to Momolu,' marvelled the headman. 'I wondered why you threw the sand into the air. It was a tribute to the eagles, wasn't it?'

Kella nodded. Before he could answer, the two young men came running back from the direction of the pile of fishing nets. Their beatific expressions were enough to tell the waiting men that the ghost no longer rode in the fishing village. A ragged cheer went up from the assembly. The headman seized Kella's hand and pumped it.

'Thank you, *aofia*,' he said fervently. 'Tonight we shall have a feast in celebration. Will you stay for it?'

Before Kella could answer, there was a cry from the crowd. One of the men pointed a tremulous finger at the sky over the island of Savo. Far away in the distance across Ironbottom Sound, the outline of a large bird soaring on a current of wind could just be made out.

'An eagle!' whispered the man. 'It is carrying the ghost of the old woman over to Momolu!'

Cries of reverent acquiescence came from the others. Kella knew that the bird was too far away to be identified. It could be a hawk, or some other small bird of prey. Or just possibly it might be an eagle carrying another tired soul to the fabled delights of the heavenly island. In any case, it was time he was leaving. There was only one more task to perform before he went. He did not expect any great results from such a long shot, but all the same he summoned the compliant headman.

'I must go,' he told him.

'Let us know if ever we can help you,' said the other man.

'Count on it,' Kella said.

He shook the other man's hand, waved farewell to him and climbed back on to the main road heading towards the town, mulling over this latest contribution. It was imperative that he get back to Malaita immediately, investigate the deaths of the two villagers and, most important of all, find out what Mayotishi had meant by a third killing.

He stopped and looked back at the village. Already life was proceeding normally. The shade of the old woman who had haunted it so recently no longer hovered over the huts. Some of the men were pushing their canoes out into the sea. Others had returned to the recently *tabu* site of the fishing nets and were starting to assess and repair them again. Older men were chattering cheerfully in groups, already embellishing and exaggerating the story of the *lau agalo* sending-off ceremony that had almost gone so badly wrong.

It was important not to have preconceptions and imperative to take nothing for granted, thought Kella. If there had only been one old villager remaining who knew the truth of the old woman's antecedents and tribal loyalties, the villagers might have investigated the matter of the eagle gods for themselves. He had only been the catalyst, looking at things through fresh eyes. Yet there was no denying the importance of his brief contribution. Kella was a modest man and he always gave the spirits their full due. As a boy he had been shown the path granted to few others. The old custom priests who had trained him in their mountain recesses had taught him how to approach the Lau gods with confidence as a go-between. The success of his recent efforts at the fishing village only underlined the importance of his continuing to use his gifts as the *aofia* to bring peace and law to Malaita.

That meant that above all he must track down and apprehend this killman who was causing so much distress on his home territory. Furthermore, he must do so without taking Chief Superintendent Grice and the other white policemen into his confidence. If he was to be free to use his literally god-given gifts for the benefit of the islanders, he could not risk being restricted by the expatriates' often inexplicable regulations, even if the results did not bode well for him in the carefully supervised and seldom deviating world of the old colonials.

'Can I give you a lift?' asked a voice.

Kella looked up. One of the capital's small fleet of ancient taxis was waiting at a lopsided angle at the side of the road. It looked as if it had been retrieved intact from a junk heap. Mayotishi the Japanese tourist was standing invitingly by the open door. He smiled thinly.

'Allow me to take you back to Malaita, Sergeant Kella,' he said, as if by some divine intervention he knew what the policeman had just decided.

Kella climbed into the back of the taxi. What part, if any, was the already ubiquitous Japanese going to play in his ongoing investigation? The sergeant knew that he would have to be circumspect in his dealings with Mayotishi.

9

RIFTS AND SCHISMS

The frightened refugees had been drifting into Ruvabi mission station since early that morning. At first they had arrived mainly singly and in pairs. Then groups and whole families had started to appear, begging for shelter and protection from the killman. Now it was noon and there were over a hundred Melanesians scattered miserably over the formerly immaculate sward. Sister Conchita saw that they were from both saltwater and bush villages. There were even a few she recognized from the last feast of the Lau Church of the Blessed Ark, when Papa Noah had been murdered in such bizarre circumstances just a few days before. The islanders must have been terrified beyond belief to leave their homes to seek sanctuary in this manner. Sister Conchita wondered why that could be. The death of the cult leader had been a dreadful thing, but these islanders lived with sudden death every day of their hard, risk-filled lives. Why were they suddenly fleeing from their homes? Could it be the fear of the unknown?

She walked across the compound from the classroom in which she had been teaching, a brisk, tiny, urgent figure in a white habit reaching to her ankles, consulting the fob watch she carried attached to the belt around her waist, next to a string of rosary beads. At the vigorous tolling of the noon bell, children and teachers emerged hungrily from the other thatched bamboo classrooms of the boarding school on the bluff above the river, shortly before it emptied into the lagoon. They headed eagerly for lunch in the long dining hut. A hundred yards away, close to the ever-encroaching tangle of bush, lay the sprawling mission house and the neat, red-roofed stone church. Scattered haphazardly about the station were the huts of those Christian families who had abandoned their villages over the years and come to live closer to the source of their faith.

Sister Conchita walked over and checked that the young blue-robed local nuns were feeding the milling newcomers from the sacks of rice she had earlier carried over from the mission store. One of the nuns looked at the unhappy islanders.

'They are frightened,' she said sadly. She lapsed into pidgin for emphasis as she hurried away to fetch another sack of rice. 'Frit too much!'

Sister Conchita nodded sympathetically. It had been a busy morning. She had risen at dawn and spent a period at silent prayer and meditation, trying to look deeply into herself, as she had promised the mother superior in Honiara. 'Concentrate on your devotions,' the old woman had warned. 'Do not have too much contact with the outside world.'

Chance would be a fine thing, thought Sister Conchita. Already it had been her limited experience that the outside world had a habit of crowding in on her, despite all her good intentions to lead a withdrawn, contemplative and hopefully placid life. This morning alone her time had been fully occupied with teaching the children and looking after the refugees, without even starting to attend to any of her administrative duties.

She checked that the food for the visitors was being cooked in large simmering tureens on stone-clustered fires all over the grass. Earlier she had held an impromptu sick call in the hospital, attending to cuts and abrasions sustained by some of the islanders in their hasty flight from their villages. Later she would have to find shelter for them all and any later arrivals who might turn up. She decided that it was also time that she looked in on Father Pierre.

The old priest was lying on the iron bedstead beneath rough blankets in his tiny simple room when the nun took him in a glass of lemonade. There was a basketwork chair on the old woven carpet. A wooden cross was suspended on bush twine from a wall. An oil lamp with a trimmed wick stood on a small table. Termite-infested books were piled everywhere on the floor.

'How are you feeling?' asked Conchita, handing her patient the glass.

'Better,' whispered the old priest unconvincingly. He was a thin, wizened man in his eighties. A few wisps of white hair were drawn across his scalp. A pair of spectacles with bottle lenses balanced precariously on his nose. For such an aged man his face was curiously smooth and untroubled, like a river pebble worn smooth by the rushing water of time. He was wearing an old-fashioned white nightgown, buttoned at the neck despite the heat. He had arrived in the Solomons from Alsace-Lorraine more than fifty years before. Over the ensuing decades he had carved Ruvabi Mission almost single-handedly from the bush.

'I wish you would let me take you to the hospital in Honiara,' said Sister Conchita as she smoothed the old priest's pillow.

'Don't fuss, girl,' said Father Pierre calmly. 'You're merely witnessing the incipient ravages of old age. My end isn't near yet. Have you heard anything more about the death of the so-called Papa Noah?'

Conchita shook her head and took the proffered half-empty glass from the old man. The best part of a week had passed since she had returned from the lethal feast at the Lau Church of the Blessed Ark. She had sent a radio message to the mission's headquarters in Honiara recounting the events she had witnessed, but so far had heard nothing in return.

'It's a strange business,' said Father Pierre, his voice growing weaker. 'These breakaway churches are usually a bit of a joke, but when someone gets murdered, that's a different matter.'

'I suppose Shem, the Tikopian, will take over the sect now,' said Sister Conchita idly.

'Who?' asked the old priest.

'You remember I told you that there was a Tikopian claiming to be Papa Noah's son? He even called himself Shem, like Noah's son in the Bible.'

'You never mentioned that he was a Tikopian,' said Father Pierre, trying to sit up. 'What did he look like?'

Sister Conchita tried to recall the features of the broad-shouldered, shambling Polynesian. She did her best to describe him to the old priest. Father Pierre listened in silence until she had finished.

'I wish you had told me this earlier,' was all he said.

'I'm sorry, I didn't think it was important,' said Sister Conchita, gently easing the distracted man back on to his pillow. She was pretty sure that she had mentioned it, but Father Pierre tended to forget things

'Of course it's important,' said Father Pierre weakly. 'It's probably the most important thing about this whole business. You must tell Ben Kella about it at once, if you haven't already done so. And while you're about it, tell that big Anglican Guadalcanal man, Brother John, too.'

'Brother John already knows,' said Sister Conchita soothingly. 'He was asking Papa Noah all sorts of questions at the feast about the future of the sect.'

'That makes it worse,' breathed Father Pierre. 'He's a shrewd fellow. So is Sergeant Kella, fortunately. You'd better send for him. That's it! Send for Ben. Tell him there's a Tikopian connection. There's trouble on Tikopia. The Anglicans thought that they'd converted the island to Christianity, but if you ask me, it didn't quite take. That's why there's going to be trouble.'

His head fell to one side and soon he was asleep. Sister Conchita smoothed his pillows once more, and looked down at the sleeping man. She admired Father Pierre more than any other man she had ever known. She had first been sent to Ruvabi at the beginning of the year as a young novice, after four years' postulant training in the USA, unsure of herself and her new vocation and already the subject of several inadvertent brushes with the church authorities. The wise and compassionate old priest had taken the impulsive new sister under his wing, treated her as an adult, allayed her fears and calmed her doubts. He had also worked her harder than she had ever been used in her life before.

Conchita had enjoyed almost every moment of her time at the mission, and knew that she would never find a better or wiser mentor than Father Pierre. She was not sure whether it was she or the mission who needed him the most. With the news of the imminent arrival of Father Kuyper on a much-heralded tour of inspection, the trick was going to lie somehow in keeping the veteran missionary, and now her close friend, in charge of Ruvabi, despite his age and lack of strength.

Sister Conchita tiptoed out of the bedroom and walked back along the corridor to the large room that served as both a lounge and a makeshift office for the mission. She sat at her desk and tried to organize her thoughts. She had a great deal on her mind. There was the mission to run during the continued incapacity of Father Pierre, and now the sudden influx of frightened islanders looking for protection from some undefined menace. There was also the death of Papa Noah to be considered.

Forget it, girl, she told herself sternly. That's none of your business. The most you can be expected to do is to act as a witness when Sergeant Kella gets back from Honiara to resume his investigations.

All the same, she thought, going through the pile of paperwork before her, it was an intriguing affair. Who could possibly want to murder such an apparently harmless old man as Papa Noah, and why select such an incongruous method of death as drowning the sect leader in a pool of water close to his ark? And who was the large Polynesian she had twice seen running out of the ark? Sister Conchita shook her head. Father Pierre had been right. This was going to be a task for Sergeant Kella to pursue with his usual mixture of logic and spurts of custom-based intuition. She must resist all temptation to become involved.

It would be nice to see the local policeman again, though, she thought. Lately Kella seemed to have spent more time globetrotting on his courses than supervising the investigation of crime on Malaita. Sister Conchita would never have admitted the fact, but she had missed the tough and shrewd but hard to fathom *aofia*.

There was a commotion in the entrance hall of the mission. Sister Conchita rose and hurried to the front door. Two harassed local nuns were supporting a screaming pregnant girl into the house.

'Put her in my room,' said Sister Conchita decisively, following them along the corridor.

She helped the young nuns place clean sheets on the floor and situate the frightened girl on her side. When the contractions started coming rapidly, she slipped a pillow under the girl's back, then watched as the young, local novices washed their hands in water from a large ewer and went to work. They were probably younger than the mother-to-be, but already had introduced many more children into the world than Conchita had.

The delivery went smoothly, and soon the lungs of a healthy baby boy were being employed at a piercing full throttle inside the mission house. A dozen female *wantoks* of the new mother who had been straining eagerly at the door now broke into the room like a cattle stampede and noisily surrounded the newest addition to the family.

Sister Conchita considered trying to maintain some form of order but decided against it. There was no point in spoiling the moment of exhausted delight on the part of the new young mother. Already the nun's clinically tidy bedroom looked as if a tidal wave bearing all manner of detritus had broken over it. The two sisters, holding the baby proudly, carried it out to the hospital building to be checked, while the vociferous relatives admiringly supported the mother up on to Sister Conchita's narrow bed.

The nun walked back along the corridor. She noticed that the whitewashed walls and scrubbed floor, which she had spent the best part of a day cleaning, were already stained and grubby. The father of the baby had obviously been informed of his new status, because, ignoring custom edicts, he came running bellowing with delight into the mission, at the head of a dozen other galloping men. Prudently Sister Conchita stood to one side to allow them to pass. She noticed with resignation that a sudden squall of rain had driven a group of mothers with their young children haphazardly into the mission lounge.

Outside, most of the other refugees were sheltering from the shower as best they could. Some had moved in to share the huts of the resident Christians, while others were clustered together for warmth under the trees at the edge of the compound. With a sinking heart, Sister Conchita realized that the mission station she had worked so hard to clean over the past few days now resembled nothing more than a rapidly deteriorating garbage dump.

She ignored the thudding rain soaking her clothing as she surveyed the shambles around her. Ever since her arrival at Ruvabi almost a year ago, she had taken a pride in rescuing the house and grounds from their previous neglected condition. Father Pierre had always been oblivious to his surroundings. Earlier in the current week she had been spurred on to even greater efforts of domesticity when she had received a bush-telegraph message informing her that the awe-inspiring Father Kuyper, he of the formidable intellect, waspish tongue and impossibly high standards, had landed at Auki and was now on his probing way to visit the mission station.

Ostensibly the bishop's right-hand man was merely dropping in to the mission on a general tour of north Malaita, but Sister Conchita already knew enough of church politics not to be fooled. She and Father Pierre had been keeping the underfunded mission going somehow or other for the best part of a year, improvising wildly and assisted only by a few willing but young and inexperienced local sisters. If word had reached Honiara that Father Pierre was unwell, the church authorities could seize the opportunity to replace the idiosyncratic old priest with a younger and more orthodox adminis- trator of their own choosing.

That meant that Conchita could eventually be recalled to Honiara or, even worse, asked to stay on at Ruvabi as a mere biddable housekeeper for a more cautious senior church organizer who would gather the reins of command closely to his chest. She seriously questioned if she could ever do biddable. One of the reasons why she had loved her time at Ruvabi so much was because of the autonomy and freedom that the old man had given her once she had earned his trust.

She did not see the familiar burly form of Brother John walking across the grass until the big man was almost upon her. As usual the Anglican missionary was wearing a lap-lap and a tattered shirt and carrying his worldly possessions in a small pack perched on his broad back.

'This is an unexpected pleasure,' said the nun approvingly, always glad to see the down-to-earth Guadalcanal man. 'Are you here because you've experienced a Damascene conversion to our cause?'

'That will be the day,' said the islander, easing his pack to the ground and wiping the sweat from his eyes as he surveyed the frenetic activity all around. 'It looks to me as if you've got your hands full with your existing members, without starting a recruiting drive.'

'Come inside and let me get you a glass of lemonade,' invited the sister.

Brother John shook his head. His glance took in the overcrowded compound and the shabby mission house, missing little. 'I can't stay at this papist temple too long,' he said. 'I might pick up something contagious.' He grew serious for a moment. 'I only came to see if you were all right after the Blessed Ark business, and to ask you a favour.'

'Why shouldn't I be all right?'

Brother John shrugged. 'Just rumours,' he said. 'There are stories that the Catholics in the Lau area are in a bit of trouble. Dissension among your village people: rifts and schisms, that sort of thing.'

'Really?' said Sister Conchita non-committally.

'Also,' went on Brother John, 'there's word about that old Father Pierre is dying.'

'Absolute nonsense!' said Sister Conchita, this time stung into a response. 'He's got a slight fever and probably a minor recurrence of his malaria, that's all. He'll soon be up and about again.'

'Good,' said the big Anglican. 'If anything happened to him, your mission would be in a right state. It's only his reputation that holds the place together. No disrespect intended.'

'I'm mortally offended,' said Sister Conchita. 'Actually, everything's fine. In fact at the moment I've got two priests for the price of one. I've heard that Father Kuyper is on his way here for a few weeks as well.'

'Now I know it's time to go,' said the Guadalcanal man, picking up his pack. 'Kuyper's a bright guy, but at heart he's an administrator. I don't think he appreciates quite how closely the various missions have to work together in the bush. He probably wouldn't even approve of us talking like this.'

'I truly believe you underestimate him,' said Sister Conchita. She changed the subject. 'Anyway, I really wanted to talk to you about Papa Noah's death.'

'You're not investigating that, are you?' asked Brother John, alarmed. 'I know what you're like when you get your teeth into a mystery.'

'No, of course not,' said the nun. She paused. 'Not really, anyway. It's just that the whole thing was so confusing. I'd like to get things straight in my own mind before I talk to Sergeant Kella. Did you see anything suspicious during or after the feast?'

'Not a thing,' said Brother John, shaking his massive head. 'The rain was coming down so hard that I could hardly see my own hand in front of me on the plateau. I helped get some of the women down the track to the safety of the village. By the time I returned to the ark, you had found Papa Noah's body, Shem had turned up from somewhere or other, and you were trying to bring the old man round.'

'What about Dr Maddy?' asked Sister Conchita. 'Did you come across her at any stage?'

Brother John screwed up his brow in concentration until the lines converged to form one deep corrugation. 'Yes, I did, as a matter of fact,' he said. 'At one point Shem was hustling the white woman across the plateau, away from the ark.'

'*Away* from the ark?' asked Sister Conchita. 'When I saw her last, she was eating at the feast with the rest of us.'

'She must have got lost in the general confusion,' said Brother John. 'You remember what it was like. It was so dark in that storm that people were wandering about all over the place. Dr Maddy must have staggered in the wrong direction until Shem found her and helped her down the path to the village.'

'I suppose so,' said Sister Conchita doubtfully. Or Shem and the American musicologist could have hurried over to the ark together in the general confusion for some reason, and were on the way back when the Anglican missionary saw them.

'There was one other thing,' she said. 'Several times Papa Noah said that he was expecting another visitor. I remember his exact words. He said that he was waiting for someone from far away to come and help. You seemed interested in that as well. In fact you tried to get him to elaborate on the remark, but he wouldn't.'

'It seemed a little odd, that was all,' said Brother John. 'As far as I knew, the Blessed Ark church was pretty much a one-man band, but old Papa Noah seemed convinced that someone was coming in to give him a hand. He was playing his cards pretty close to his chest, though. He wouldn't tell me anything.'

Sister Conchita nodded. 'You mentioned that you wanted a favour from me.'

'As a matter of fact it's about Papa Noah,' said Brother John. 'He's being buried on one of the artificial islands early tomorrow morning.

I've got to see someone else so can't be there. I was wondering if you could attend in my place. With Father Pierre being laid up, you're the only expatriate missionary in the Lau region at the moment. It would be a sign of respect and inter-church cooperation if one of us could be there.'

The big man was trying to appear casual, but his words did not ring true. Sister Conchita wondered why he really wanted her to attend the funeral. Still, he had helped her enough times during her early days in the Solomons, and most of the different missions tried to assist one another when they could. Why should this be an exception?

'Sure,' she said. 'I'll regard it as a mandatory church parade.'

Brother John nodded and raised a hand in thanks before padding away like a graceful bear. Within a few minutes he was out of sight among the trees. Sister Conchita turned to walk across to the classrooms. Considering the time she had left before the afternoon school bell rang, she would have to forgo lunch and eat that evening when matters had calmed down a little.

At that moment she heard screams coming from the islanders encamped under the trees where the main track wound through the bush into the mission area. As she hurried in the direction of the din, she sensed that something bad was about to happen. She increased her pace to a stumbling half-run across the ridges of mud. Dignity, always dignity, she told herself wryly, hitching up her habit. By the time she arrived at the trees, she was approaching a wild gallop and panting for breath.

A big golden-skinned man was rampaging among a group of seated islanders, pulling them to their feet and pushing them roughly into lines, urging them towards the bush track through the jungle. As she drew closer, Sister Conchita recognized him as Shem, who had claimed to be Papa Noah's son at the Lau Church of the Blessed Ark. The islanders being bullied into place were cowering, making no effort to fight back. Their eyes were dilated with terror. Sister Conchita had never seen a group of Melanesians so subdued.

'Stop that at once!' she panted, standing in front of the furious Tikopian. Shem glared at her, his large hands clenching and unclenching spasmodically.

'Go away, Praying Mary!' he growled. 'These are my people now that Papa Noah is no longer with us. I'm taking them back to the ark where they belong.'

'They came here for sanctuary,' the nun told him. 'They're frightened and confused. They don't know what to do.' She took a deep breath. 'They are under the protection of this mission as long as they wish to remain here. Please leave them alone and go away.'

'I must take them!' shouted Shem. 'Three members of my church have been murdered!'

Conchita did not know what the man meant, but she tried to outstare the Tikopian, desperate not to show the man how frightened she was, and determined to stand her ground no matter what the consequences. Shem spat something in his own language at her and turned away to start manhandling his former followers again. Before she had time to think, Sister Conchita darted forward and pulled him away from the group. Taken by surprise, he staggered back a few inches. Then he turned on the nun with a roar. It had started to rain harder. She wondered what sort of sight she must be presenting to the gaping islanders, soaking wet and bedraggled in the tropical downpour as she struggled with an infuriated man twice her size. None of the terrified refugees moved forward to help her. For a moment the nun wondered if she was going to meet an incongruous end amid the clinging mud of this corner of her cherished mission. For some reason she fleetingly recalled the awful circumstances surrounding the death of Papa Noah outside his ark, with his soaked, rag-doll-helpless body and face immersed in the flooding rock pool as she tried to revive him.

She realized that Shem had stopped struggling, and peered confusedly through the tropical downfall. The big man was paying no attention to her. He was facing the trees, trembling. Another

Tikopian was standing on the track under the foliage. He was not as wide as Shem, but taller and older. He wore a loincloth with a leather belt around his waist. A long knife was thrust into the belt. The effect on Shem was dramatic. He gave a half-despairing grunt and then ran quickly past the second Tikopian and was lost to sight among the trees. The other Tikopian looked expressionlessly at Sister Conchita, and then turned and glided easily after Shem, his right hand cupped over the knife in the belt.

Feeling sick, the nun tried to control her trembling limbs. She wondered how close she had just come to death. Shem had been enraged almost beyond endurance, there was no doubt about that. But what had the second Tikopian been doing? Conchita was convinced that he was the same man she had now encountered twice in the ark. She would have to consider matters carefully when she had more time to spare. She started to walk towards the remaining islanders to comfort and reassure them, but they scattered like skittish horses into the trees at her approach.

Sister Conchita took a few steps along the track, begging the islanders to return. She heard approaching footsteps around a tangled corner in the jungle path. Could it be Shem returning to try once more to fetch his former adherents from her mission? Over her dead body, decided Sister Conchita, with a rush of adrenalin.

'I'm not going to move from this path,' she called out, only too aware of the quaver in her voice. 'If you make any attempt to enter the mission, it will be over my dead body!'

'And good afternoon to you too, Sister Conchita,' came a cool, modulated response from the trees.

Unkempt, drenched, sweat-stained and mud-encrusted, Sister Conchita peered through the undergrowth. For the first time since she had encountered Shem that afternoon, she allowed a moan of genuine despair to escape her lips. Rounding the corner was the self-possessed, immaculate and somehow, despite the downpour, apparently dry form of Father Kuyper, the bishop's feared inspector.

10

THE SPIRIT OF THE ISLANDS

The Spirit of the Islands had left Honiara the previous evening and now was only a few miles from Kella's home in the Lau Lagoon. Sitting on the deck next to the wheelhouse, Kella wondered how much it had cost the mysterious Mr Mayotishi to charter even such an admittedly decrepit vessel.

Kella studied the ship around him without enchantment. It was a familiar sight about the islands. He had been a deck passenger on too many of its incarnations to be enthused by the prospect of travelling on the precarious old tub once again, even on the short journey between Honiara and Malaita. Before the war, the ship had been a fishing trawler, until it had piled on to a reef off the island of Santa Isabel and been abandoned by its owner and the surviving members of its crew. It had lain neglected on the coral rocks throughout the war years before, in 1945, an enterprising and bored Australian beachcomber had utilized his sober and sometimes his drunken moments to crudely restore the vessel, using a variety of spare parts cannibalized from ships and vehicles left behind by the retreating Japanese forces, and a few hunks of metal and components stolen at night from neglectful, poorly guarded US bases and dumps.

The resultant hybrid had been surprising seaworthy, and for a time the alcoholic owner had even scraped a precarious and hazardous living delivering supplies and mail to remote plantations, missions and government stations among the islands. Then one night, emboldened by alcohol, he had foolishly tried to outrun a storm on the Weather Coast of Guadalcanal. As a result, *The Spirit of the Islands* had been hurled up on to the shore like a crumpled toy, to join the vast ghost fleet of unwanted sunken and beached Japanese and American vessels now rusting on islands and atolls all over the post-war Solomons.

Yet again a saviour had been on hand to salvage the indomitable ship. A Chinese company based in Honiara had decided to increase its fleet of battered cargo ships collecting copra from the coastal villages. Its engineers paid salvage rates for the tortured assemblage of wood and metal, towed the wreckage to Honiara and set out on the second reconstruction job in its eventful thirty-year history. Once again *The Spirit of the Islands* was hammered and cajoled into a variety of fresh shapes, emerging a little elongated and considerably wider in the beam, as a combined cargo vessel and inter-island ferry boat, with room for forty deck passengers. Below there were three cabins, a stuffy stateroom, a galley, two fairly capacious holds, fuel storage tanks and an engine room with a reconstructed pair of diesel engines.

To the surprise of many, including its owners and crew, the renovated and now extremely ugly *Spirit of the Islands* emerged as a tenacious and courageous battler in the roughest of seas, and had become a familiar sight dragging its rusted carcass around the islands. Today Kella was the only passenger. He had been offered a passage back to Malaita by the ubiquitous Japanese as he left the fishing village the previous afternoon, and had accepted unhesitatingly.

Kella stood up and walked to the ship's rail. In the distance he could make out the reefs surrounding his lagoon. He would spend the night in the *beu* at Sulufou, and then visit the ark early the following morning. He did not expect to find much of use there. From long experience he knew that there were rarely such things as productive crime scenes among the islands. Earlier in the week, when he had visited the sites of the killman's first two murders, not only had both decomposing bodies been buried already, but the areas of the deaths had been trampled by dozens of curious visitors.

He would have to rely upon the evidence of eyewitnesses like Sister Conchita, Brother John and Dr Florence Maddy. Perhaps Shem, the Tikopian, might volunteer some information, but as he was heir apparent to the church, with its presumably munificent coffers, he would hardly be an impartial witness.

'The bosun tells me that we will be putting you ashore in less than an hour,' said Mayotishi, his head emerging above the companion-way. 'Could you spare me a few minutes before then, Sergeant Kella?'

Kella followed the Japanese down the steps into the stateroom. Like Mayotishi himself, the cabin was small and tidy. A table was clamped to the floor in the middle of the room. Mayotishi ushered the sergeant into one of the wooden chairs around the table and took another one opposite him.

'Thanks for the lift across,' Kella said. 'I might have had to wait a week for a boat from Honiara.'

'I'm afraid I had an ulterior motive,' said the Japanese. 'But you will already have guessed that, Sergeant Kella. You have the reputation of being a very shrewd man. You also speak very good English. I believe that you acted as an official interpreter during the war. You must have been very young then.'

'They brought me back from my secondary school in Fiji to help with the liaison between the Americans and the islanders in 1942. I found it boring, so I got a job on a coast-watcher's raiding boat in the Roviana Lagoon.' Kella hesitated, but it was important that the foreigner knew the truth. 'You accused me yesterday of being anti-Japanese. I don't think I am, but I have killed Japanese soldiers.'

'We all did our duty. I did my insignificant share of fighting too.'

'Here in the Solomons?'

Mayotishi shook his head. 'The Philippines,' he said. 'I served on a destroyer.'

'What exactly are you doing in the Solomons now, Mr Mayotishi?'

asked Kella, deciding that it was time to stop pussyfooting around. 'We don't get many tourists on this part of Malaita.'

Mayotishi took his time over replying. He seemed almost embarrassed. When he spoke, he kept his eyes on the table in front of him.

'To be absolutely frank with you, I'm not a tourist, although my visa may say so,' he said. From his wallet he produced a blue embossed warrant card bearing his photograph. 'I'm an official of the Hikiage Engo Kyoku – the Bureau of Repatriate Welfare in Tokyo. It is the duty of my department to investigate reports of Japanese soldiers believed still to be surviving in former Pacific battle areas. I'm here in an official capacity, although I have not yet reported my presence to the authorities in your capital, an omission for which I can only apologize.'

'Aren't you a little late getting here?' asked Kella, while his mind worked on the information. 'The war ended fifteen years ago. Most of the Japanese pulled out in 1943 and went home.'

'Would that that were true,' sighed the Japanese. 'It might surprise you to know that we suspect that even today there might still be dozens of Japanese survivors of World War Two scattered about the islands of the South Pacific. There have been a number of such cases since 1945, I can assure you. My colleagues and I are still coming across troops of the Imperial Japanese Army who do not yet know that the war is over.'

'That sounds rather self-absorbed,' Kella said.

Mayotishi did not react to his tone of levity. 'Let me give you a few examples. On the island of Peleliu in 1947, thirty-four Japanese holdouts actually attacked a peacetime US Marine garrison. Several years later, in 1949, two of our machine-gunners finally surrendered on Iwo Jima. One of our corporals was killed by Philippine soldiers on Lubang in 1954. Earlier this year, in May, Sergeant Tadashi Ito and Private Bunzo Minagawa finally surrendered on Guam. They are just a few of the brave soldiers of the emperor who chose to fight on after 1945. It is the responsibility of my department to find each survivor, inform him of the true situation and bring him home as swiftly and safely as possible.'

'And you think that some of these could be here on Malaita?' asked Kella.

'It is possible,' nodded the Japanese. 'Doubtless you are aware of the rumours to that effect. I am here to enquire into the matter. Often these reports turn out to be unfounded, but sometimes not. It is my duty to carry out a thorough investigation into all aspects of the sightings.'

Kella wondered how Mayotishi could have heard about the Japanese bayonet being abandoned after the attack on the islander in the territory of Basiana. It was a sign of how much money the Japanese government was prepared to back their agent with. Or perhaps it merely indicated how poor most Solomon Islanders were that Mayotishi could afford to recruit a network of spies with such ease.

'And where do I come into this?' Kella asked.

'I've been searching for you rigorously for several days, ever since I arrived in Honiara,' said Mayotishi. 'I need your help, Sergeant Kella.'

'How?'

'The situation is a delicate one,' Mayotishi said. 'As I intimated, there have been examples on other islands in the Pacific of Japanese soldiers actually attacking villages and military installations, under the misconception that they were still fighting in the war. In some cases, unfortunately, there have been deaths. If that happens, we prefer to find our nationals quietly and smuggle them home to save diplomatic embarrassment. In this case, I could hardly conduct an official enquiry with the backing of the Protectorate's officials if, the gods forbid, it was to result in a Japanese citizen being arrested for murder. You can see my dilemma. The presence of the Japanese in these islands is still an emotive matter, as you must know. After all, seven thousand US troops and thirty-two thousand Japanese soldiers were killed in the Solomons in 1942. Nobody knows how many islanders died.'

'Of course they don't,' said Kella. 'Why should they?'

Mayotishi gestured impatiently. 'I didn't mean that their lives were unimportant, just that no records were kept.'

Kella let it go. 'You still haven't told me why you've been looking for me,' he said, although by now he had a pretty good idea.

'Isn't it obvious? I made enquiries and I was told that you were almost certainly the best policeman and tracker on Malaita,' said the Japanese. 'That you knew the island better than anyone else, and that you were a man of influence in the local tribal structure. You are also generally held to be a man of considerable independence of mind. Who wouldn't want to have you on his side? I need you to help me hunt down this killman and ascertain whether or not he is a former Japanese soldier who doesn't know that the war is over. If it transpires that the killer is not Japanese, then you can arrest him in the normal way and take him back to Honiara.'

'And if he *is* Japanese, Mr Mayotishi?'

'Then the matter will be taken out of our hands and transferred to a higher diplomatic level,' said Mayotishi. 'I'm not asking you to hush anything up. I just want the initial stages of the enquiry carried out by an expert, in my presence. I do not come entirely empty-handed. I have chartered this vessel and its crew. I am prepared to put them at at your full disposal if you will use them in the search for this alleged Japanese soldier. I imagine it will be better than trudging all over Malaita on foot.' Mayotishi took a map from a drawer in the table. 'I am told that the island is a hundred miles long and twenty-three miles wide, and that the central jungle is almost impenetrable, with a mountain range rising to a height of three thousand feet. Using *The Spirit of the Islands* will at least provide us with a comfortable and reasonably fast-moving base to take us round the coast. What do you say?'

He looked expectantly across the table. Kella tried to seem inscrutable, although he was probably wasting his time. He had the feeling that he was playing poker against an expert. He had to admit that the idea of conducting an investigation in some sort of comfort and at a reasonable speed for once was a tempting one. On the other hand, Chief Superintendent Grice and the other expatriate administrators were unlikely to look kindly on what was in effect a moonlighting operation on his part, should they find out what he had been doing. However, if eventually the end was to justify the means, that might make up for the trouble he would undoubtedly get into. There was no denying that Mayotishi's proposal might fit in handily with other plans that were beginning to formulate in the policeman's mind.

'The authorities won't like it if I conduct an investigation without informing them,' he said.

'Do the authorities matter?' asked Mayotishi. 'The British won't be here much longer anyway. Soon an independent Solomon Islands will be dealing directly with Japan.'

'You're suggesting that I cut out the middleman,' Kella said. 'Some might consider that a touch premature.'

'The decision is yours,' said Mayotishi. 'The general opinion is that you will be an important man on Malaita when the colonial era ends. That will entail making decisions. Why not get a little practice in now?'

'Only when you start telling me the truth,' said Kella. 'You're not a civil servant. You wouldn't have access to the type of research that would identify me as the *aofia*, or the sort of money that could afford to charter this old tub.'

'What am I, then?' asked Mayotishi

'Intelligence, I'd say,' Kella said. 'Either the Japanese Cabinet Intelligence and Research Office or the Public Security Intelligence Agency.'

'You're remarkably well informed, Sergeant Kella. I was told that you moved in a number of different worlds.'

'Put it down to my diffuse training,' Kella said. 'These days I'm more of a professional student than a policeman. I imagine that you've been sent to keep things smooth in the Solomons. From what I hear, your country is trying to move in to the islands in a big way – fishing, canning, logging. You don't want to run the risk of a half-crazed Japanese soldier running amok and spoiling negotiations. You want to find him and ship him home as quickly and as quietly as you can.'

'No comment,' said Mayotishi. He paused. 'Are you going to report your suspicions to your superiors?'

'I didn't say that,' Kella said. 'I've never been offered a whole boat as a bribe before. I must be moving up in the world.' He stood up. You mentioned three deaths on my island,' he said.

'Of course,' said Mayotishi. 'There were the two villagers and Papa Noah himself.'

Kella hoped that his face was not betraying his feelings. If the head of the Church of the Blessed Ark had been killed as well, the possible repercussions were terrifying.

11

ANOTHER CANOE, ANOTHER SHORE

Sister Conchita cut out the engine of her canoe. She had not been the first to arrive for the funeral of Papa Noah. Already there were several hundred canoes in the lagoon ahead of her, all lying motionless. The armada varied from simple dugouts with a single occupant to large, plank-built craft containing whole families. Apart from the occasional cry of a baby there was no sound on the water. The eyes of all the islanders were on a small collection of rocks rising ahead of them among the larger artificial islands.

A single narrow channel of water had been left between the massed canoes. Sister Conchita paddled down it towards the tiny island known as Foubebe, where she had been told that the burial of Papa Noah was to take place. She could see only three islanders already crowded together on the normally uninhabited patch of rock. It was a few yards across in diameter and consisted of nothing but a small thatched hutch that served as an Anglican church. Two of the waiting men were wearing loincloths. A third, older man was clad in a ceremonial grass skirt, with markings in white lime drawn across his face and body. He was squatting cross-legged on the hard ground, apparently in a trance.

The nun brought her canoe alongside. The islanders on the rock ignored her, but as far as Sister Conchita could make out, they did not look actively hostile. No one offered to help her up on to the island, so she tethered her canoe to an outcrop and scrambled up as best she could, greeting the others as she took her place among them. Although they were pressed together like seeds in a pomegranate, no one bothered to reply. On the far side of the artificial island Sister Conchita could see even more canoes in the lagoon, forming a huge shifting carpet of brown and grey on the water for as far as the eye could make out.

The creepers covering the entrance to the church were brushed clumsily aside and a plump, worried face peered out of the hut. After a pause, unwillingly a fourth man emerged. With something approaching relief, Sister Conchita recognized the latest arrival as Brother Baddeley, a local Anglican pastor who sometimes assisted Brother John in his local missionary duties. He was a small, tubby, inoffensive Guadalcanal man, wearing a tattered brown cassock and carrying a well-used Bible. He nodded to the sister, looked apprehensively at the other hulking Melanesians and in silence led the watchful group in single file round to the back of the church.

Behind the hut lay the body of Papa Noah. His torso had been wrapped in talo bark and sago palm leaves roughly in the shape of a fish, leaving only his head and face exposed. A rectangle of rock on the ground, about six feet in length, had been excavated and replaced with sand to a depth of three or four feet. A hole had been dug in this sand and the loosened material had been placed in a mound running along the sides of the grave. Effortlessly the two younger Melanesians lifted the emaciated corpse and placed it at the bottom of the newly formed cavity. Brother Baddeley looked uneasily at the man daubed with lime, who gave no sign of recognition. The Anglican missionary cleared his throat and began rattling through the burial service.

'*I am the resurrection and the life . . .*' he gabbled in an unnaturally high-pitched tone.

Somehow the squat Guadalcanal man stumbled through the

ceremony, looking up often to glance fearfully at the three islanders on the compacted rocks. Sister Conchita wondered why he was so frightened of the other men. She could only conclude that the painted older one was a custom priest and his burly companions were two of his acolytes. It was accepted that most of the older Solomon Islanders and many of the younger ones followed a tortuous mixture of Christianity and traditional pagan ancestor worship, but she had never before witnessed a funeral service in which both faiths were represented officially at the same time.

Was that why Brother John had asked her to attend? Perhaps he was worried that without an expatriate present, the custom priest would have taken advantage of Brother Baddeley's manifest timidity.

'*Blessed be the name of the Lord,*' the Melanesian Mission representative gibbered to a conclusion. Almost before the words were out of his mouth the custom priest had shouldered the inoffensive Guadalcanal man out of his way. He picked up a length of *taba* wood lying at his feet and placed it over the body of Papa Noah.

'*Noni diena,*' he cried in a piercing eldritch screech heard right across the lagoon, peering into the grave. A collective sigh went up from the distant canoes.

Sister Conchita edged closer to the still petrified Brother Baddeley. 'What does that mean?' she whispered.

'He is welcoming the dead man to the pagan paradise,' muttered the missionary. 'He is telling him that he will soon be going in another canoe to another shore.'

'I thought that was our line,' said Sister Conchita disapprovingly, deciding that it was not her place to interfere, much as she disapproved of the form the strange ceremony seemed to be taking. This was one of Brother John's churches; he should be here to maintain a seemly form of order of service on the island.

Taking his time, the custom priest stepped aside disdainfully. His two followers each picked up a large clam shell from a heap placed by the side of the grave and started shovelling sand from the piles along the side back into the hole. Brother Baddeley made the sign of the cross in the air before him, and ineffectually tried to help, using his bare hands to move the sand. Within minutes the grave had been filled in, without any substantial aid from the Anglican cleric. The custom priest shouldered Brother Baddeley aside again, and the Anglican minister stumbled and almost fell. Sister Conchita changed her mind about interfering. Impetuously she stepped forward to the side of the grave and intoned the Latin prayer for the dead. The words rang out over the lagoon in her small, clear voice:

'*De profundis clamavi ad te, Domine. Domine. Exaudi vocem meam.*'

One of the large Melanesians started towards her, but the custom priest called him back. The old man stared hard at Sister Conchita. She met his gaze unflinchingly. God stay with me now; I know you will, she thought. The custom priest continued to regard her. A flicker of something shaded his rheumy eyes before he turned away. Surely it could not have been respect, thought the nun.

The custom priest leapt into a canoe, followed by the other two islanders, who picked up their paddles. Slowly the massed canoes began to disperse in the wake of the priest's, their occupants paddling away in silence. Soon, as the logjam broke up, most of them were being propelled energetically across the lagoon back towards the main island. Only when the mourners were well away from the small artificial island did Brother Baddeley relax and take out a handkerchief to wipe the sweat from his glistening face.

'What was that all about?' asked Sister Conchita.

Baddeley shuddered. 'Bad magic,' he said fervently. The rotund man was beginning to recover from his fright. 'All finished now,' he said.

'But why were they here?' asked Sister Conchita. 'Did Brother John know that they were going to try to hijack the funeral?'

'Oh yes,' said Brother Baddeley. 'That's why he wanted you to be here. Brother John knew that even the custom priest would not harm a *neenu* under the protection of Sergeant Kella.'

Sister Conchita was aware of a pang of annoyance. She had hoped that she had been invited to the ceremony in her own right, not because the ubiquitous policeman seemed to have taken her under his wing.

'Sergeant Kella has bigger magic than the custom priest,' said Baddeley slightly desperately, as if trying to convince himself. 'Bigger than anybody.'

Sister Conchita looked at the newly filled-in grave. 'What happens now?' she asked. 'Will Papa Noah's body remain here?'

Brother Baddeley shook his head. 'They call this the Big Man's Island,' he told her. 'If a great chief or priest of any tribe or religion dies in Lau, he is buried here on Foubebe. His body lies in the sand for six months. Then it will be dug up. After that his *wantoks* may collect his bones and take them back to bury them in his own village.'

'I can't get over the number of mourners here this morning,' marvelled Sister Conchita.

'They were members of the Lau Church of the Blessed Ark,' Baddeley told her, his plump, guileless face creased with worry lines. 'They were representing many more. It was just becoming an important religion when Papa Noah was killed. It is all very vexatious!'

He shook Sister Conchita's hand and walked back into the church. Sister Conchita turned towards her canoe. She lifted her eyes to the cloudless sky.

'I never doubted for a moment,' she said.

12

THE GAMMON MAN

Carefully Kella steered his dugout towards the artificial island belonging to the Gammon Man. Most of those canoes that had been tethered off Foubebe for the burial of Papa Noah that morning were being paddled away. Across the lagoon he caught a glimpse of Sister Conchita crouched deep in thought over the outboard motor of her canoe as she headed back to Ruvabi, but he made no attempt to attract her attention. He wondered why Brother John had not been present at the ceremony. The Guadalcanal man had been pursuing his own secret agenda lately.

He tethered his dugout to the jetty and climbed up on to the carefully raked and weeded shingle. The island was a small one, designed and constructed for the needs of a single family.

The Gammon Man came out of his house yawning to greet Kella. He was squat, muscular and broad-shouldered, with a wide, bland face and shrewd eyes. He had a large but firm stomach, attached like an extra slab of muscle to his body. 'You woke me up, Sergeant,' he complained mildly. 'What sort of time do you call this?'

'I'm sorry,' said Kella unrepentantly. 'We can't all work gentleman's hours.'

The Gammon Man grunted, unimpressed, and led the sergeant back into the house. Inside it was divided by a partition into a living room and sleeping quarters. In the former there was a wooden table bearing an unlit oil lamp, and several basketwork chairs. There were piles of carefully dusted books, each wrapped in a large protective plastic bag, on mats covering the beaten-earth floor. Kella knew that most of them would contain acknowledgements to the Gammon Man, inscribed gratefully to him by their authors. Usually the islander would take several copies of these books in their transparent wrappings on his travels and display them proudly to all he met, especially expatriates who might be a source of employment.

The Gammon Man's wife, a handsome Lau woman a decade younger than her husband, hurried out of the sleeping quarters. Sinuously she swayed her way to the kitchen attachment. She averted her gaze politely from the visitor as she passed.

'A cup of tea?' asked the Gammon Man. 'Something to eat, maybe? My wife can cook an English breakfast if that's what you're used to these days. Ham and eggs, that sort of thing.'

'No thanks,' said Kella. 'I tend to have my breakfast in the morning. I just want to ask you a few questions about the death of Papa Noah.'

The Gammon Man nodded and pointed to one of the chairs. He sat opposite Kella and regarded the policeman expressionlessly. The Gammon Man's real name was Wainoni. He had received his nickname through his fluency in English, acquired at a mission school, an apparently built-in high degree of self-confidence in his dealings with expatriates, and a matchless ability to lie fluently and expressively about any local topics that interested foreign academic researchers visiting Malaita.

Wainoni had embarked upon what was to become an increasingly lucrative career soon after the war, when his fluency in English had led to his being recruited as a guide by a visiting professor of anthropology. After a cautious start, he had realized that the gullible Australian researcher was prepared to accept as the gospel truth almost everything his loquacious native escort told him, and that it was much easier to make up his own stories about the history and customs of the jungle around them than it was to go to the trouble of visiting inconvenient and possibly dangerous regions of the hinterland to find out the truth. In pidgin 'gammon' meant to lie fluently.

From this relatively inauspicious start, he soon found his reputation growing in the enclosed world of Melanesian scholarship. Soon he was being passed on reverently from one overseas scholar to another like a family heirloom, treated as a source of all indigenous knowledge, as well as being a willing, skilled and apparently fearless bush scout and counsellor.

Less articulate fellow islanders had looked on with increasing awe and wonder as Wainoni had parlayed his linguistic fluency, ingratiating manner and total disregard for the truth into a one-man business. Thesis after published thesis in Australasia, the USA and even parts of Europe owed their inception to his practised guiding hand and utter indifference to reality. No matter how wild or outlandish the theory being pursued by the latest grant-aided university visitor to Malaita, the Gammon Man could be relied upon, for a suitable fee, to provide the so-called facts that would eventually substantiate it in an eighty-thousand-word volume designed to languish neglected in some sunless college library.

'You wouldn't be thinking of spoiling things for me, would you, Sergeant?' asked Wainoni, smiling thinly.

'Hardly,' said Kella with genuine respect. 'You're probably the only Solomon Islander ever to make a decent living out of whitey without actually stealing from him. We've all got to admire real talent when we see it in action.'

Wainoni relaxed perceptibly. 'In that case, how may I help you?' he asked.

'Your latest protégée, or victim, Dr Maddy, was there when Papa Noah was killed outside the ark. How did she get there, and what was she supposed to be doing?'

'That's easy,' the Gammon Man said promptly. 'Dr Maddy is a musicologist. She's come to make a study of pidgin songs about the Second World War.'

'But the Americans and the Japanese hardly touched Malaita,' said Kella. 'Most of the fighting in 1942 was done on Guadalcanal and in the west, hundreds of miles away.'

Wainoni regarded the policeman like a teacher dealing with an obtuse pupil. 'You know that and I know that,' he said. 'Fortunately, Dr Maddy doesn't know it – yet.'

'But it's a matter of record,' Kella said, startled for once out of his equilibrium. 'People have written whole books about the war in the islands.'

'You mustn't believe everything you read,' said Wainoni sententiously. 'That's one of the first things I always tell my clients. Written history is bunk. The truth lies in industrious personal research on the part of conscientious scholars, preferably guided on a previously negotiated daily stipend by me.'

'Of course,' said Kella. 'Forgive me for doubting you. I should have known that you would have given this matter deep and proper thought. So you're helping this misguided young woman to conduct an investigation into something that never happened?'

'Hardly. I'm helping Dr Maddy with her groundwork into the unknown. Isn't that what scholarship is supposed to be about? Anyway, one or two Japanese are rumoured to have taken up residence in hiding on Malaita after the war.'

'Perhaps, but I doubt very much if they had the time or the inclination to compose pidgin songs about their predicament.'

'On the whole, I'm inclined to agree with you,' said Wainoni judiciously, 'but surely that's the point of scientific investigation? Learned people must study these matters, and it is the duty of the less gifted among us to help and guide them according to our abilities.'

'For a fee.'

'Exactly, Sergeant Kella! The labourer is worthy of his hire. You display a unique gift for getting to the heart of a problem. I shall have to watch out. I sense a potential rival.'

'Remind me never to buy Government House in Honiara from

you, should you offer to sell it to me,' said Kella. Negotiating with the Gammon Man was like wading through treacle. 'All right, why did you arrange for Dr Maddy to attend the feast at the Lau Church of the Blessed Ark last week?'

The Gammon Man frowned. 'That was a bit strange,' he admitted. 'Of course I had heard that the celebration was going to include a choir of virgins from the main island singing "Japani Ha Ha!". People passing through the lagoon were talking of nothing else but the church choir practising the *tue tue* dance and then singing that stupid little pidgin song, but it never occurred to me to pass on the information to Dr Maddy.'

'Probably that was because you couldn't think of a way of making a profit out of the transaction. Go on, who *did* take her to the celebration?'

'It was the Tikopian called Shem, the one who claims to be Papa Noah's spiritual heir. Somehow he contacted her and invited her to the feast. I don't know why. I told Dr Maddy that it would be an unprecedented opportunity for her to record "Japani Ha Ha!" and maybe other songs relating to the war. On the day of the ceremony, I took her over by canoe to the saltwater village and delivered her to Shem, who was waiting on the beach. I left them and he accompanied her up to the plateau. The next thing I know, a couple of women from Sulufou brought her back here late that same night. Dr Maddy was in a considerable state of shock, but all she would tell me was that there had been a dreadful accident at the feast. I imagine that she was referring to the death of Papa Noah.'

'And then you washed your hands of her?'

'She had no more call upon my services. I had fulfilled my contractual obligations to the letter,' said Wainoni with dignity.

'But you still did nothing to look after her in her distressed state?'

'It's not my job to protect her,' said Wainoni indignantly. 'I'm not her father!' A spasm of genuine alarm fluttered his jowls. He put a beseeching hand on the other man's arm. 'Whatever you do, don't frighten her away, Sergeant Kella. That woman is a humble businessman's dream. She's got half the dollars from her scholarship grant and weeks of trusting innocence left in her yet.'

'Stop it!' said Kella, rising. 'If I listen to any more of your fraudulence, you'll have me believing that you're as pure as a Sikaiana maiden. Take me to this island for which you are probably charging Dr Maddy an extortionate rent.'

The Gammon Man leered at him. 'It's only fifty yards away,' he said mischievously. 'Why do you need me?'

Kella hoped that his face was expressionless. 'The last time Dr Maddy and I met, it was under slightly unfortunate circumstances.'

Wainoni grinned lasciviously. 'Yes, she told me about that,' he chuckled. 'It's all right, Sergeant Kella. I assured her that to the best of my knowledge you were not a peeping Tom. Indeed, I know for a fact that you have always adopted a more hands-on approach with the ladies. When it comes to sexual encounters, you waste more chances than I've ever had.'

'Are you going to take me over or not?' asked Kella, standing up.

Wainoni looked at his watch. 'She won't be there,' he said triumphantly. 'She said that she was going to Tabuna village at first light this morning to record some pidgin songs from a man who worked for the Americans unloading cargo during the war.' He saw the expression on Kella's face. 'What's wrong with that?'

'Don't you know anything?' asked Kella, heading for the door. 'The men of Tabuna are the laziest on Malaita and a bunch of thieving villains into the bargain. None of them would risk breaking into a sweat unloading cargo, and as sure as your corrupt soul is bound to rot in the deepest pit of hell at Ano Gwou, where it will be condemned eternally to eat the ghosts of your ancestors, not one of them ever went near the war!'

'Is that so?' sighed Wainoni smugly. 'There is so much duplicity around these days. My trouble is that I'm too trusting. Why, sometimes in my darker moments I fancy that some of my informants even lie to me.'

Kella walked back to his canoe, shaking his head resignedly. Think what you liked of Wainoni, you had to admit that he was good at what he did. As he untied his dugout, the sergeant noticed that a small lean-to hut on the island was full of green bananas. For some reason Wainoni had recently started ploughing some of his profits into this usually unprofitable trading venture. He was buying bananas from the bush people and transporting them to the market in Honiara. It was a shrewd enough move, thought Kella. After rice, wheat and corn, bananas provided the most lucrative cash crop in the South Pacific. The only problem lay in the fact that it was proving difficult to export them to overseas markets before they ripened. Perhaps the Gammon Man was planning for the future, the sergeant thought. One day, when Lau had become sated with academics and finally there were no more abstruse subjects to be twisted out of shape and put into books, the venal Wainoni might have to look for a real job.

13

DIFFICULT TIMES FOR THE CHURCH

Later Sister Conchita assured herself vehemently that she had not meant to eavesdrop on Father Kuyper's conversation with the recumbent Father Pierre in the latter's bedroom that morning. She would have done better to stay well away. As it turned out, events were to be even more frightening than the visiting priest's predictions.

She had been about to enter the room to take the old priest's temperature when she heard the august visitor to the mission conversing with the invalid in an unhurried undertone. She paused in the half-open doorway. Father Kuyper was sitting by the side of the bed, talking as much to himself as to the elderly man lying there. Father Pierre's eyes were closed and he was breathing regularly but shallowly.

Sister Conchita was concerned. As far as she could tell, from the occasional snatch of conversation she had caught, for the past few days the Dutch priest had been telling Father Pierre everything about the troubles forming like storm clouds outside the mission. Several times she had heard him discussing the unexplained killings in the district. How much of it Father Pierre was taking in, the nun could not be sure.

'Difficult times, old friend,' murmured Kuyper, his hand clasped over that of the veteran priest. 'There are big changes in store. Pope

John says he wants to open the windows of the church to allow in fresh air. Let us hope that he does not throw them open too wide and admit a tempest! They're already forming commissions to prepare for the Second Vatican Council. How that will affect us in these islands, so far from the centre of things, heaven only knows – literally. One thing is certain, Father Pierre. Whatever happens at these meetings, the Catholic faith as we know it will never be the same again. We must guard the pass – if only we can ascertain where it is situated and with what weapons we have been issued.'

The bishop's inspector looked up to see the nun hovering uncertainly in the doorway. His face betrayed no feeling, although Conchita suspected that he was disconcerted to have displayed such uncharacteristic vulnerability in his recently concluded monologue.

'Come in, Sister,' he said, rising, in control of his emotions again. 'You have your duties to carry out. Don't let me stop you.'

He walked out without looking back. Sister Conchita took the old priest's temperature and smoothed his pillow before leaving. Father Kuyper was standing at the lounge window when she entered the room. 'What is your diagnosis?' he asked.

'Father Pierre has a temperature and is tired, that's all,' said the nun.

'I hope so,' said Father Kuyper abstractedly, without turning round. 'He's not a young man any more.'

'He's fine,' said Sister Conchita in a tone that brooked no contradiction. 'He will soon be ready to resume charge of the mission again, I assure you, Father.'

Father Kuyper almost smiled at the spirited response. He was a slight, silent man in his forties, with a head of cropped yellow hair. He was not given to shows of emotion and maintained a watchful, almost disapproving air to those few aspects of the world that seemed to interest him. He was the principal of a small teacher-training college a few miles outside Honiara. Every six months, forty or fifty students would arrive from rural senior primary schools to undergo a rudimentary course intended to send them back to their home areas as unqualified grade-four teachers. Officially his educational establishment was called Bethlehem, but conditions there were so bleak that it was known as Bush College. Only Father Kuyper's sheer determination and force of will had kept it struggling along for the past few years.

'If you say so, Sister,' he murmured, returning his attention to the compound. He seemed reluctant to leave his vantage point at the window, as if he was waiting for someone. Sister Conchita had noticed the priest operating the mission's two-way radio on several occasions since his arrival.

'This is getting out of hand,' Kuyper said, staring out of the window at the rain sweeping across the ground. Several hundred islanders were huddling for shelter in makeshift windbreaks and hastily constructed canvas tents. Inside the mission house, women and children were camping in every available recess. The noise was indescribable. In the kitchen, half a dozen local sisters were working relentlessly around the clock to provide a steady supply of food for the hordes of visitors now descending in increasing numbers upon Ruvabi. Only this lounge, at Father Kuyper's insistence, had been set aside as a final refuge for the staff of the mission.

'We can hardly turn people away,' said Sister Conchita, again speaking with more emphasis than she had intended. 'They've come here to seek the protection of the church.'

'They've come here because they've been scared by this spate of senseless killings,' said the slight priest. 'Perhaps that's what the deaths are intended to do.'

'Do you mean that someone is murdering people just to frighten everyone?' asked the nun with a shudder. 'That's a horrible thought.'

'It could be worse than that,' said Father Kuyper, knocking the dottle out of his pipe on the lounge table. 'Have you thought that this could be part of a plan to make your parishioners lose faith in the church itself? Indeed, could the murder of Papa Noah have been intended as some sort of a catalyst?'

For once Sister Conchita did not know what to say. In the few days he had been at the station, the bishop's inspector had not conformed to her expectations in any way. For a start, the notoriously direct and energetic Father Kuyper had seemed distracted, as if his mind was on something else. Almost automatically he had collected in her housekeeping accounts and started to study the daily timetable of the mission, but his heart had not seemed to be in either investigation.

Sometimes Father Kuyper had engaged in long, rambling discussions with the older priest, but more often, as Conchita had just witnessed, he seemed to welcome the opportunity to put his own thoughts in order as he talked quietly and insistently to himself in the comatose Father Pierre's presence. She wondered if he had hoped for some sort of assistance or interjection from the older man, and whether she should pass on Father Pierre's cryptic remark about the island of Tikopia being central to what was going on around them. She decided to wait until she had had a chance to talk to Father Pierre again.

'You can't mean that,' she said weakly. 'The church has been preaching the faith on Malaita for a century.'

'And have we done more than scratch the surface?' asked the priest, still looking out of the window. 'Have any of the missions? Most islanders practise the Christian faith only in tandem with their old pagan beliefs. You have cause to know that better than most, Sister Conchita.'

'What do you mean?' asked the nun.

'It is well known within the faith that Father Pierre thinks so highly of your potential that he even encouraged you on one occasion to encounter the so-called Lau gods, to see how you would cope with the concept of many faiths in these islands. Whether he should have introduced someone so young in years and in the doctrine to such a complicated matter is another matter. However, it is certainly a sign of the regard in which he holds you.'

Sister Conchita thought back to the day many months before when Father Pierre had sent her on her own to the remote mountainous Lau settlement outside Honiara. Here she had encountered the girl known as the dream-maker who had enabled her to help Sergeant Kella. She had not known that any other expatriate was aware of that story. However, it was commonly acknowledged that Father Kuyper knew everything that happened relating to the Catholic Church in the Solomons, among its chain of a thousand islands.

'Sergeant Kella is back on Malaita,' she said. 'He'll be looking into the matter, I'm sure.'

'Ben Kella is a very interesting man,' said the priest. 'He was head boy here at Ruvabi mission school some years ago, you know. He is a good detective and a dedicated pagan priest. But we must always remember that he no longer owes any duty to our faith. There is no reason for him to extend us any latitude in the course of his work. In that case he can hardly expect us to bother him with our doubts and fears at this stage. As you intimate, with his track record, Kella will probably discover everything that there is to know soon enough. Still, you're aware of that. You know him better than I do.' He paused. 'Tell me, Sister, is it true that once in order to allow Sergeant Kella to escape from Point Cruz wharf, you created a diversion by taking a group of elderly nuns on to an American cruise ship?'

'The story has grown in the telling,' Conchita said.

'Anyway,' said the priest unexpectedly, 'I've been looking forward to meeting you, Sister Conchita. Although from your name I was expecting, if I may say so, someone perhaps a little more . . . sultry.'

Sister Conchita felt herself blushing. Could the remote Father Kuyper actually be teasing her? Surely not! 'An error of geography,' she said stiffly. 'When I finished my training I thought I was going to be sent to South America, so I selected a name that I thought would be more in keeping with my calling in that part of the world.'

'But they sent you to the South Pacific instead,' said Father

Kuyper. 'Fate can be cruel. Not that there's anything wrong with the name Conchita,' he added.

'It's just that you don't expect it on an irascible Boston-Irish girl only three generations away from her shanty-town antecedents, I know,' said Conchita, walking towards the door.

'There is one thing,' said the priest. 'If it is decided that matters here are becoming unsafe, it might be necessary to send you back to Honiara, until the situation eases. I'm just giving you advance notice. Don't worry. Something miraculous might occur and the trouble will all blow over.'

Sister Conchita resisted the impulse to argue. Was this the thin end of the wedge? Obedience, she told herself; obedience and humility.

'Very well,' she said. 'Now if you'll excuse me, Father, while we're on the subject of miracles, I must attempt to see to the feeding of the five thousand.'

14

WHICHWAY NOW?

After he left Wainoni, the Gammon Man, it took Kella over an hour to reach the saltwater village of Tabuna. He paddled several miles down the Lau Lagoon, between the artificial islands, then made a detour and dragged his canoe up on to the beach a mile to the north of his destination. He hurried into the coastal fringe of trees, so that he would not be observed from the open sea.

As soon as he had rounded the headland in his canoe, he had noticed the government vessel at anchor outside the reef. From a distance it looked like the *Commissioner*, forty feet long, with six cabins and space for eighty deck passengers. Every three months it made a heavily subsidized seven-day trip to the tiny remote island of Tikopia, carrying essential supplies for the Polynesian inhabitants there. Throughout the Solomons, government vessels competed with commercial ones for freight cargoes, generally a source of dismay to the Chinese traders. However, no private vessels wanted the dangerous and unproductive Tikopian run.

A small dinghy, rowed by two Melanesian seamen and containing four bulky lighter-skinned Polynesians perched on top of a pile of casks, was nosing its way into the lagoon through a gap in the jagged coral wall of the reef. Presumably the six men were going to gather water for their long sea voyage, filling their casks from the river skirting the village of Tabuna. The Tikopians were probably passengers going home on holiday after a stint working as labourers on one of the logging plantations in the western islands.

Kella hurried bent double into the trees skirting the beach, hoping that he had not been seen from the rowing boat. He was wearing the red beret of his police uniform, and that was not always a symbol universally accepted by the notoriously rebellious and feckless Tikopians. He found and followed a trampled strand of track leading through the bush towards the collection of thatched huts.

It was strangely quiet among the trees. A narrow overgrown path had been worn away between the haphazard riot of coconut palms, banana plants, canarium and iron trees and the thousands of different weeds and brambles clutching haphazardly at one another and almost blotting out the sun in a great colourful dappled tapestry. Scarlet and yellow orchids sprayed from the branches. Fallen trees littered the path, lying across carpets of scarlet hibiscus flowers, their rotting wood almost obscured by thousands of disciplined marching red and black ants.

Dominating this part of the jungle were the mighty hardwood evergreen banyan trees with their red berries and drooping branches. When these branches touched the ground, they would often take root and form additional reinforcing trunks, so that the trees were growing horizontally as well as vertically in a series of great moss-covered hoops. Because of this constant renewal, the banyan trees were regarded as signs of eternal life. Wherever possible villagers would hold their meetings in their shadows, to guarantee wisdom for their deliberations. Today, however, there were none of the usual urgent hunting parties of men looking for wild pigs, no groups of cheerfully chattering women on the way to their gardens in the clearings along the jungle tracks. Even the birds and animals seemed subdued.

Closer to the houses he encountered a thick curtain of creepers hanging from the upper reaches of the trees. They fell to the mossy ground in great accumulations of green, brown and black. Something among the living trellis looked wrong. Kella stopped for a few moments and tugged thoughtfully at some of the long fronds, gazing up at the higher branches of the trees. After a few minutes he realized what was out of synchronization. Then he continued through the jungle.

He passed the outer circle of huts and emerged in the village square between two rows of thatched homes. Most of the villagers were looking on as a dozen young Melanesians surrounded the six men from the *Commissioner*. The four Polynesians and the two seamen from the government vessel were standing apprehensively shoulder to shoulder on the bank of the river where it widened and slowed down before disgorging its water into the lagoon.

'Whichway now?' Kella asked, using the standard pidgin form of initial police enquiry to ask what was going on. It was a long-held ambition of his to substitute this one day with the phrase 'Hello, hello, hello', which he had admired in the television reruns of *Dixon of Dock Green* on his visit to London.

One of the Tikopians recognized Kella's uniform and cried out unconvincingly in English: 'Help us, Sergeant! They will not let us take water from the river.'

'They are thieves! They will not pay!' shouted one of the village men.

'Guard us while we fill our barrels, policeman,' demanded the Tikopian who had spoken first.

Kella paused, while both groups looked at him waiting for his reaction. Finally the sergeant shrugged indifferently and turned away.

'Beat the crap out of each other if you like,' he said. 'I don't care.'

One of the villagers who could speak English translated for the benefit of his companions. The men around him grunted indignantly and broke into a dozen separate conversations.

'Are you going to allow these strangers to invade our village?' demanded their spokesman.

'Why shouldn't I?' yawned Kella. 'All you're doing is *biboimim*. If I want to see play-acting, I'll go to the Point Cruz cinema and watch John Wayne at work on the screen. Come with me, all of you.'

He walked confidently back into the trees without looking round to see if he was being followed. When he reached the nest of overhanging creepers, he came to a halt. As he had hoped, the men from the ship and the villagers were all at his heels. Behind them most of the women and children from the village were also gathering hopefully, in case the latest visitor to their settlement was about to prove to be some sort of source of entertainment to break up the long, boring day for them.

Kella indicated one of the darker strands cascading to the ground. 'Pull hard on the end of that,' he said in the Lau dialect to the nearest villager, a young, broad-shouldered man. The islander looked frightened and eyed his companions furtively for guidance. Kella transferred his attention to the nearest Tikopian. 'All right,' he sighed, switching to English. 'You do it, then.' The Polynesian shook his head sullenly, his downcast eyes studying the ground with sudden interest. Kella nodded.

'I thought not,' he said. 'You've got some sort of precious cargo stored away up there, haven't you? Something that could break if it was brought down too violently. Bottles of hooch, perhaps? My guess would be Australian whisky from a Chinese store in Honiara. Am I right?'

No one answered. Kella reached out to give the strand a tug. There was a howl of anguished protest from the men in both groups. Kella let go of the creeper and stood back. He looked enquiringly at the group. One of the villagers shuffled forward.

'Mefella fetchim,' he muttered.

For the next quarter of an hour, three of the younger villagers went up the tree from various sides, climbing agilely hand over hand. Each returned from every journey with three bottles of Australian Sullivan's Cove malt whisky cradled compassionately in his arms. After four trips for each man, Kella counted more than thirty full bottles on the ground before him. The villagers and visitors from the ship looked at him like errant schoolboys.

'Let me guess,' said the sergeant. 'You Tikopians came to the end of your contracts as labourers in the Roviana Lagoon or somewhere like that, and invested a chunk of your savings in this whisky in Honiara. You then had it transported by truck along the road to this village, while you travelled down on the government ship. Am I right so far?'

'We have not broken the law,' growled one of the Tikopians.

'Not yet,' agreed Kella. 'That was to come next. You knew that the *Commissioner* would put in here at Tabuna, so you came to an arrangement with the men of the village. They would hide the bottles until you arrived, for a price, and then hand them over to you. You bribed these two seamen from the *Commissioner* and volunteered to come ashore with them, ostensibly to fill the water casks from the river. In fact, of course, you were going to hide the whisky bottles in some of the barrels and smuggle them ashore when you arrived at Tikopia. *That* would be against the law, because the four hereditary chiefs of Tikopia have banned the import of alcohol to their island.'

'You forget,' offered one of the Tikopians hopefully. 'The men of the village threatened to attack us when we arrived.'

'No they didn't,' scoffed Kella. 'Even the peace-loving men of Tabuna would have made a better job of an ambush than the pathetic attempt I just had the misfortune to witness. What really happened was that one of the villagers saw me heading for the village in my uniform and you all hastily concocted the attack story in the hope that I would be fooled and maintain the peace and look on while you loaded the whisky on to the ship.'

There was a pause.

'How did you know about the whisky?' asked the oldest villager.

'Because your work was sloppy,' said Kella. 'You didn't expect anyone in authority to turn up, so you just put the bottles in a fishing net and suspended it from the top branches of one of the trees. However, you had to make sure that you knew which was the right tree among all the others in this wilderness, so you dangled one of the strands of the net to the ground, among all the other creepers. As I walked through the bush, I saw that one of the strands was much darker than the other fronds. When I touched it, I could feel that it was manufactured from nylon, probably in Taiwan, and was not a real creeper. So I guessed that something was being hidden in a net above my head.'

'Are you going to arrest us?' asked one of the Tikopians uneasily.

'Certainly not,' said Kella. 'As I said, you haven't broken any laws yet, and will not have done so until you attempt to smuggle these bottles on board the *Commissioner*.'

Besides which, he thought, there could be another twenty bloody-minded Tikopians involved in the smuggling racket and spoiling for a fight waiting on board the government vessel outside the reef. There was no way in which a single policeman could assert any authority over such a potentially dangerous bunch.

'What will happen to the whisky?' asked a voice from the men from the ship.

'That's the first sensible question I've heard from you. I suggest that you leave it here in Tabuna until you sail back for your next logging job in six months' time,' Kella said. 'You won't make a fortune from it, but you can still have a hell of a party upon your return.'

The Tikopians and the two Melanesian seamen who had rowed them ashore conferred in undertones. The man who had done most of the talking so far stepped forward.

'How do we know that the men of this village will not drink it first?' he asked.

'For two reasons,' said Kella. 'The first is that they are afraid of you Tikopians.'

'And what is the second reason?'

'They're afraid of me, too.'

The Tikopian spoke quickly to the others again and then nodded. 'Very well,' he said. 'We trust you and will leave the matter with you, Sergeant.'

'I'm glad that's settled,' Kella told them. 'Now perhaps I can get on with my real work. I'm looking for the American woman who collects songs. Who can show me where she is?'

The relieved islanders conducted him back to the centre of the village, where the Tikopians and the seamen resumed filling the casks, moving much more swiftly this time. Kella wondered what the villagers had made of the musicologist with her tape recorder. On the whole, the islanders were accustomed to the apparent eccentricities of the occasional touring expatriates and paid little attention to them. In years past, one government geologist had been famed for his proclivity towards teaching bush schoolchildren to sing 'She'll Be Coming Round the Mountain' in Esperanto, while a driven district administrator had spent years constructing a seaplane out of materials jettisoned by the Japanese. When after several attempts it had failed to take off in one of the bays, he had attacked it wildly with an axe and reduced it to matchwood.

Florence Maddy, wiry and alert, permanently ready to go on to the defensive, was standing outside one of the huts with a number of the village women. She was wearing shorts and a T-shirt. She recognized the police sergeant without any obvious sign of warmth, brushing an errant strand of hair back from her face with a nervously trembling hand as she greeted him.

'Sergeant Kella,' she said with a slight nod. 'I believe you're looking for me again. What is it this time?'

The emphasis on the last two words indicated that their last encounter on her artificial island still loomed in her mind. Taking his cue from her brusque greeting Kella got straight down to business.

'I'm investigating the death of the islander known as Papa Noah last week,' he said. 'I believe that you were present at the church feast by the waterfall. Can you tell me what you saw there?'

'Nothing of any help to you in your official capacity, I'm sure,' Florence said stiffly. 'I attended the feast because I heard that the choir would be singing songs of interest to me in my research project. In fact they only sang one such song. Then the storm blew up and some of the women present helped me down the slope to shelter in the village.'

'Did you see anything of Papa Noah during this time?'

'I had spoken briefly to him earlier to express my disappointment that only one pidgin song had been sung, but he seemed preoccupied over some visitor he was expecting. Then the storm came and everything became chaotic. I could hardly see an inch in front of my nose. As I told you, at this juncture some of the local women bundled me away to safety through the storm, and that's all I know.'

'But who invited you to the feast in the first place?' persisted Kella.

'I really can't remember,' said the musicologist. 'Does it matter? Excuse me, I have work to do.'

Reluctantly Kella turned aside. As he did so, he noticed a backpack and several suitcases inside the door of one of the adjacent huts. They were half hidden beneath a number of woven mats.

'Are you going somewhere, Dr Maddy?' he asked.

The musicologist flushed. Too late Kella heard someone walking up behind him. He half turned, instinctively raising his hands to protect himself. Something very hard descended with force upon the back of his head, and suddenly he seemed to be falling forward helplessly into a very deep, very dark and apparently endless chasm. Before he was completely enclosed in darkness, the sergeant thought how misguided he had been ever to turn his back on a group as temperamental as the Tikopians.

15

THE KOROKORO BIRD

Kella wondered how long he had been unconscious. The sun was almost directly overhead, which meant that about an hour had passed since he had been attacked from behind. He heaved himself to his feet and limped down to the water's edge. As he had expected, the *Commissioner* was no longer in sight. The government vessel must have weighed anchor and sailed round the headland while he was lying senseless on the ground. Apart from a few stops to take on water, the ship would be out of touch for the best part of a week on its way to Tikopia.

He turned back and searched the village. It was empty. The islanders would have fled to the safety of the bush after a police officer had been assaulted within its boundaries. It would be several days before they dared to return, if they came back at all. With rumours of the activities of the killman still percolating, many of them might choose the safety of one of the missions in the area. Kella bore them no animosity. None of them would have hit him. It would have been one of the irresponsible, heedless water-gathering Tikopians who would have struck the blow, before fleeing with the others for the safety of the ship, almost certainly taking Florence Maddy with them.

Dazedly Kella wondered what was happening. The musicologist must have gone with the Tikopians of her own free will, or the captain of the *Commissioner* would never have allowed her on board when she arrived with the returning water-gathering party. Anyway, she had packed enough bags for a long voyage, so she must have been expecting to be taken on board the *Commissioner*.

Why on earth would Dr Maddy have wanted to go to the remotest island in the group? The government vessel would not put in at any island containing a radio, so it would virtually be out of touch with the world until it reached its final destination. The ship would have a transceiver, but by the time Kella could get himself back to the police radio service in Auki, the *Commissioner* would have dropped its passengers off at Tikopia and would be making its way back to Honiara. There was no way in which he could get in contact with the ship or Florence Maddy in time to find out what was going on.

Kella tried to go through things in his mind. He had been set up, he was sure of that. All the events leading up to the attack pointed to that conclusion. For some reason of her own, Florence Maddy had made her way to Tabuna to pick up the *Commissioner* and sail on to Tikopia. The Tikopia passengers refilling the water casks at the river had been sent ashore to pick up the musicologist and take her out to the waiting government vessel. But by whom and for what reason? As a subsidiary money-making venture they had also hidden away a cache of whisky to smuggle down to Tikopia from the village of Tabuna. When they had seen Kella approaching, they must have thought quickly and made sure that the strand leading to the net containing the bottles was easy to spot in order to divert him from Florence Maddy. Kella had fallen for the trick and assembled everyone under the trees, thus wasting more time.

While he had been doing this, other islanders had been getting ready to smuggle Dr Maddy out to the waiting *Commissioner*. Unfortunately for them, and for himself as it had transpired, the sergeant had come back to the village too soon, before the musicologist had been able to leave. Someone, presumably one of the Tikopia, had knocked him unconscious, giving the others time to hurry the American academic out to the government vessel.

Kella walked into the jungle. His mind was made up. It was bad enough being fooled in his capacity of policeman; it was much worse seeing the role of the *aofia* being scorned and challenged in the manner that had just occurred, even by a bunch of irresponsible larrikins like the Tikopia. He owed it to the gods and to himself to see that there was payback, and that it was made in full.

He spent half an hour in a small glade, preparing for his next venture. First he said a prayer to the tree gods, before picking up a fallen branch to serve as his sacrificial offering. Then he smeared his face with white clay from the riverbank as a sign to any passers-by that he was about to commune with the spirits and must not be deflected from his purpose by anyone. When he was ready for his great encounter, he started to walk through the trees down to the beach.

On his way down he heard a *korokoro* bird singing up in the higher branches. He took this as a good sign. A single croak from the tiny bird indicated that it would be a bad time to start new ventures, but continual chattering meant that a long and dangerous journey might profitably be undertaken. Close to the shore, a ring of coral stones taken from the beach had been placed around a tree as a sign that a holy shrine lay close at hand on the reef.

Some women from the artificial islands who had climbed the slope to work in their gardens on the mainland had left their canoes on the beach when Kella emerged from the fringe of trees. With one hand he dragged one of the dugouts down to the water and started paddling out into the lagoon.

Shore birds swooped around his dugout as he headed south – white cockatoos, black wagtails, sandpipers, fish hawks and others. They were sensible to spend so much of their time close to land, decided the sergeant. No sane animal or man would embark upon a long sea voyage in the perilous island waters without a strong motive. There were too many things that he still did not know. He would have to take advice from the highest possible source. He did not like bothering the sleeping souls of his ancestors in this fashion, but if a priest could not appeal to the gods, who could?

He paddled for half an hour, until he was approaching the southern end of the lagoon, away from the majority of the artificial islands. There were no other canoes in sight. This was a holy place. Unless an islander had urgent business here, he would pass the area as quickly as he could, averting his eyes from the rocks in the lagoon wall. Eventually Kella stopped paddling opposite a single jagged white rock protruding from the reef. He picked up the branch from the bottom of the dugout and threw it into the lagoon, and watched it float towards the white rock.

'*Lau ann e doo!*' he cried, begging the sacred spirits of the rock to catch his soul and nurture it. This was one of the Lau shrines to the shark gods. Tradition had it that beneath the surface of the water, on the seaward side of the shrine, there was a large cave where dwelt those famous ancestors of his clan who had been rewarded for their mighty deeds on earth by being turned into sharks when they died. No shark-worshipper had ever dared to dive beneath the waves to ascertain the truth of this belief, while any strangers who approached the reef would be killed at once, which was bad luck for anyone from other tribes whose canoes were overturned out at sea and who were swept ashore in the vicinity.

Kella waited for the shark god who supervised deep-sea journeys to faraway places to be roused in order to listen to the *aofia*'s plea. Passively he sat while the god found time to put aside other matters with which he was dealing. Then he implored the spirit to tell him if the gods wished him to travel to Tikopia and save the white woman he had seen leaving on the *Commissioner*. Apologetically he gave the silent, lowering unseen god some background on the case that had brought him into contact with the American musicologist.

'It's like this, Grandfather,' he said humbly. 'There have been three deaths on Malaita over the past few days. The leader of the Lau Church of the Blessed Ark has been murdered and two converts to the sect have also been found dead. Whatever is happening seems to be connected to Papa Noah's breakaway church. The two men murdered in the bush had nothing in common except that they belonged to Papa Noah's sect, and they both drowned in an area in which there was no supply of water. It's all very puzzling. Oh yes, and I've also lost a white woman, a *neena* who should have been under my protection.'

Kella looked hopefully at the rock, waiting for an answer. None was forthcoming. Perhaps the notoriously demanding and indecisive god of the ocean wall needed more information before making up his mind. Kella did not blame him

'The third murder was that of Papa Noah,' he went on. 'He was drowned as well, but in a more straightforward manner. He was knocked on the back of the head and then his face was held under the surface of a rock pool until he died. Did the same man murder Papa Noah who also killed the two men in the bush? Although all three drowned, Papa's death was different because it had no element of magic about it. It was almost certainly improvised on the spot.' Kella paused again. Still there was no response from the reef. The *aofia* decided that he had better keep talking. 'The storm was so bad at the time of Papa Noah's death', he went on, 'that no one could really see what was happening. Sister Conchita thinks that she saw a Tikopian in the ark. Before he died, Papa Noah said that he was waiting for an important visitor, someone who was coming from a long way away. He also said something about becoming rich soon. Oh yes, and as well as that, I've run across a Japanese official called Mayotishi, who wants me to search Malaita in case the killman might be a surviving Japanese soldier.'

Put like that, it sounded even more confusing. Kella hoped that the shark god was making more sense of it all than he was. But he had started now, so he had better continue.

'Shem, the second in command of the ark, who had most to inherit from the old man's death, claims to have been busy guiding frightened women and children down to the safety of the village. The truth of the matter seems to be that almost anybody who wanted to could have crept up behind Papa Noah at the height of the storm and killed him. Oh, and I haven't mentioned any of this to Superintendent Grice or the government authorities. They don't even know about the killman yet. I've only just had time to tell you.'

The sergeant had to admit to himself that his actions over the past week did seem pretty amateurish, and definitely career-threatening. This time Kella gave the god of the reef several more minutes in which to cogitate and come up with an answer. The waves continued to lap lethargically. A breeze carried several small relaxed soaring birds out to sea, like shuttlecocks driven with long, lazy strokes through the air.

'The person who worries me the most', Kella ploughed on, 'is the white woman, Dr Maddy. She seems ordinary enough, highly strung, single-minded, wrapped up in her research. She was at the feast, where she had a row with Papa Noah because he wouldn't let the choir sing any more songs. What happened to her when the storm started is a bit confusing. She claims that she went straight down the hill to the village, but no one has been able to confirm that yet.'

Several bottlenose dolphins made their way languidly into the lagoon through a gap in the reef wall. They lifted their snouts and opened their mouths in their trademark inane grins. Kella sat still. He was a shark-worshipper, but dolphins also had their adherents, which made their presence in the shark lagoon puzzling. The two blue-grey mammals altered course and started nosing at Kella's canoe. They withdrew and then launched themselves at him with greater force, like enormous torpedoes. The dugout rocked and almost went over.

Kella made no attempt to right it. He dared not pit his strength against the power of the spirits, even if these were ones he did not worship. All the same, he knew that one more attack from them would smash his flimsy craft. At last the dolphins seemed to sense that they were approaching a human domain. Banging their tails against the water, they turned and dived back to the comparative safety of the open sea. Kella did not follow their progress with his eyes. The last warning joust had spun his canoe completely around, so that he was facing the shore. A plump middle-aged islander with a sweet, innocent face and wearing only a loincloth was walking along the beach. He had a small woven bag suspended from one shoulder and was carrying a long pole. The man stopped for a few seconds, watching the dolphins cavorting out of the lagoon into the endless sea. Then he turned his attention to Kella and nodded. The *aofia* raised a hand. The plump man continued on his unhurried way, heading south. With a few strokes of his paddle, Kella turned the canoe back to face the shrine.

'It's Dr Maddy that I've really come to see you about,' he said, returning to the reef god, shaken more than he cared to admit by his fleeting encounter with the walker on the shore. The place was getting positively crowded with spirits. 'For some reason that I can't fathom, she's gone to Tikopia. She was helped on her way by a group of Tikopians who knocked me unconscious. When I came round, she was already on her way there.' A large wave hurdled the top of the reef and churned in a foaming, disgusted mass in front of his dugout. Pieces of debris floated forward from it shyly, as if being offered at a market by a tentative salesman. 'Yes, I know,' muttered the shamefaced sergeant. 'You don't have to tell me. I should have been more alert. You don't want your priests getting you a bad name because of their sloppiness. Is that why the dolphins have just been threatening me on your behalf? Anyway, it's done now, and I'm sorry. What I want to know is what should I do next? Why has Dr Maddy gone to Tikopia? Will she be safe there? Above all, should I try to get down there to fetch her back? She is a *neena* and so under my sworn protection. But if I spend a long time getting to Tikopia, what might the killman get up to here on Malaita? Is it fair to persuade Mr Mayotishi to take me all the way down to Tikopia in the ship he's hired? And there's always the possibility that if I stay away too long, even the whiteys in their offices in Honiara will notice that something is wrong. They'll come blundering over from Guadalcanal and stir up all sorts of trouble. Please, will you give me a sign as to whether I should try to get to Tikopia or not?'

For a long minute nothing happened. Then, although the surface of the water had returned to its former state of smoothness and Kella had made no movement, his canoe started to rock gently from side to side. The swaying continued for some time. Then the dugout was still again. Kella bowed his head. If the *agalo geu*, the spirit of journeys, did indeed wish him to travel so far, then he was assured of a certain amount of protection.

Unless, of course, the pagan gods of Tikopia were stronger than the Lau spirits, thought Kella as he paddled back to the main island. He wished that the ocean-reef god had been more forthcoming. The *agalo geu* had certainly given the sergeant permission to travel across the great sea, but it had displayed remarkably little enthusiasm for the whole venture, and the dolphins, on their unusual visit to the lagoon, had demonstrated outright hostility to him. Added to which was the appearance of the walker on the shore.

If there was one thing that worried Kella, it was the sponsorship of a silent and therefore presumably dubious god.

16

FORCE MAJEURE

It was quite late at night when Father Kuyper sent for Sister Conchita. She had been sitting with the sleeping Father Pierre in his room, occasionally mopping the perspiration from the old man's brow and struggling not to fall asleep in her chair by his bed. Occasionally Father Pierre would mutter something incoherent. She would lean forward to try to hear him, but she could catch nothing but the odd meaningless word.

After she had been summoned by one of the local sisters, Conchita picked her way along the crowded corridors of the mission, stepping over the sleeping bodies of the islanders who had crept inside the building for warmth once darkness had fallen. She knew that outside in the compound, hundreds of shadowy figures would still be moving around as the refugees prepared for the night.

When she entered the lounge, she was surprised to see Sergeant Kella sitting with the priest. The policeman seemed embarrassed at her presence and did not meet her eyes or return her nod of greeting.

'Do we really need the sister here?' he asked in a low tone. 'This is a delicate situation. The fewer people involved the better at this stage. No offence, Sister Conchita.'

'None taken,' replied the nun impassively. She had not often seen Kella ill at ease like this. It was an oddly satisfying sight. It would do the normally omniscient policeman no harm to squirm, even if she could not yet discern the source of his mortification. She decided to turn the screw just a little

'You're quite a stranger, Sergeant,' she said. 'Will you be off on your overseas tours again soon?'

'Alaska, they tell me,' grunted Kella.

Sister Conchita widened her eyes theatrically. 'Alaska?' she repeated. 'Very cold, I believe. Well, they say that travel broadens the mind.'

'I have asked Sister Conchita to join us this evening because I need her input,' said Father Kuyper, ignoring the interchange. He gestured the nun to an adjacent hard-backed chair. 'I'm a stranger to this part of the Solomons, and poor Father Pierre is too ill to be of much use to anyone, despite his experience. He keeps drifting in and out of a coma. In the short time that I have been at Ruvabi, I have had time to see Sister Conchita at work and to get to know her a little. She has been here less than a year, but it's evident that already she has immersed herself in the lives of the islanders in her pastoral care. In this case I have decided to rely upon her undoubted talent for observation.'

'*Force majeure*,' murmured Sister Conchita. Father Kuyper raised an impatient eyebrow. 'In the country of the blind the one-eyed nun is queen,' she elaborated hastily.

'Thank you, Sister, but the repetition of several hackneyed shibboleths was not the sort of contribution I was hoping for on this occasion,' Father Kuyper snapped.

The nun muttered an apology, then darted a dark glance at Kella when the police sergeant snorted in amusement in the stillness that ensued. She ordered herself to keep quiet. Father Kuyper's recent grudging accolade had been about the only kind words she had received from the priest since his arrival. Perhaps that was because she had not yet deserved his praise, nor anyone else's, she admonished herself.

'Perhaps you would like to tell us the purpose of your visit this evening and give us your take on current circumstances, Sergeant

Kella,' said the priest. 'You usually manage to surprise me. Why should tonight be any different?'

Kella nodded. He had been prepared for this, although he had hoped to avoid the involvement of Sister Conchita. She had a knack for getting to the crux of any problem with an objective directness that could be unsettling. Plus she usually managed to infiltrate herself into any situation she regarded as interesting, no matter what inherent dangers might be in the offing. He started to pick his words with care, aware of the calibre of Father Kuyper's highly attuned antennae.

Kella was one of the few people outside the church hierarchy who was aware of the Dutch priest's position in the local church. Kuyper had a honed intellect. He had worked for five years in the Vatican for the Congregation of the Doctrine of Faith before coming to the Solomons. It had soon become common practice for him to be used by his South Pacific superiors for any complex task requiring mental dexterity and utter discretion. He was known to the irreverent, and indeed to many of the reverent, as the bishop's fixer.

'In the past week or so, three members of the Church of the Blessed Ark have been murdered,' Kella said. 'As you know, this has caused a great deal of upheaval in the Lau district and beyond. Many of the islanders are terrified at the prospect of a professional killman being on the rampage. One of the chiefs has even used the phrase *vautuutuni oka.*'

'You must bear with me,' said Father Kuyper coldly. 'I don't speak the local dialects.'

'*Vautuutuni oka* means a religious war.'

Two tiny red spots glowed like hot coals on the priest's pale cheeks. He grew tense. 'I find that hard to believe, Sergeant Kella,' he said. 'Very hard indeed. Go on!'

Carefully Kella gave his now attentive audience an edited version of what he had discovered or assumed over the last few days. For some reason he did not mention his encounters with Mayotishi, the Japanese official. As a general rule he preferred to keep at least one card up his sleeve in any dealings with expatriates. He had learned that most of them had their own built-in forms of deviousness.

'Hmm,' said Father Kuyper non-committally when the policeman had finished. 'It certainly looks very much as if everything is centred on this Blessed Ark cult. Sister Conchita, I understand that you were present at the feast at which Papa Noah was killed. You'd better tell the sergeant what you saw there.'

In as few words as possible, Sister Conchita recounted all that she could remember about the details of the bizarre afternoon in the storm at the feast by the waterfall. When she had finished, Kella leant forward.

'The Tikopian you saw in the ark and again briefly in the mission grounds, could it have been Shem, Papa Noah's assistant?' he asked.

'No, I'm sure it wasn't. I only caught a couple of glimpses of the second man, but I'm sure that he was older and taller than Shem.'

'Could you tell me about the knife he was carrying?'

The nun did her best to describe the fearsome-looking weapon she had glimpsed so briefly.

'It could have been a Japanese bayonet, I suppose,' Kella said.

'It could have been practically anything,' snorted Father Kuyper. 'Please don't twist the facts to fit in with any theories you may be developing, Sergeant. Do you have anything further for the sister?'

Kella shook his head. 'No, I don't, not at the moment,' he said, sitting back.

'There is one other thing,' Sister Conchita said. 'I don't know if it's relevant.'

Trying not to be intimidated by her two listeners, the nun described the incongruous joint efforts of Brother Baddeley and the custom priest to provide a joint burial service for the old man on the artificial island. As she spoke, Father Kuyper's expression grew more and more sombre.

'At last, something reasonably relevant,' he said when she had finished. 'What do you make of that, Kella?'

'It seems pretty certain that the Church of the Blessed Ark is a bit of a mishmash of beliefs,' said the sergeant slowly. 'They've taken bits and bobs from a number of sects, including several pagan ones, as well as Christianity. As a result, it looks as if the Melanesian Mission and the custom people were both struggling to claim Papa Noah as one of their own at his funeral.'

'Nothing unusual about that,' commented Father Kuyper. 'As I was telling Sister Conchita, Christianity and the pagan faiths have been competing in this area of Malaita for almost a hundred years.'

'You're right, there isn't. But judging from the sister's account, the Lau Church of the Blessed Ark is a flourishing concern. To be able to fill most of the lagoon with the canoes of the mourners, well, I've never seen anything like that. So we have a new, independent cult with a lot of adherents and quite a bit of money, from what I've heard. And suddenly it's thrown out of balance because its leader has been murdered.'

'And what do you think are the implications of that?' asked the priest.

'It depends on who the new sect leader is going to be. It looks as if Shem is making a bid, and there are probably others with the same ambition, including this mysterious visitor who was due to turn up at Papa Noah's last feast, before the old man was murdered. Was he the same man Sister Conchita saw in the ark that afternoon? If there are a number of candidates wanting to become the next head of the Church of the Blessed Ark, they might be trying to outdo one another to impress the members. That may have been why Papa Noah was murdered in the first place.'

'Do you also think that this is why the would-be new high priest might have killed two other members of the sect recently?'

'I don't know what to think,' Kella confessed. 'It's certainly a possibility. If you ask me, at least one of the candidates for the job is a zealot who is prepared to start a religious war between Christians and pagans in the Lau area. We've got to stop that before it gets out of hand.'

'How do you propose to do that?'

Kella hesitated. 'It seems to me that the answers to a lot of the questions we're asking are to be found on the island of Tikopia,' he said. 'The Blessed Ark cult has a large number of Tikopians in it.'

'That's just what Father Pierre thinks!' burst out Sister Conchita before she could stop herself. She was aware of Father Kuyper's disapproving glance and clasped her hands demurely in her lap, determined again to say no more unless she was asked.

'There isn't much that the father doesn't know about Lau,' nodded Kella. 'He probably understands more about the sect and its members than I do. From what I can see, the Church of the Blessed Ark has a number of connections with the island. There's Shem, for a start, and the man that Sister Conchita caught a glimpse of before she discovered Papa Noah's body. He was a Tikopian.'

'And Shem ran away to hide in the bush outside the mission when he saw another Tikopian,' said Sister Conchita, unable, despite all her efforts, to adhere to her self-imposed silence for more than a minute.

'What about Dr Maddy?' asked Father Kuyper. 'Where does she come into this?'

Kella shrugged. 'She certainly seemed interested in the Church of the Blessed Ark,' he said. 'She was recording music at the feast and she appeared to have struck up some sort of relationship with Shem. Later, she seemed to go to a great deal of trouble to get herself to Tikopia. She was assisted in her endeavours by the group of Tikopians going home on the *Commissioner*, as I found out to my cost. I've got to get down to that island and make sure she's all right. At the same time I can try to find out if the events surrounding Papa Noah's sect had their origins on Tikopia. After all, they were still having disputes there between the pagans and the Christian converts up until a few years ago.'

'How do you intend getting there?' asked the priest. 'There won't be another government ship going to the eastern islands for three months at least.'

'I think I can handle that,' said Kella, avoiding giving a direct answer. 'I've got to find Brother John and take him with me as well. The Melanesian Mission runs the Anglican Church on the island, and they'll need to be kept in the picture. Anyway, Brother John's a useful guy to have around if there's a likelihood of trouble.'

'What puzzles me', said Sister Conchita, who was following her own train of thought, 'is why Brother John didn't attend Papa Noah's funeral himself.'

'He certainly must have had urgent reasons not to be there,' said Kella. 'I think Brother John probably knows more about this affair than he's letting on.'

'Perhaps,' said Father Kuyper. 'We all have our secrets; even you, Sergeant Kella.'

'And perhaps you, Father Kuyper.'

Suddenly there was more testosterone in the lounge than in a boxing ring, thought Sister Conchita. Rashly she tried to defuse the situation by bringing the combined wrath of both antagonists down upon her own head.

'May I make a suggestion?' she ventured. Father Kuyper nodded. 'Why don't I go down to Tikopia with Sergeant Kella?' she asked.

'Certainly not,' said Kella immediately.

Bad move, thought Sister Conchita with subdued triumph. As things stood at the moment, anything meeting with the policeman's disapproval might automatically recommend itself to the bishop's visitor. She waited for Father Kuyper's response. The priest raised his eyebrows.

'Why should you do that?' he asked.

'If the source of the religious strife is on Tikopia, a representative of the Catholic faith ought to be there with Sergeant Kella and Brother John,' said the nun. She thought before she went on, wondering if she was going too far. 'There's something else as well.'

'Go on,' said Father Kuyper.

'You told me some time ago that you were worried about my

presence at the mission,' said Sister Conchita. 'You said that you were considering sending me back to Honiara for my safety's sake. Why not send me to Tikopia with Sergeant Kella instead? I'd be safer there than I would be at Ruvabi under the present unsettled conditions, and I might be of some use reporting back to you at first hand about what's happening down there.'

Father Kuyper was beginning to nod judicially. Sister Conchita waited for Sergeant Kella's detonation of protest. It came almost at once.

'That's out of the question,' said the sergeant.

'Well, if I'm not wanted . . .' said Sister Conchita, judging that this should spur Father Kuyper into a suitably inflamed response.

She was right. The priest waved them both into silence and stood up with a briskness that brooked no interference. 'I admit that I am sceptical about the possibility of a religious uprising,' he said. 'However, as I am in charge at Ruvabi during the illness of Father Pierre, I must take into account the sergeant's advice. You may well be right in your assumption about Tikopia being the centre of all that is going wrong at the moment. We won't know until you've been down there to see for yourself. But this is more than a criminal matter; it's a religious one as well. You are, forgive me, a pagan, Sergeant. It's important that you be accompanied by Christians on your mission. As you say, you ought to find Brother John and persuade him to represent the Anglicans. Sister Conchita, in this case you must be the bishop's delegate.'

'It might be dangerous,' Kella warned desperately, although he could sense that beneath her impassive countenance the nun was thrilled at the prospect of the proposed action.

'It is also vitally important that the Christian faith be preserved on Malaita. Sergeant Kella, I guess that you are operating on your own in this matter, as usual. Would I be correct in assuming that you have not informed your superiors of your intention of going to Tikopia?' Kella did not answer. A grimace of satisfaction creased Father

Kuyper's face. 'Exactly,' he said. 'Well, if you are not accompanied on this expedition of yours by two adherents of different Christian faiths upon whom I can depend, namely Sister Conchita and Brother John, then I shall be forced to radio Honiara and inform the police authorities of your intentions. I imagine that you will be recalled to the capital at once.' He raised a hand. 'Enough!' he said sternly. 'There is no more to be said on the matter.'

For a minute or so Sister Conchita had been aware of a disturbance in the mission compound outside the lounge window. Now the confused babble swelled to screams. The nun wondered if a few of the islanders could be engaged in some incongruous ritual. She stood up and moved towards the door of the lounge to look into the cause of the sudden disturbance. Before she could go out, she heard the outer door of the building being thrown open and then two sets of heavy footsteps thudding along the corridor towards them. The lounge door hurtled open, and two big men staggered into the room. One of them was Brother John. The missionary was supporting Shem the Tikopian, who was bruised and bleeding.

Sister Conchita hurried over to inspect the injury. Father Kuyper got to the reeling Polynesian before her and helped Brother John lower the Tikopian into a chair. Shem seemed dazed. Father Kuyper examined him quickly.

'It doesn't look too bad,' he told the nun. 'Let's take him over to the hospital, just to be on the safe side.'

The priest and the nun supported Shem out of the lounge. Brother John made as if to lumber after them, but Kella put a restraining hand on his arm.

'He'll be looked after,' he said. 'Sit down and tell me what happened.'

'There's nothing much to tell,' said the missionary, sinking into one of the armchairs. 'I was walking along the track in the dark and I heard the sounds of a struggle ahead of me. Then I saw that Shem was fighting another Tikopian. The attacker ran off into the bush when he saw me coming. I brought Shem here to get patched up.'

'Where was Shem going?'

'I don't know. If you ask me, he was probably coming to the mission under the cover of night to persuade some of the members of his cult to return to the ark.'

'Did you recognize the attacker?'

'No, except, like I said, that he was a Tikopian.'

'Do you think it could have been the killman?'

'Who knows? You know what things are like all over north Malaita. Anybody who shoves somebody else in a queue at a trading post is accused of being the murderer these days. If you ask me, this looked like a good old-fashioned knock-'em-down-and-drag-'em-out fight to me, not an attempt at an assassination.'

This was not good, thought Kella. There was no point in continuing to question Brother John. Kella was more convinced than ever that the wandering Anglican preacher knew more than he was admitting about a lot of things.

'Let's see how Shem is getting on,' he said.

The two men left the mission building and crossed the compound. Word of the attack on the Tikopian had spread. Most of the islanders claiming sanctuary at the station had woken up and were standing talking agitatedly. Kella noticed how shabby and dilapidated the mission looked after only a few days. Coping with several hundred itinerant islanders had taken its toll on the fabric of the building. When he had been a student here twenty years ago, the place had shone like a polished pearl necklace.

Kella and Brother John entered the hospital building. Shem's wounds had been treated, and the big man was looking much better.

'Don't tell me,' Kella said to Shem resignedly. 'You saw nothing and you've no idea who attacked you.'

'It's the truth,' said the Tikopian aggrievedly. 'Somebody jumped out of the bush and started hitting me. I fought back, but if Brother John had not come along, I would have been hurt.'

'Of course I believe you,' Kella told the Tikopian sceptically. The sergeant had to admit that he could not fathom Shem. Most of the time he was sure that the big man was just another happy-go-lucky Polynesian, living strictly for the day. Yet Shem had got himself involved with the Church of the Blessed Ark and might even have been implicated in the death of Papa Noah. It all seemed so out of character. Was there a darker side to the man than was obvious on the surface, or had he just suddenly found himself out of his depth?

'Anyway, I've got news for the pair of you,' Kella told Brother John and Shem. 'I'm going down to Tikopia to make sure that Dr Maddy is all right. At the same time I want to find out if the killman is linked with Papa Noah and the Church of the Blessed Ark in some way, and why so many Tikopia are connected with the cult. I suspect that you both know far more about this connection than you're letting on, but for some reason neither of you is telling me what you know. All right, this is what I'm going to do. I'm taking the pair of you down to Tikopia with me, so that I can keep an eye on you and find out what you've really been up to. Or we can all wait here while I send for a police patrol from Auki and lock you up in the cells there until I get back from the outer islands. Which is it going to be?'

Neither of the men he was addressing seemed thrilled by the alternatives put before them so bluntly. Shem shuffled his feet and looked at the ground. Brother John scowled, his habitual affability wiped away for the moment as if by a sponge.

'What grounds have you got for arresting me?' he asked.

'Delivering tedious sermons at inordinate length, for starters,' Kella said. 'I'll think of something better later. Well?'

Brother John hesitated, and then nodded. 'But I'm only coming because I want to know what's happening to our mission on Tikopia,' he said. 'Otherwise, you'd better double the usual size of that police patrol you're going to send for if you hope to get me inside a cell.'

'Whatever,' said Kella. 'Shem, how about you?'

Shem shuffled his enormous bare feet. 'I have much to do at the church here on Malaita,' he said.

'You won't be able to do it from Auki police station, that's for certain,' said Kella. 'At the moment, that's your only other option.'

'In that case, I'll come with you,' Shem said fatalistically. 'After all, I haven't been home for five years.' He stretched and yawned.

'Keep still!' ordered Sister Conchita. She threw a swab into a waste basket. 'There, that's finished. You can sit down, while I look for beds for the night for you and Brother John.'

'Why would the killman want to attack me?' Shem wondered aloud.

'It was dark,' said Kella. 'Perhaps he was waiting for Brother John instead.'

As she hurried across the compound on her errand, the nun wondered why Father Kuyper was so keen on sending her to Tikopia with Sergeant Kella and Brother John. Was he really entrusting her with representing the Catholic faith on that faraway island, could he be concerned about her safety on Malaita, or was there some other reason for his behaviour? She also thought about Sergeant Kella. She had practically invited herself on the trip to Tikopia. How would the witch-doctor policeman react to that?

17

LANDFALL

Dozens of canoes were putting out from the shore of Tikopia as the government vessel *Commissioner* dropped anchor in the harbour. Islanders were already scrambling up the rope ladders dropped over the sides and swarming all over the decks, animatedly greeting those friends and relatives who were returning from work on the plantations of Malaita, Kira Kira and the Russell Islands.

Florence Maddy stood on the main deck of the passenger boat, her baggage at her feet. It had been a strange voyage. Ever since she had left Malaita, she had been the only white person on board. The Tikopians around her on the voyage had been perfectly friendly but had maintained a discreet distance as she had sat reading the long hours away in a deckchair in the bows of the ship. Even when she had tried to talk to some of the children on board, they had scampered off giggling, hiding behind their mothers' skirts.

She remembered with envy the Roman Catholic Sister Conchita just before the dreadful storm at the feast of the Church of the Blessed Ark. Compact, attractive, self-possessed and comfortable with herself, the nun had seemed capable of talking to everyone she met without a trace of condescension. Compared with Conchita Florence guessed that she must have resembled a tongue-tied country cousin from a particularly remote village in the Ozarks. Still, the nun would probably not know too much about the critical theory of Theodor

Adorno. Nor would she want to if she had any sense, thought Florence.

Again she wondered if she had made a mistake in embarking on such a speculative trip at short notice. It was true that she had been getting nowhere with her research on Malaita, but had her sense of desperation motivated her to jump out of the frying pan into the fire by coming to this lovely but isolated island? Back at the Department of Fine Arts at her university, it had seemed such a good idea when her trip to the Solomons had first been mooted. After all, how much was known at first hand about the music of the Pacific? Jane Freeman Moulin of the University of Hawaii had studied in the Marquesas, and David Fanshawe had used the University of the South Pacific as a base for his indigenous recordings in Fiji, but still there had seemed much more scope for study in the region.

That was before she had grown to appreciate the difficulties of communication among the islands, the vast distances to be travelled at a snail's pace under the broiling sun and the constant damage caused by the heat and rapacious insects to her recording apparatus. As she checked that her tape recorder was at her feet with the rest of her baggage, a hand was placed on her shoulder. Florence looked up to see a tall, lean, grey-haired Tikopian standing next to her. He stooped and picked up her grips, walking off with them to the ship's rail. Florence dithered and then scuttled helplessly after him.

'I'm Dr Maddy,' she gasped to the man's back as he shouldered his way to the side of the vessel. 'Have you come to meet me?'

The tall man did not answer. He dropped Florence's baggage over the rail to a couple of islanders waiting below in a canoe at the side of the *Commissioner*. Then he gestured to the musicologist to climb down the rope ladder into the canoe, and followed her down into the swaying dugout.

As soon as Florence and the tall man reached the canoe, the other men started paddling towards the shore. They moved at an angle to most of the other canoes, which were heading for the nearest beach.

121

Florence sat in the prow of the dugout, clutching the sides as the craft skimmed across the surface of the lagoon towards an expanse of white sand a mile or so to the west of the main landing area. Reaching their destination, the islanders who had been paddling dragged the canoe up on to the isolated shore. Florence climbed out uncertainly. The three islanders who had brought her ashore picked up her grips and gestured to her to follow them at a run across the beach.

They kept moving at a fast pace until they reached a group of trees at the edge of the sand. A group of four women wearing only tapa cloth skirts were waiting there. They took Florence's bags from the men and hurried on ahead, while the three men fanned out watchfully as they loped through the undergrowth.

'Where are you taking me?' gasped Florence.

No one answered her until they reached a small village in a clearing. Without pausing, the group hurried towards a thatched hut at the end of the single row. The grey-haired man threw open the door and indicated that Florence should go inside.

'Quick time!' he urged.

Florence stumbled into the solitary room. The women put her bags on the floor and hurried out. The musicologist turned to ask the grey-haired man what was happening, but saw that the single room of the hut was now empty. She hurried towards the door. It swung shut on her. At the same time she heard a heavy bar being slotted into place across the entrance. In vain she tried to force the door open. It would not move.

Florence started to scream.

18

PAYBACK

The moon was rising over the lagoon and the coastal fringe of mangroves with their tortured exposed roots on the main island of Malaita. The killman lay among the trees, his eyes fixed on his target. He could hear the bullfrogs croaking hoarsely in the undergrowth. He had been lying there for several hours on a patch of mauve and scarlet bougainvillaea, as the twilight had shaded into darkness. Now it was so cool that he was no longer sweating. Automatically he checked his weapons again: the bolt-operated Arisaka rifle loaded with a clip of five rounds and bearing the impression of the chrysanthemum with sixteen petals, the symbol of the emperor. Attached to his webbing belt he carried a Type 30 bayonet in a frayed scabbard, and four Type 97 hand grenades. Carefully wrapped in palm leaves in the canvas pack on his back were four sticks of dynamite.

He could see no one, but he knew that the enemy lay before him. They were always there, pretending to go about their everyday business but constantly on the lookout for him. By ignoring him they hoped that he would go away, never to encroach upon their comfortable lives again. He would never do that. On Malaita he was as permanent as a conscience. What once had been for him little more than a task to be endured had developed over the years into a nurtured, hatred-fuelled and inescapable mission.

He checked again that he had done everything correctly. He had hidden his canoe securely in the undergrowth a hundred yards up the beach. He had skirted the still almost deserted village and had climbed the path to his target, stopping every few yards to ensure that he was alone. He had chosen his position among the trees and waited for several hours. In all that time no one had appeared within his line of vision. He had found his objective, conquered the terrain and outflanked the enemy. All that remained now was to breach and destroy the obstacle.

The killman decided that the time had come. In his mind he went over the three main duties of a lone infantry raider: to surprise and confuse the enemy, to ransack the location and to destroy goods. He wished, as he always did on such occasions, that he possessed the luxury of the firepower and personnel of a typical Japanese squad at its peak: the machine-gunner, the sniper and the light mortar carrier. He remembered the final instructions to any infantryman: to close with and destroy the enemy.

He muttered the mantra of the survivor – 'You must leave your farms and become soldiers' – then picked up his rifle and ran across the intervening ground towards his destination. He reached the building and kicked open the door. He paused, took out a torch, switched it on and placed his rifle against the wall. Then he removed the four sticks of dynamite from his backpack and deposited them along the length of the construction. He had visited it several weeks ago and knew exactly where to place them. He lit the fuses, retrieved his rifle and ran back towards the shelter of the trees.

The dynamite exploded as he reached the edge of the jungle. From some distance away he could hear the shouts of startled men and women in the village below. The killman leant his rifle against a tree and scooped up the first of the percussion-initiated grenades he had left there on the ground. He tapped it on the trunk of the tree and lobbed it across the intervening ground into the heart of the blazing construction. He followed it with the three remaining grenades, each delivered accurately and exploding with a yellow flash, adding to the general conflagration. Then he turned and hurried away through the trees.

19

THE MONKEY ISLAND

Kella was waiting as darkness began to fall over the endless sea. He had been biding his time for the entire five days of the voyage, ever since *The Spirit of the Islands* had left Malaita. Casually he made a play of checking the fishing line he had cast over the bow of the cargo vessel, while his eyes raked the deck. He accepted that there were a few qualities that applied to both the *aofia* and a twentieth-century policeman. One of them was the ability to wait and then, at the right moment, to move, hopefully in the right direction. All his instincts, developed in both the worlds he inhabited, told him that the time to act decisively was almost upon him. His eyes searched for the sacred areca nut he had secured to the deck with gum at the beginning of the voyage. It was still in place and should guarantee them a safe landing. When the vessel returned to Malaita, Kella would retrieve the nut, give thanks and place it in the sacred *beu aabu* on his home island of Sulufou, as an offering to the gods.

Mayotishi had made no demur to taking his chartered vessel to Tikopia, once Kella had assured him that the origins of the killman's activities might be found on the tiny island. The sergeant suspected that the Japanese was as much in thrall to his fates as Kella was to his. He had promised the fatalistic official that as soon as they returned to Malaita he would devote all his energies to tracking down the murderer and, in the process, ascertaining whether or not the man was a Japanese soldier.

After the attack on the track outside the mission, neither Brother John nor Shem had made any further objections to travelling to the relative safety of the remote eastern island. Indeed both men seemed quite relieved for the time being to be in a comparative limbo away from Malaita.

Earlier in the week, the vessel had put in at the islands of Utupua and Vanikoro to take on water and fresh fruit and vegetables. For the past three days it had been shuddering briskly across the open sea. So far the weather had been fine, except for a few refreshing squalls of rain. Mayotishi had recruited only a skeleton crew of half a dozen seamen, in addition to the bosun commanding the vessel, the engineer and a Chinese cook. Kella had approved. When he had supported Tottenham Hotspur during his sojourn at the London School of Economics, he had subscribed to the theory that in the same way that any good First Division side needed a spine of a striker, a centre half and a goalkeeper, so an inter-islands vessel in order to thrive required a steersman, a mechanic and a hash-slinger.

He had been further heartened to discover that the bosun, a grizzled, uncommunicative middle-aged man, was a *wantok* from the Lau district, as was the young, cheerful and decidedly friskier engineer.

The vessel, without a cargo and with only a few tons of rusted pig iron as ballast, bobbed easily enough on the surface of the water. Below deck, one of the two small, airless cabins was occupied by Mayotishi, and the other by Sister Conchita. Kella and Brother John were sleeping on mattresses on the deck, moving into the stateroom when it rained. Shem was sleeping in the crew's quarters. That evening they had dined off bonito fish and taro in the stateroom, and now most of the passengers and crew were scattered about the vessel, enjoying the serene night air before it was time to sleep.

Mayotishi was sitting under a canvas awning, reading a book by the light of a hurricane lamp placed on a small table next to him. Rimless spectacles perched on his nose gave him the appearance of a studious weasel. The last Kella had seen of Sister Conchita, she had been saying her evening prayers in her cabin. Brother John was performing effortless push-ups next to the enclosed wheelhouse. At the wheel, the bosun was peering anxiously at the magnetic compass. This was situated on the roof above his head, free from the influence of any magnetic materials on the ship. Its location was commonly referred to as the monkey island. The helmsman was able to study the compass through a twisted periscope coiling up before him. Like all Melanesian navigators, he would much rather steer towards a fixed secure point close to the horizon, but this far out at sea, such an option was denied him. If the vessel should overshoot the tiny speck of an island they were heading for, the next landfall would not be until the coast of the New Hebrides group was reached, by which time *The Spirit of the Islands'* supplies of water and fuel would have been used up long ago and its crew and passengers would almost certainly have died of thirst.

Kella studied the sea with a wary eye. There were signs of an approaching black squall. The waves breaking against the bows of the vessel were growing more and more phosphorescent, and he could see in the sky six of the *togo o ni*, the group of maidens that the white people called the Pleiades cluster. He caught the helmsman's eye. The bosun shook his head resignedly.

Not far from Kella, most of the crew members had been gambling and squabbling noisily for the last hour over an oilskin crown-and-anchor chart on the deck. Shem, the Tikopian, was prominent among them. So far he had kept to himself on the voyage, but tonight he had joined the Melanesians in their gaming, like an indolent, lazily smiling shark that had been following a shoal of small fish hungrily for days. The seamen around him cursed and cheered alternately as the dice were propelled from the shaker and the stakeholder raked in the money and paid out the winners. As Kella watched, the game broke up in some dissension. He was at Shem's side almost before the Polynesian had got to his feet.

'Did you win?' asked the sergeant.

'Against Melanesians? What do you think?' grinned Shem evilly, opening and closing a callused fist to reveal a fleeting glimpse of a wad of crumpled Australian dollars.

'Congratulations! Have you thought any more about the time when Papa Noah was killed?'

Shem sighed, but answered readily enough. 'Oh, that! I've told you all I know. There was a big storm. Everything grew so dark and the rain came down so hard that you could hardly see anything. I did what I could to get people away from the exposed feast ground and down to the shelter of the village. By the time I came back up again, Sister Conchita was trying to revive Papa Noah. I helped her, but it was too late. Papa was dead.' The Tikopian stared defiantly at the policeman. 'Are you satisfied now?' he asked truculently.

'Not yet,' said Kella. 'Now I want to go back a while. Tell me about the feast. What was it being held for?'

The Tikopian sighed, but surprised Kella by giving a fairly comprehensive answer to his question. The feast had been Papa Noah's idea from the start, to mark the first anniversary of the dream in which he had been told to build his ark. The old man had left the actual organization of the celebration to his acolytes, but had personally invited the guests by walking many miles into the bush and along the shore and reefs to summon the converts to his cult living in the villages along his route. He had also invited Sister Conchita and Brother John, although Shem did not know why. Neither did the Tikopian have any idea who the mysterious guest referred to by the old man could have been.

'What about Dr Maddy, the white professor?' asked Kella. 'Did Papa Noah invite her as well?'

Shem looked embarrassed. 'Not exactly,' he said. 'Wainoni the Gammon Man came to see me about her. He told me that the white woman was upset because she could not find enough pidgin songs about the war. Wainoni was afraid that she might leave without paying him all the money she had left. He wanted to keep her among the artificial islands for a little longer. He knew that the church choir would be singing at the tra-la-la, so he asked me if it would be possible to include "Japani Ha Ha!" and maybe a couple of other war songs for her to record on her machine. Papa Noah had been rehearsing these with the girls' choir for days, so he had no objection, and he included her in the invitation.'

'At a price, I fancy,' said Kella.

'The Gammon Man was prepared to make a contribution to church funds,' said Shem.

'I bet he was,' said Kella. 'Dr Maddy was his milch cow. Wainoni didn't want her drying up on him. Talking of money, what happened to Papa Noah's?'

'I don't know what you mean,' said the Tikopian. 'What money?'

'Come on,' said Kella. 'Everybody knows that anyone wanting to join the Lau Church of the Blessed Ark had to pay an entrance fee of two strings of custom shell money. The church had over a thousand adherents. Where are all those shells now?'

'I don't know,' said Shem. 'Papa Noah took care of the finances.'

As far as Kella could tell, the Tikopian was telling the truth. Papa Noah and Shem had both lived in ordinary leaf houses in the village below the ark. They did not appear to own even a canoe between them. Neither had ever shown any sign of being wealthy. That meant that a lot of valuable custom money was lying around somewhere. Could that have been a motive for the murder of Papa Noah?

'What about the others?' Shem demanded, suddenly going on the attack.

'What others?' asked Kella.

'The killman has now murdered three members of the Church of the Blessed Ark on Malaita. He killed Papa Noah, a young man hunting for wild pigs, and another man preparing a new garden.'

Kella remembered the details given to him by the tribal chiefs meeting on the artificial island of Sulufou. He had noted that the killings had taken place many miles apart. Was the fact that three members of the Ark cult had been murdered an important link, or just a coincidence?

He doubted that it could have been the latter, but he said nothing. It was obvious that Shem was frightened of something. At the same time Kella noticed that the seamen on deck were beginning to cast apprehensive glances at the lowering sky. The ship started to buck irritably, like a pawing horse preparing to unseat its rider. One of the Melanesians shouted an abrupt warning. The others started running for the companionway leading below.

'Big rain!' cried one of the deckhands, pushing the sergeant towards the steps.

Kella followed the others down to the narrow passage below. Shem and Brother John were just ahead of him. They stopped in the ship's corridor and glowered at one another. There was no love lost between these two, thought the sergeant. Then Shem stepped back and shouldered his way along to the crew's quarters. Attracted by the disturbance, Sister Conchita opened the door of her cabin and looked out enquiringly.

'We're running into a squall,' Kella told her. 'I should stay where you are if I were you.'

'Come in,' said the nun, retreating into the cabin. She sat on the single bunk and indicated that the sergeant should take a narrow bench attached to the wall beneath the porthole. Gingerly Kella lowered himself on to the flimsy seat.

'I haven't seen much of you on the voyage so far,' he said. It was true. The sister had hardly left her cabin.

'There were things I wanted to think and pray about,' Sister Conchita replied.

'Snap!' said Kella.

The nun smiled weakly. She and the sergeant rarely discussed the divergences in their faiths and beliefs. Their skills complemented one another and both of them were content to leave it at that. There were some subjects a pagan priest did not discuss with a Christian nun, even one who had become a close friend like Sister Conchita.

'While I'm here, may I ask you some questions about the death of Papa Noah?' he asked. 'They're mainly background ones.' Sister Conchita nodded. She was composed now, her hands folded in her lap. 'Basically I'm interested in why you went to the feast in the first place,' he went on. 'The Church of the Blessed Ark is a very new arrival on Malaita. It hasn't had time to get established yet, so it hardly presents itself as a rival to the Catholic missions. Why did someone as busy as you bother to attend a ceremony of such a minor sect?'

'That's what I said. It was Father Pierre's idea. For some reason he was particularly interested in Papa Noah and his church. He thought it was becoming an important one. He asked me to attend and keep my eyes open.'

'Who better?' said Kella. Outside, the rain was coming down hard now, hammering down on the deck above them like thousands of tiny tacks being driven relentlessly into the weather-beaten planks by a phalanx of industrious gods. More rain rattled interrogatively against the glass of the porthole. *The Spirit of the Islands* was suddenly making hard work of its passage, running breathlessly up waves and then plunging recklessly down the far side of them like a frolicsome elderly aunt paddling at the seaside.

'Thank you, Ben,' said the nun composedly. 'I'm aware of my reputation for being a nosy young biddy. However, I really can lay most of the blame at Father Pierre's door on this occasion. I'd hardly heard of Papa Noah and his church, but the father seemed really worried about it.'

'I wonder why,' said Kella lightly. 'The old boy's seen off a fair few sects on Malaita in his time. What was so different about this one?'

'I don't know; he wouldn't tell me.' The nun hesitated. 'I got the impression that Father Pierre wasn't so much worried about what the ark church *was*. He seemed more concerned about what it might become.'

'What do you mean?'

Sister Conchita selected her words with precision. 'Once when we were discussing my trip to the feast, he said something to the effect that he wished that Papa Noah had chosen almost anything but an ark as the symbol for his cult. He said that it had too many connotations with the great canoe. In the wrong hands it could lead to dreadful trouble.'

Kella leant forward. 'Can you remember his exact words?' he asked.

The nun closed her eyes in concentration. 'I believe', she said slowly, 'that he said: *the ark and the great canoe; there's very little difference between them.*' She opened her eyes. 'Yes, that's right, the great canoe. Is that of any help to you, Ben?'

'Not much,' admitted Kella.

The two sat in puzzled silence. What sort of sect was the Lau Church of the Blessed Ark? pondered the sergeant. He had assumed that it was just another unimportant minor cult, like dozens of others that had sprung up and then withered on the vine in the course of his lifetime on Malaita. Most of them had been founded by zealots who claimed to have had a dream or a vision in which they were commanded to establish a new church. The resulting conglomerations had usually consisted of a few bewildered adherents following a haphazard mixture of Christian and pagan practices. Their average lifespans were usually less than twelve months.

It was beginning to look as if the ark church was going to be different. For a start, the venerable Father Pierre had expressed his misgivings about it. The priest had once been Kella's headmaster at Ruvabi mission school. Even then he had been noted for his tolerance and acceptance of the diverse pagan faiths often being followed in tandem with the Catholic religion in his far-flung parish. When the young schoolboy had informed him that he was leaving the mission to take up the arduous training of the *aofia*, Father Pierre had made little attempt to deter him. 'Follow your path as it has been appointed,' was all the sad priest had said. They had remained friends ever since. If Father Pierre was concerned about the Lau Church of the Blessed Ark, then almost certainly there was a great deal to be worried about. But what? It was time to bring Sister Conchita into the equation. Her opinion was always worth having. Kella opened his mouth, but the nun's thoughts seemed to be running on parallel lines and she forestalled him with a sympathetic smile.

'It's a matter of symbols, isn't it?' she asked. 'Papa Noah selected the ark as the icon for his cult. It must resemble the symbol of some other sort of religion. Somehow Father Pierre is afraid that the two icons will merge in one dangerous faith.'

'I was hoping that the father would have explained more about that before you left Ruvabi,' said Kella.

Sister Conchita did not answer. Her silence only intensified the noise of the squall gathering outside. Father Pierre had been too ill to tell her anything. She wondered if he would ever be fit enough to run his mission again. The drumming of the rain was now being reinforced by the screaming of the wind and the monotonous thud of waves slapping against the sides of the ship. Sister Conchita guessed that by the standards of the Solomons, this would not be considered a major storm. Certainly Kella was not reacting to it in any visible form. He was sitting impassively on the bench, not even squirming round to glance out of the porthole behind him. Not for the first time, Sister Conchita thought that he looked like a deeply tanned and even more battered version of the film star Jack Palance in urgent need of a haircut. He must have aroused her unease.

'The bosun's still heading into the wind,' he said, 'which means that he's not too worried yet. If he was, he'd turn and run before the storm.'

'Is *The Spirit of the Islands* fast enough to outrun the bad weather?' Sister Conchita asked, hoping for a positive response.

'Probably not,' Kella said.

They heard the sound of footsteps running up the companionway to the deck. The ship began to rise and plunge in even greater parabolas. Water was coming in under the door of the cabin from the passage outside.

'The crew is going up to lash everything down to stop it being swept away,' Kella told her.

Dismayed shouts came from the deck. Kella frowned and stood up. He opened the door, allowing more water to gush in. He stood out in the passage, straining to hear.

'Wait here,' he ordered, and started running up towards the deck. Sister Conchita hesitated, and then, disregarding his instructions, followed the police sergeant closely. Mayotishi emerged from his cabin and joined the small group.

When they reached the deck, the ship was rolling and plunging deeply from side to side. The wind screamed in from the west. The rain was hurtling almost horizontally in solid sheets. For the first time since she had come to the Solomons, Sister Conchita was really cold. The seamen were milling around the wheelhouse. The usually imperturbable bosun had thrown the door open and was shouting desperately to the crew. With difficulty, Sister Conchita and Mayotishi followed Kella across the slippery planks of the deck. As Kella engaged the bosun in a dialogue in the Lau language, the fear was apparent in the older Melanesian's tone.

'What's the matter?' Sister Conchita shouted, above the noise of the wind and rain.

'Apparently the magnetic compass has broken,' said Kella. 'There's no course for the bosun to follow. We're travelling blind.'

'What's wrong with the instrument?' asked Mayotishi. He was wearing yellow oilskins. The Japanese seemed to have an outfit for every occasion.

'There's only one way to find out,' Kella said.

He groped for the rope ladder swinging against the side of the wheelhouse and started climbing. The ladder crashed against the wheelhouse in the wind, and the rain thudded down, but it was only a few spray-soaked and slippery rungs to the flat roof, and he was able to swing himself up on to his stomach. Pausing to get his breath back, he ran stooped against the wind across to the compass situated in a protective wooden casing next to the rail. It was illuminated by the flickering light of an oil lamp, mounted on one side. As he approached, he could see that the glass face of the compass had been shattered into hundreds of shards and that the magnetic needle had been wrenched off and thrown away.

'What's wrong?' Brother John shouted from below.

Kella looked down at the group of worried faces staring up at him. 'It's smashed,' he said briefly, climbing back down to rejoin the others.

'Storm big too much,' said the bosun, who had handed over the wheel to one of the seamen. 'Compass himi bugger-up big time. No lookim long Tikopia. Me go turnaround quick time.'

'What's he saying?' asked Mayotishi worriedly from the edge of the gathering.

'We can't find an island as small as Tikopia without a compass. We'd just sail into nothingness,' said Brother John. 'He wants to turn round and head back for Malaita. I must say that he's got a point. If we return the way we came, sooner or later we're bound to find one of the islands in the main group. If we go plunging on blindly like this . . .' He shrugged.

Those members of the crew who understood English muttered their agreement. Shem shouldered his way through the crowd. He towered above the other seamen. He seemed to have changed since Kella had last seen him. There was a new air of purpose, almost of determination about the Tikopian.

'We don't have to turn back,' he said, raising his voice. 'I can guide you to my home!'

Murmurs of dissent spread among the crew. They faded away beneath the Tikopian's imperious gaze. Shem turned his attention to the bosun. The Lau man hesitated, and then nodded reluctantly.

'Try littlebit,' he grunted, and went back to his wheel.

Shem took up a place in the prow of the vessel. He looked up at the stars, thought for a few moments and then pointed into the darkness.

'That way,' he said.

The bosun spun his wheel and edged *The Spirit of the Islands* round to its new course. Sister Conchita looked uncertainly at Kella.

'Are we . . .' she began.

'We're fine,' Kella told her. 'Shem's guiding us home.'

He watched the nun and Mayotishi return down the companion-way to their cabins. Then he walked over to the immobile hulk that was Shem.

'Why are you doing this?' he asked. 'You don't really want to go home, do you?'

Shem did not look at him. 'It is my karma,' he said.

Kella had not finished for the night. He moved between the slowly dispersing and still dubious seamen to Brother John, who was standing on his own by the rail. The big man nodded remotely when the police sergeant joined him.

'For a man of God, you get on my nerves considerably,' said Kella.

'How so?' asked the missionary.

'Do you want to tell me why you did it?'

'Did what?' responded Brother John.

'Smashed the compass on the monkey island, of course,' Kella said.

Several moments passed before Brother John responded.

'How did you know I did that?' he asked.

'You overdid it,' Kella told him. 'The magnetic needle had been torn sheer away from the face of the compass. Only three men on board would have been strong enough to do that – you, me and Shem. It wasn't me, and Shem wanted to get home so badly that he's just volunteered to go three days and nights without sleep in order to try to steer us to Tikopia. He says that it's his fate to do so. That only left you. I assume that you wanted to delay us on our voyage, or better still abandon the trip altogether. Do you want to tell me why?'

'It's the *mata matangi*,' said Brother John after a moment.

'A ceremony?' guessed Kella.

Brother John nodded. 'It means the eyes of the wind,' he said. 'It's a Tikopian pagan ritual to bless homes and possessions. It's due to take place at the end of the week.'

'I thought Tikopia was a Christian island now,' Kella said.

'Only in theory,' said Brother John. 'The last pagan chief died on the island in 1953, and everyone said that Christianity was now going to be the sole religion of Tikopia. But the pagan faith only went underground. Lately it's been resurfacing in quite a big way. In the Melanesian Mission we've been afraid for some time that there might be attempts to bring the old religion back by force. We've kept our eyes on events and even infiltrated a couple of agents into Papa Noah's breakaway church. What really concerned us was the number of Tikopians affiliated to the Church of the Blessed Ark on Malaita. I hear that Father Pierre noticed that as well. There's plainly some link between Papa Noah's group and the pagans on Tikopia.'

'So you guessed that the date of this pagan ceremony – the eyes of the wind – might be used as an occasion to revitalize the pagan faith on Tikopia,' said Kella. 'You knew the date of the ceremony and feared that it might be dangerous if a group of strangers from the outside world were to turn up at the island at such an important time for the pagans on Tikopia. You hoped that without a working compass on board our progress would slow down considerably, or even be abandoned altogether. You didn't reckon on Shem's determination to reach home in time.'

'You're right, of course. The island's on a knife edge and has been for the best part of a year. If the pagans take over, it will be years before the Melanesian Mission gains a footing there once more. That could mean a religious war on the island, persecution, and all sorts of trouble.'

'What about your minister on the island?'

'That's the problem. His name is Abalolo, and he's disappeared.'
'Disappeared?'
Brother John nodded. 'Bearing that in mind,' he said, 'I think that we will have to be very careful when we make landfall on Tikopia.'
'If we get there at all,' said Kella.

20

THE SAVO MEGAPODE FIELDS

On a large, sloping patch of black sand on the tiny island of Savo stood a group consisting of a dozen fascinated, perspiring tourists from a cruise ship, Welchman Buna, the Legislative Council member for the Roviana Lagoon, and a tall, stooped, grey-haired man whose name was Sanders and who worked for the US State Department in a capacity never defined on his infrequent visits to the Solomon Islands but whose occasional presence in Honiara was always sufficient to cause awe and unease among the highest echelons of the government's expatriate administrative officers.

The two men stood a little apart from the others. Both were smartly dressed. Sanders wore a tan lightweight suit while Buna's dark slacks were sharply pressed and, despite the humidity, his white shirt hung stiffly at attention from his torso. The female tourists were in print dresses while the men favoured shorts and Hawaiian shirts. The launch that had brought them on the fourteen-mile journey from the capital across Ironbottom Sound was anchored a hundred yards off the white sands of the shore. A little way along the beach, four Melanesian crew members, now off duty, smoked roll-up cigarettes around the dinghy in which they had rowed the visitors ashore. The official tour guide, a cheerful Guadalcanal man, was wielding a megaphone with all the flourishes of a silent movie director.

The tourists were looking in amazement at the sight before them.

On the wide patch of sand, hundreds of scrawny, big-footed brown and black birds about the size of chickens were scrabbling out holes several feet deep. When each hole was large enough, the bird would roll a recently laid egg into it with its feet and then start kicking sand back into the hole until the egg was covered.

'The megapode birds – the *ngeros* – will never see their eggs again,' announced the tour guide proudly. 'They leave them here in the holes. The sand is warmed by the volcano in the centre of the island. This is enough to hatch out the young birds in about three weeks. They will dig their way up through the sand and start running about immediately. After an hour or two these young birds will fly away into the trees over there.'

'The ones that aren't killed by dogs or pigs or whose eggs haven't been dug up for food by the islanders,' murmured Buna.

'Nature red in tooth and claw,' said Sanders. He touched the other man on the shoulder as a sign that they should stroll away from the main group. 'Could you tell me exactly what is going on with our mutual friend Sergeant Kella?' he asked.

'Nothing, as far as I know,' said the politician, with a sinking feeling in his stomach. How was it that mention of the ubiquitous police sergeant never seemed to herald the onset of good news? 'In fact, the last time I saw him he specifically assured me that matters were quiet over on Malaita. I did hear that he exorcized a ghost somewhere on Guadalcanal the other day, but that's par for the course for our Ben. He can almost do it in his sleep. Why, what has happened?'

'It's complicated,' Sanders said. 'Well, complicated enough to bring me back to these islands. As far as we can ascertain, a professional murderer is at large on Malaita, and Sergeant Kella is trying to find him.'

'It's what he's paid to do,' Welchman Buna said.

'Granted, but it seems that he hasn't told his superiors what he's up to.'

'So what else is new?' Buna asked. 'You know Kella. His enquiry probably clashes with some tribal *tabu*, so he's keeping things quiet until he's got everything sorted and in harmony. Our Ben is very keen on getting things in harmony.'

'Furthermore,' went on the American, as if he had not heard the other man, 'there are rumours that the killer is a Japanese survivor from the Second World War pursuing a private campaign on Malaita.'

'Oh, dear God!' said Buna.

'My sentiments entirely,' said Sanders. 'My latest information is that Sergeant Kella has linked up with an official Japanese investigator and an Anglican priest called Brother John, and that they are looking for this soldier. There are some weird stories that a nun has gone with them as well. They're all on a chartered vessel called *The Spirit of the Islands*. I don't have to tell you what that could entail. The Japanese are looking for a way back into the Solomons big-time. They're having an economic revival in the Pacific these days, and that worries my superiors. As we understand it, they're considering starting logging and fishing industries in this part of the world. The people that I work for would rather they kept their distance. *I* would rather they kept away too. It would be most unfortunate if an iconic figure like Kella were to link up with the Japanese. Heaven knows what those missionaries are doing going with him.'

'Kella fought the Japanese during the war,' Buna pointed out. 'As a teenager he was a scout with John Deacon's guerrilla raiders. I can't see him teaming up with his old enemies.'

'Alliances are strange affairs. They can change direction with the prevailing wind,' said the American, pausing under the shade of a group of palm trees curtseying with brief grace in the breeze. 'As we both know, Mr Buna.'

Buna did not reply at once. He had been in the pay of the Americans ever since he had attracted their attention with his enterprising efforts to rescue the young John F. Kennedy after the latter's PT boat had been sunk in the Roviana Lagoon in 1942. Along with several other prospects he had been selected for his potential as a big man in the islands and supplied by the Americans with enough clandestine money to embark him upon his political career. However, he realized that lately he had been worrying his backers with his signs of striking out for independence, culminating only recently when he and Ben Kella had combined to put three FBI operatives in hospital with serious injuries sustained on the island of Olasana. 'What do you want me to do?' he asked.

'Keep an eye on things and let me know what you find out,' the American told him. 'And keep all this under your hat. It's strictly confidential at this stage. That's why I wanted to meet you away from prying eyes in Honiara.'

'Does Chief Superintendent Grice know what Kella is up to?' asked the politician.

'Apparently not. Just how bright is Grice?'

Buna remembered a favourite phrase of a salty American master sergeant who had trained his wartime guerrilla group. When the politician spoke, the words were at a variance with the prim, buttoned-up exterior he chose to present to the world.

'I doubt he could pour piss out of a boot that had instructions printed on the heel,' he said.

Down by the megapode field, things were stirring. The tour guide was leading his party down to the beach. The seamen with the dinghy were discarding half-smoked cigarettes and preparing to ferry the visitors back to the passenger liner moored at the Point Cruz wharf. In a rare show of conviviality, Sanders walked down to join the crowd on the shore. Buna followed at a slower, more contemplative pace. The most important factor in the information provided by the man from the State Department was not the hunt for the alleged Japanese killman. Rumours like that were always sweeping the bush and eventually reached the capital in a confused form.

What was much more interesting was the sudden grouping of three such disparate characters on the chartered ship. The missionaries on

Malaita got on well enough, but they seldom united to work together on projects in the remote areas. There was little doubt in his mind that the nun Sanders had mentioned would be Sister Conchita from Ruvabi Mission. She was the only white sister on the island. Besides which, if anything interesting, untoward or possibly dangerous was happening in the remote jungle, the redoubtable young sister would be drawn to it like an ant to honey, to see if she could help.

With the tough and experienced Brother John of the Melanesian Mission, the idiosyncratic and driven Sergeant Kella, the pagan *aofia*, and this unknown Japanese official with pockets presumably limitless enough to be able to charter the rust-bucket that was *The Spirit of the Islands*, a very strange company seemed to be putting to sea. It was a group that would only band together under the most exigent of circumstances. Buna only wished that he knew what these were. One thing was certain. He did not envy them their prospective voyage, whatever its destination.

Unbidden, a fragment of poetry entered his mind, verse he had been taught what seemed a lifetime ago, after he had been identified by the Methodist church in the western islands as a potential academic high-flyer and fast-tracked as a student to the church's prestigious Goldie College.

'*They went to sea in a sieve,*' he murmured.

Sanders' ears were sharp. He glanced back. 'What was that?' he asked.

'Nothing,' said Welchman Buna, increasing his pace towards the dinghy. 'I was just showing off my Western-style mission education.'

Sanders frowned. 'I hope you're not treating this lightly, Buna. My people would not wish Sergeant Kella any harm, but if he moves contrary to the interests of the USA, we might be forced to take extreme executive action against him.'

Buna surveyed the American almost with pity in his eyes. 'That is your prerogative, Mr Sanders. All I would say in reply is that when, all those years ago, the council of tribal elders chose Ben Kella to be the new *aofia*, it wasn't just because he came from a line of great Lau warriors and the signs indicated that he was destined by the gods to be the next custom-law enforcer on Malaita. He was also selected because they could see even at that early age that he was extremely tough and really smart.'

'Your point being?'

'I'm saying', said Buna, and he meant every word of it, 'that if you take on Kella on his own territory, you'd better be prepared for a hell of a fight.' For the second time that afternoon he resorted with some relish to outdated American idiom.

'He might not beat you, but he'll come in the best second you ever saw.'

'Perhaps I should employ this paragon of yours,' said Sanders. 'You know what they say – if you can't beat 'em, join 'em!'

'You couldn't do it. There's one big difference between Ben Kella and me.'

'Oh, what's that?'

'He's not corruptible,' said Welchman Buna sadly.

21

WHERE WILL HE HIDE?

Sister Conchita stood with Kella and Brother John outside the hut of Atanga, one of the four paramount chiefs of Tikopia. Dozens of interested old Polynesian men sat on the white sand of the village around her, taking in every detail of her appearance and costume but making no attempt to talk to her. Many of them chewed betel nut or smoked pipes.

The visitors had landed on the island several hours ago. Before that, for three days and nights, Shem had sat stoically, without sleep, in the bows of *The Spirit of the Islands*, steering by the tides and stars. At last some of the seamen had seen coconuts floating in the water. At about ten o'clock that morning, the Polynesian had suddenly come to life and pointed, and the others had crowded to the rails for their first glimpse of their long-awaited destination.

At first Tikopia had been a mere child's unformed pencil smudge on the flat far edge of the sea. As the ship drew nearer, the vague land form filled out to reveal sandy beaches, a thickly forested interior and a central volcanic mountain. The outline of a lake shimmered at the foot of the volcano. Flocks of grey ducks floated lethargically over its surface, while pied cormorants flapped watchfully overhead, looking for shoals of mullet in the brackish water. A guidebook had informed Sister Conchita that the whole island was only three miles long and about half that wide.

After the ship had anchored just outside the reef on the western side of Tikopia, there had been a surprisingly long wait before canoes had put out from the shore to take the visitors ashore. The islanders in the outriggers were silent. There were none of the customary excited, screaming children who had greeted *The Spirit of the Islands* at other stops on their journey.

The Melanesian crew members to a man sensed the unwelcoming atmosphere and refused sullenly to go ashore. Mayotishi had joined them in their caution.

'Never go in anywhere unless you are certain of the way out,' was all the Japanese would say as he watched Sister Conchita, Kella, Brother John and Shem descend a rope ladder to the waiting canoes. He was holding a rifle. 'I'll keep the engines running,' he had called after them. 'If you have to get back here quickly, we'll be ready to weigh anchor.'

There had been a few Polynesians waiting for them on the shore, but they drifted apart expressionlessly to allow the visitors to enter the village at the top of the steeply sloping beach littered with coral pebbles and boulders. Shem had indicated the hut belonging to Atanga, the district chieftain. It was larger than the others, with a roof of woven coconut palm tiles. Sister Conchita had heard that the bones of the chief's celebrated ancestors were buried beneath the floor. The most prominent feature of the dwelling was the front door. It was only three feet high and not as wide.

'The chief is waiting inside,' Shem had said. 'Anyone who enters his house must approach him on their hands and knees like this.'

He had suited his action to his words and entered the hut on all fours, leaving the others outside. He was gone for almost an hour. Conchita had spent the time watching an industrious group of bare-breasted young women wearing only bark-cloth loincloths gathering molluscs out on the reefs. Some of them had hibiscus flowers behind their ears. She guessed that most of the younger men would be fishing somewhere in fleets of canoes among the great breaking waves far out at sea.

Once the nun heard a voice raised in anger from the hut. It did not sound like Shem's. When the young Polynesian at last came out, his face was strained. Without looking at the others, he hurried out of the village along a track into the trees. From inside the hut a muffled voice barked out some sort of instruction to the waiting group.

Kella and Brother John moved forward to go in. Sister Conchita started to follow them. Kella put a hand on her arm.

'Not you,' he said with a shake of his head. She thought he had a faint triumphant twinkle in his eye. 'Women aren't allowed in the chief's hut.'

Well, pardon me for living, thought Sister Conchita. She watched the sergeant and the missionary crawling through the low doorway. Both Kella and Brother John were rational, sympathetic men, but neither of them seemed to question for a moment the edict forbidding her to enter the presence of the chief. They lived in a different world, she decided, not for the first time. Still, she thought, there was one advantage of being an invisible entity. As long as she kept away from any *tabu* areas, no one would care what she did or where she went.

She followed the track taken a few minutes earlier by Shem, doing her best to appear to be strolling casually. Soon the trees were crowding in over her head, but the path at her feet had been well maintained, with only a dusting of goat's-foot creepers to obstruct the scuttling hermit crabs intent on their tasks. Brown needles from casuarina trees had fallen in clumps. Springs of clear water gurgled happily as if sharing a common joke. Sister Conchita passed several squares of land that had been completely cleared to allow taro and sugar cane to be cultivated in tidy clusters. She thought that this would be one of the few parts of the island from which it was not possible to see the ocean. She remembered that Kella had told her that the villagers never used the terms left or right but preferred instead to mark the direction of objects as inland or seawards.

'Christian?' asked a woman's voice from behind her.

Sister Conchita turned. An old woman wearing only a grass skirt walked out of the trees. Her grey hair was long and stringy. Deep lines furrowed her face.

She indicated the nun's habit.

'Mary bilong Jesus?' she asked.

'Him now. Mefella Praying Mary,' Sister Conchita said.

The old woman nodded in satisfaction. She led the way through the trees away from the path. Ten minutes later she stopped in front of a solitary hut in an overgrown clearing. The hut had a neglected appearance. There were gaping holes in the woven walls and roof. Sister Conchita looked inside the dilapidated construction. The floor and walls were bare. Anything of value had been taken. In one corner she saw a heap of empty scallop shells. Without quite knowing why, she picked one up and put it in her pocket. The old woman gestured to her to leave the hut.

'By'm by. Maybe tumera,' she said. Almost as an afterthought she added: 'Christian help.'

The woman led the puzzled nun back through the trees and pointed out a way past a sluggish stream and a regimented row of sago palms ahead of them before stepping once more into the shadows of the bush. Sister Conchita walked carefully past the palms until she rejoined the original track. After another twenty minutes she found Shem standing in a long hollow trench with smoothed-out sides. He was holding a long stick with a sharp shell point. His placid, gentle face revealed nothing of his thoughts.

'You must be tired,' said the nun. 'You haven't slept for a long time.'

'It's nice to be home,' said the Tikopian. 'There will be time enough for a long sleep later.' He lifted the stick. '*Tika*,' he said. 'It's a game we play here. Outsiders call it Tikopian darts. I'm good at it. Have you seen it played?' The nun shook her head. Shem hefted the stick in his hand and held it close to his cheek, as if judging its weight. Then he took a short run along the trench and hurled the barbed stick with impressive, muscle-pumping strength. It struck the baked ground and hurtled in a series of bounces along the trench, slithering to a stop like a snake rigid with venom many yards away at the far end of the channel. The Tikopian looked up at Sister Conchita.

'It would be nice', he said, 'to dance again with pretty girls and play *tika* and drink *kava*.'

The nun wondered what he was trying to tell her. 'You can do all those things now that you have come home,' she said.

The Tikopian shook his head so that the long hair brushed across his shoulders. 'Haven't you heard?' he asked. 'The Christians have stopped us growing the pepper plant with which we make our drink.'

'Us?' asked Sister Conchita. 'You're a pagan, then?'

'Oh yes,' said Shem. A faint twinkle coruscated in his eyes. 'Like your friend Sergeant Kella,' he added.

'I wasn't sure,' said Sister Conchita, ignoring the reference to the policeman. 'The Church of the Blessed Ark took some of its beliefs from the Christian faith and some from the old ways.'

'And some from both,' said Shem. 'That is why it was so important – and so dangerous.'

'How was it dangerous?' asked Sister Conchita. She sensed that she was about to be told something important, if only she could work out its value. But Shem smiled sadly and shook his head.

'Is that why you joined Papa Noah's sect?' she asked. 'You wanted to belong to a pagan church that reminded you of the old ways here on Tikopia?'

'Don't you understand?' asked Shem, chiding her gently. 'I didn't want to join any church. I still don't. I was young. I wanted to sail on the Chinese ships and drink beer in the bars at Kira Kira and Gizo and pay to go with the Guadalcanal girls in the jig-jig houses in Honiara. And maybe, when I had done all that, when I had drunk much beer and had many women, I would have come back here and become an old *tautai*, a sea expert respected because he could still take his canoe as far as Anuta and Fatutaka and back.'

'Then why . . .'

'My father is Atanga, the high chief and priest of this district,' said Shem, a harsh, almost metallic tinge to his voice. 'He sent word to me that I must join Papa Noah's church, so I did. I stayed with him for a year, learning all I could about the old man's ways, according to my instructions. That meant that all the other Tikopians in the area came as well.'

'So you wanted to take over the Church of the Blessed Ark after Papa Noah was killed?' said Sister Conchita.

'Don't you see?' asked Shem. 'The last thing in the world I wanted to do was to take over any church! Papa Noah was a good and kind man. He wanted his church to help people, not to become a battlefield between the Christians and the pagans. I couldn't use what he had built for sinful ends. I have just told my father that.'

'What did he say?'

'What I knew he would say. He told me to go to my land, the sea.' A wry smile twisted Shem's lips. 'My people have a saying: "If a chief is angry with a man, where will he hide?" Even now he is waiting for a sign from the old gods. Sometimes, in times of great trouble, they visit Tikopia and appear on the top of Mount Reani. The lesser ones can take the form of animals and move among us bearing messages for those gifted with the sight to see them and ears to hear. Tomorrow my father will go to wait for the gods' decision at Somosomo, the site of the ancient ceremonies.'

Abruptly, as if he could keep still no longer, the Polynesian started running gracefully along the trench. At the far end he stooped and without stopping picked up the pointed stick. Then he leapt up on to the track and soon became a blurred figure, mingling with the branches of the trees.

Sister Conchita wondered what to do. It was all very well being put in a position to garner all sorts of different experiences in the Solomons, but the down side was that it meant she was doing many things for the first time in her life and was never sure that she was doing them the right way. Right now she was convinced that something bad was about to happen. She hurried along the track in the direction taken by Shem. Some way ahead of her she heard a woman's scream. Sister Conchita started running.

It took her several minutes to reach Shem. When she did so, he was sitting slumped against a tree. A group of weeping Tikopian women were standing around him. At first Sister Conchita thought that Shem was only resting. Then she saw the blood pouring down his throat and chest.

22

SWEET BURIAL

'What happens next?' asked Sister Conchita.

'They will give Shem a sweet burial,' said Kella.

'What does that mean?' asked the nun.

'It's the description given to any Tikopian who dies at sea,' Kella told her. 'It is the best sort of death possible for one of them. They will send Shem's body out alone into the ocean.'

They were standing on a small headland overlooking the beach. Hundreds of men and women had gathered on the shore below them. The previous evening, canoes had taken Sister Conchita, Kella and Brother John back to *The Spirit of the Islands*. They had spent the night on board. In the morning, the ship's dinghy had brought them as far as the reef and then pulled back hastily to the safety of the anchored vessel. Brother John had left them as soon as they reached the island, hurrying in the direction of Mount Reani.

'So Shem killed himself?' asked Sister Conchita.

'No doubt about it,' Kella said. 'Soon after he left you he sat down under the tree and plunged the point of the *tika* dart into his throat. He was a strong man. The arrow would have gone a long way in. He died immediately.'

'I had no idea that he was thinking of taking his own life,' said the nun in a small voice.

'He didn't have much choice,' said the sergeant. 'He told you that he didn't want to be a priest. He had already told his father Atanga the same thing. If he hadn't killed himself, some of the *marau*, the pagan priests, would have murdered him instead.'

'But why?' asked Sister Conchita.

'He told you,' said Kella. 'You just didn't make the correct deductions. How could you? His father is the only pagan chief left on Tikopia. The other three paramount leaders have all been Christians for some time. I think that Atanga has been plotting for years to launch a coup to make Tikopia a pagan island again, maybe with himself as the sole chief and high priest. Shem was already working in the Solomons. For some reason Atanga ordered him to join Papa Noah's sect and work his way up in the hierarchy of the Church of the Blessed Ark. Shem managed to do that and to persuade a lot of other Tikopians working on Malaita to join Papa Noah's sect as well.'

'Why?' asked Sister Conchita.

'I don't know yet,' said the sergeant. 'What is obvious is that while Shem was working as Papa Noah's so-called son, he discovered several things about himself.'

'That he liked Papa Noah very much, and that he had no vocation to be a priest – pagan or otherwise,' said the nun, relieved at not having to ask yet another question.

'Exactly,' Kella said. 'Perhaps you have been paying attention after all. After Papa Noah was murdered, Shem decided to return to Tikopia to tell his father that he would not – could not – be a pagan priest. I suspect that Atanga gave his son an ultimatum – either to go through with his plans or be disowned as his heir.'

'Atanga certainly quarrelled with Shem,' said the nun. 'Shem was very shaken when I spoke to him. He said something that I didn't understand. He said that his father had told him to go to his land, the sea.'

'That's what happened, then,' said Kella. 'That's the traditional Tikopian curse of disownment. If a chief tells any members of his tribe to go to sea, it means that the islander is banished from the chief's land for ever. He has nowhere else to go but the great ocean.'

'But that means death,' said Sister Conchita.

'Oh yes,' said Kella, almost matter-of-factly. 'It does. That's why Shem killed himself. He'd already been sentenced.'

Sister Conchita shook her head in bewilderment. 'Where's Brother John?' she asked, almost at random, as she tried to marshal her thoughts.

'He's just started looking for Abalolo, the island's Christian minister,' said Kella. 'No one seems to know what's happened to him. Or if they do know, they're not telling us.'

He craned his head forward. There was more intensified movement on the beach below. The crowd parted slightly to allow four islanders to carry an improvised stretcher bearing Shem's body down to the water's edge. They deposited the framework on the sand and stood to one side. Then the crowd swirled apart as a dozen men appeared over the brow of the beach pushing a large canoe down the incline towards the lagoon over a series of rounded tree trunks acting as rollers. The vessel was decorated with leis and garlands. Its guardians were big and strong, but the canoe was so solidly built that they could only inch it over the tree trunks.

'*Vaka tapu*, the big canoe,' said Kella. 'I thought there was only one left, in a museum in Auckland. The pagans on Tikopia must have spent years making that replica down there. They were probably going to unveil it at the eyes of the wind ceremony to mark the resurgence of their religion on the island next week. But with Shem dead, all they can use it for is burying him.'

'Why can't Chief Atanga revive the faith by himself?' asked Sister Conchita.

Kella said nothing, merely pointed towards the beach.

A second litter borne by half a dozen islanders was being lowered on to the sand. It was covered by a roof of sago palms, with fronds hanging down the sides. The fronds were brushed aside and a very big and extremely old man stepped painfully out. He stood trying to balance himself, brushing aside offers of help from his retainers. Then very slowly he hobbled with excruciating precision down to the bier, pausing every few feet to rest, swaying like a stricken tree in a gale every time he did so.

'That's Atanga,' said Kella. 'He's too old to launch anything except his son's final canoe journey. He's probably only been keeping himself alive until Shem returned to take over as high priest. Yet all the time Shem didn't want the job.'

'But for Shem to have to kill himself because he couldn't live up to his father's expectations . . .'

'Custom,' said Kella, as if that explained everything.

Far below them, four men were lifting Shem's body into the long canoe.

Six more Tikopians climbed into the outrigger and picked up their paddles. In a few minutes they were propelling the canoe towards the coral reef, while a great wailing emanated from the mass on the beach. The canoe headed for a narrow channel leading out to the open sea. The men navigated the aperture and steadied the rocking vessel with their paddles just outside the reef, while two of them erected a mast and a tapa-cloth sail on a joist in the centre of the canoe. Then all six islanders dived over the side, splashed their way back through the channel and began swimming easily across the lagoon to the crowd on the sand.

A paroxysm of wind filled the sail and started taking the canoe and its solitary occupant out to sea. The dugout was the only object above the level of the water as far as the hazy, wavering horizon. Sister Conchita watched the vessel's progress with all the concentration she could muster. She thought she knew why Shem had spent so much time in the Church of the Blessed Ark, but this was not the moment to voice her suspicions.

Brother John emerged from the bushes behind Kella and Sister Conchita. He shook his head as he joined them.

'No one claims to know what happened to Abalolo,' he said. 'Not

even the islanders in the Christian sections of Tikopia. One minute
he was here; the next he seems to have disappeared.'

'What do you think?' asked Kella.

'I think he's probably dead,' said Brother John briefly. 'If Atanga
intended reviving the old pagan faith, the first thing he would do
would be to get rid of the leading Christian minister on the island.'
He looked out to sea. 'No one will move from the beach until the
canoe is taken over the horizon by the wind,' he said. 'After that,
there's no telling what Atanga might get up to. We really ought to
be getting back to our ship and putting as much distance between us
and Tikopia as possible.'

'You take Sister Conchita back,' said Kella. 'I've still got to find Dr
Maddy.'

'I'd better stay with you,' Sister Conchita said. She returned the
forbidding looks of the other two with something approaching
defiance. Then she cleared her throat nervously. 'Actually, I think I
know where she might be,' she said.

The nun led her two sceptical but mercifully for the moment silent
companions into the trees. Doing her best to steer by the golden darts
of sunlight piercing the foliage, she was relieved to stumble across the
track she had followed the day before and then the line of sago palms
leading to the sluggish stream.

'Where now?' asked Kella.

'There's a broken-down hut round the next corner,' said Sister
Conchita. 'I think it's the remains of a Christian church.'

'What makes you believe that?' asked Brother John

Sister Conchita fumbled in the pockets of her robe and produced
the scallop shell she had picked up from the floor of the hut the
previous afternoon.

'I found this inside,' she said. 'Obviously no one thought it was
worth stealing.'

'They had a point,' Brother John said. 'What's the purpose of an
empty scallop shell?'

'It was the symbol of St James, the son of Zebedee,' the nun told him. 'In medieval Spain, any Christian pilgrim who could produce such an object would be given shelter and provided with as much food as would cover the surface of the shell. I imagine that the first Spanish Catholic priests who came ashore and preached in the Solomons in 1568 might have mentioned the importance of local symbols like shells to their religion. As the centuries passed, other Christian denominations among the islands might have taken up the same common emblem, including the minister at that church over there.'

As she led the group, she told them about her meeting with the old woman. By now they had turned a corner on the bank of the stream and were standing in front of the remains of the hut. Brother John approached what was left of the front door.

'That old woman was a Christian,' he said. 'She recognized Sister Conchita's habit and told her that she was going to hand Dr Maddy over to her today in what remains of the Christian church building in Chief Atanga's territory.'

The sergeant pulled hard on the door. It sagged to one side, allowing sunlight into the hut. Sitting on the floor, her hands sheltering her eyes from the glare, was Florence Maddy. She was wearing the same shorts and T-shirt that she had had on when Kella had last seen her on Malaita. As usual, her tape recorder was cradled protectively in her arms. She struggled to her feet when she saw the others, her eyes widening.

'Are you all right?' asked Kella, entering the hut.

Dr Maddy nodded confusedly. She seemed to be experiencing difficulty in speaking. Sister Conchita guided her by the elbow towards the door.

'We don't have too much time left,' she said, trying to sound reassuring. 'Do you think you can get as far as the reef with us? We'll be all right then.'

The musicologist inclined her head again and stumbled out of the old church with them. While Sister Conchita supported the other woman, Brother John took over the leadership of the party, heading through the trees parallel to the coast.

'We'll be in one of the Christian territories in a minute,' he told them, panting. 'We'll head down to the beach there and try to get back on board *The Spirit of the Islands*. I'm not saying that Chief Atanga will necessarily come looking for us with bad intentions once Shem's canoe has taken him over the horizon, but he's an old-fashioned leader. He could decide to exact retribution for the death of his son. As soon as he can no longer see Shem's canoe out at sea, he will be carried to Mount Reani to be instructed by his gods. That gives us a little time.'

A quarter of an hour later, Brother John led them out of the trees and on to the beach. There was no sign of any village. To their right, a headland topped by cliffs and holed with the dark mouths of caves cut off their view of Chief Atanga's beach and its mourners. On the solitary expanse of beach immediately ahead of them, one old Tikopian was sitting next to his outrigger at the water's edge, mending a fishing net. Out beyond the reef, *The Spirit of the Islands* lay sedately at anchor.

'How are we going to contact Mr Mayotishi?' asked Sister Conchita.

Wordlessly Kella produced a small hand mirror from the pack he carried on his back. Cupping it in his hand, he trapped the rays of the sun and started to flash a message out to the waiting vessel. Either the lookout on board the ship was alert, or Mayotishi was standing over him. Almost immediately the rusted anchor of *The Spirit of the Islands* groaned up on to the deck of the vessel and the ship began to move cautiously forward to the very edge of the exterior of the reef. It was a difficult and dangerous manoeuvre. The vessel could easily have been holed beneath the waterline on the jagged lumps of coral against which it was now bumping. It was completely out of character for the bosun to risk *The Spirit of the Islands* in this manner. The vessel altered course a little, and Kella was able to see, as he had expected, that Mayotishi was at the wheel, handling the ship with considerable confidence. It almost looked as if the sombre Japanese was enjoying himself for once. The ship glided with surprising dexterity into place alongside the wall of rock before the anchor was lowered again.

'We need to get out to that reef,' said Brother John, running down to the old man mending his nets and engaging him in a lively and apparently fruitless dialogue accompanied by hand gestures on both sides and ending with the Tikopian shrugging and then shaking his head firmly.

There was something that Kella had to know. He turned to Florence. 'What made you come to Tikopia?' he asked.

'Shem saw that I was disappointed not to have recorded more pidgin war songs at the feast,' said the musicologist. 'He told me that he could arrange for me to go to Tikopia, where there was a famous song about an American bomber crashing during the war. He arranged for me to get a passage on the government boat.'

'But no one speaks pidgin on Tikopia,' Kella said.

'Nobody told me that,' said Florence, tight-lipped.

'Then what happened?' asked Sister Conchita.

'It was crazy,' said the other woman with a shudder. 'When the *Commissioner* put in at Tikopia, a group of islanders met me and hustled me ashore. Ever since I got here, I've been moved from one village to another.'

'It seems to me', said Kella, 'that somebody wanted to get Dr Maddy away from Malaita for some reason. It might have been Shem, or the person concerned might have paid Shem to tell her the story about the American bomber song.'

'Why would anyone want to do that?' asked Florence. 'What harm could I be to anyone on Malaita?'

'I don't know yet,' Kella said. 'Anyway, I reckon that on the voyage to Tikopia, some of the Christian passengers on board the ship realized that Dr Maddy was being lured to their island by pagan

Tikopian members of the Church of the Blessed Ark. This alarmed them, because they didn't know what Shem and the others wanted with Dr Maddy, so when the ship anchored they arranged for her to be smuggled ashore. Ever since Dr Maddy arrived, she's been moved from place to place on the Christian areas of the island, so that the pagans couldn't find her.'

Brother John trudged back up the beach, shaking his head. 'It's no use; he won't take us out to the reef,' he said.

Kella sighed impatiently and brushed Brother John aside. With something of a flourish he walked over and offered the old man the mirror with which he had been signalling. The sergeant pointed first at the dugout and then at the distant reef. The canoe owner accepted the looking glass judiciously, admired his reflection in it and placed it carefully at the bottom of his dugout before, with maddening precision, putting aside his net and pushing the canoe out into the lagoon.

Sister Conchita, Florence Maddy, Kella and Brother John clambered into the now crowded dugout as its owner started paddling his passengers effortlessly towards the coral wall. As they drew closer to *The Spirit of the Islands*, Sister Conchita looked out beyond the cargo ship. In the distance she could see the great canoe with its sail distended still carrying Shem steadily towards the horizon. A school of dolphins had surrounded it and seemed to be swimming on either side. One or two of them even appeared to be nudging the canoe forward with their heads. From their truncated round snouts, she guessed that the placid mammals were bottlenoses, reputed to be the cleverest and most adaptable of the whole species. Although some of the fully grown ones were up to eight feet long, it was difficult to make them out with their dark grey backs merging into the blue of the ocean. They seemed to be providing a strangely dignified escort for the canoe. It was quite a coincidence that they should have turned up at this particular moment.

Or was it such an unforeseen event? Sister Conchita wondered. A number of frayed fibres in her mind seemed to weave into place in one strong single strand. She leaned forward and tapped Sergeant Kella on the shoulder.

'I know why the Tikopians have linked up with the Church of the Blessed Ark,' she said.

23

EYES OF THE WIND ·

The dinghy from *The Spirit of the Islands* put the four of them ashore on the main island of Malaita at a spot roughly halfway between the site of the burnt-out ark and Sulufou shortly after dawn. Kella, Sister Conchita, Brother John and Florence Maddy stood uncertainly on the beach, as if reluctant to leave after the long but uneventful voyage back from Tikopia.

'The parting of the ways,' Kella said, wishing that he could have thought of something more original. 'Are you sure you want to go up to the ark, Sister Conchita?'

'I'd like to see what is left of it,' said the nun. News of the destruction of the edifice had come to them over the local pidgin news on the radio.

Kella knew that Sister Conchita had more definite plans than that but that she would only reveal them in her own good time. He looked at Brother John, who was standing with Florence Maddy. He had deputed the Guadalcanal man to escort the musicologist along the coastal path back to her island. Brother John had appeared reluctant to accept the commission but had known better than to dispute the matter with Kella.

'The sect of the ark will probably dwindle now that Papa Noah and Shem are dead,' the young nun went on. 'After all, as I told Sergeant Kella, there was only one main connection between the cult and Tikopia. It came to me as I watched Shem's canoe taking him out to sea. Papa Noah based his cult on the story of Noah. He even built his own ark. The pagan Tikopians noticed that. Their own faith was based on the *vaka tapu*, the great canoe. When most of them became Christians, they gave this canoe to an overseas museum, as a relic of the past. But when Atanga and his followers started their revival of the pagan faith, they secretly built another *vaka tapu*.'

'The one Shem was buried in,' said Brother John.

'Exactly,' said Sister Conchita. 'The Tikopian pagans decided to take over the Church of the Blessed Ark because it was based on the same icon as their own faith – a ship. The cult would give them a foothold on other islands, especially if Shem took over the church after Papa Noah's death.'

'That would give Shem a reason for killing Papa Noah,' said Brother John.

'Are you saying it was Shem who murdered Papa Noah?' asked Sister Conchita. 'It seems so out of character.'

'Who else could it have been?' Brother John asked.

We only have to accuse Shem if we want to direct attention away from the real killer, thought Kella, wondering why Brother John was being so bellicose. Aloud he said: 'I don't buy Shem as the killer. He wasn't a fighting man. That's why he wouldn't become the high priest.'

'All those Tikopians are hard men,' said Brother John with conviction. 'Some of them must have murdered Abalolo, the Christian minister on Tikopia, and hidden his body.'

'Oh, no!' said Florence. She coloured when she saw everyone looking at her, but cleared her throat and continued gamely. 'I mean, Abalolo isn't dead,' she said. 'Some of the Christian women looking after me told me about him. They said that he had left Tikopia suddenly on a government boat six months ago, without giving any reason.'

No one in the group reacted visibly or said much after that. Soon afterwards they started taking their individual paths away from the beach. Kella watched them go. Apart from Florence Maddy, each of them was being secretive about his or her mission. He had no idea why Sister Conchita was heading for the site of the ark, and he was sure that Brother John had his own destinations as well. Mind, he himself was just as bad, thought the sergeant. The news that Brother Abalolo had probably been on Malaita for months meant that Kella was going to have to change his plans. He searched in his mind for an appropriate expression from the British crime movies he enjoyed watching so much at the Point Cruz cinema, claiming that they helped him with his understanding of colloquial English. Finally he settled on one.

'I must see one of my snouts,' he said, in what he hoped was an imitation of Leslie Dwyer, one of his favourite actors, and started walking towards the mountains.

24

THE TREE SHOUTER

The tree shouter had already started his work by the time Kella arrived at the clearing amid the forest of red-brown *akwa* trees on the side of the mountain, struggling to survive amid the choking cliffs of orchid-strewn vegetation in the Kwaio district of Malaita. The old man nodded almost imperceptibly in recognition as Kella entered the glade. The policeman examined the ground for signs of centipedes and scorpions before sitting on a tree trunk to enjoy the performance. He had noticed on his way up that most of the villages were still disappointingly desolate and empty, as their inhabitants continued to seek sanctuary from the killman in the bush.

This was high country, the home of the bushmen, the traditional enemies of the saltwater coastal dwellers. Kella examined Giosa, the tree shouter. For years the bushman had been turning the onset of old age into an art form, as carefully cultivated as the way some people embraced and embellished the prospect of death. Prematurely wrinkled, he grew his straggly, matted hair long to his shoulders and constantly renewed the darkest of dyes to emphasize the tattoos slashed across his hunched torso in an attempt to make them resemble natural corrugations of the flesh. The two upper teeth remaining in his slack mouth drooped loosely like badly set green pendants. Legs as thin as filaments of brown vine straggled dispiritedly from his discoloured loincloth.

165

As Kella looked on, Giosa worked the crowd with all the concentrated skill and attention to detail of an Indian fakir the sergeant had once watched entertaining passengers at Benares airport. The tree shouter was circling the tree that the villagers had called upon him to weaken, muttering ferociously, like an athlete psyching himself up before an event.

The *akwa* was enormous, twelve feet in circumference and a hundred feet high, with huge leaf-encrusted branches burgeoning from its sides. The villagers had been clearing the area for new gardens, but this particular tree was throwing too much shade over the coveted fertile ground. Efforts to fell the giant with axes had so far been beyond them, and so the village headman had called in the tree shouter.

When he was ready, Giosa walked away from the trunk and stood on the charred stubble of the slashed and burnt garden land. Packs of terns swooped over the clearing into the spears of sunshine piercing the surrounding trees. The old man finished limbering up and faced the *akwa* before going to work flamboyantly, while the wondering villagers looked on. Kella had to admit that Giosa always gave value for money. For the next thirty minutes he howled threats and imprecations at the tree, trying to make it comprehend that it was no longer wanted in this part of the jungle. He interspersed these warnings with menacing wails and growls from the animal denizens of this particular part of the bush area. He hissed like a snake and a crocodile, squawked like a flying fox, squealed like a wild pig and screeched like a parrot. Sometimes he even sang hoarse, tuneless snatches from custom songs, involving the ancient gods in his struggle with nature.

Kella studied the artistry of the tree shouter with dispassionate admiration. Giosa was one of only half a dozen of his kind left on Malaita. Because of his reputation he was one of the few islanders with free access to every region of the island, encouraged to ply his trade in return for gifts of shell money and dolphins' teeth. As a result, he was a font of news and gossip.

Kella had known the old man for some time. Before the war, Giosa had belonged to a family famed for its ability in savage internecine brawls. Some of its members were even rumoured to present themselves as potential hired muscle to less aggressive tribes who nevertheless had scores to settle with neighbours. Giosa himself, despite his lack of size, had played a prominent part in a number of affrays in areas not then patrolled by expatriate district officers. His cunning and speed of hand made up for any lack of bulk.

A few years ago one of Giosa's recalcitrant sons, carrying on the family tradition, had badly injured a Toambaita man in an inter-tribal squabble. Kella had tracked down and arrested the youth and after his trial had escorted him to Honiara prison to serve his sentence, which by virtue of his family's reputation for violence was more severe than it might otherwise have been. He had also used his influence to ensure that Giosa's son had been left alone by a squad of Toambaita men who were also doing time in the same gaol for a variety of offences and who might have been tempted to exact vengeance for their stricken *wantok*'s injuries. Giosa, who by this time had abandoned violence in favour of the more lucrative and less painful tree shouting, had appreciated the policeman's efforts and afterwards was usually prepared to share his accumulated information with Kella upon request.

The Kwaio men were ruthless fighters. Their paramount chief Pazabozi had laid the bones curse on Kella only a few months before, but had since died of old age. The pointing of the cursed bones at the sergeant had not worked, mainly because the old chief's powers had been waning. Kella, aided by an American anthropologist, had killed Hita, his heir apparent, and a form of uneasy peace had spread over the district like a tattered blanket, until the recent arrival of the killman to upset the equilibrium once again.

In the centre of the glade Giosa had completed his stream of invective and stood in silence at last, his chest heaving, waving with the mock modesty of a flamboyant Victorian actor manager in acknowledgement of the appreciative cries of his small audience. Then, as half a dozen of the village men picked up axes and attacked the tree, he walked over and sat down next to Kella, who offered the perspiring old man his water bottle. Giosa drank long from it.

'You're back from Tikopia, then,' he said, using the Lau dialect.

'I'm looking for the man who killed Papa Noah and two members of the Church of the Blessed Ark,' Kella said.

'I should hope so,' said Giosa self-righteously. 'That idiot, whoever he is, is very bad for business. People can't be building gardens and paying me to shout at their trees if they're away cowering in the bush somewhere.'

'Nevertheless, some say that he is a killman and so to be feared.'

'Then they don't know what they're talking about,' said Giosa, spitting scornfully and with enormous trajectory at an undeterred line of red ants. 'This man who kills is nothing like one of the old *ramos*. He is only a boy compared with the real killers we used to have.'

'Who says?' Kella asked.

'I do. A *ramo* or a killman, whichever you call him, was a professional killer,' said Giosa. 'I grew up among them, so I know. The man who is murdering now is an amateur.' Irritably the old man elaborated on his theme. 'There have been three killings,' he explained, ticking them off on his fingers. 'Papa Noah was murdered outside his ark in a pool of water. The other two were also drowned, but no one knows how. It's all too complicated. A professional killman used to take pride in his work. He would leave his signature, if you like, so that everyone would know that he had accomplished the task he had been paid to do. He would not make a children's puzzle of his killings like this. A true *ramo* would strangle a victim in a particular way, or use a stone club that always left the same mark on his prey's head, and so on. This would be his sign, known to all. That way he would gain a reputation and get more paid assignments. The man they're calling a killman today is doing none of these things. He's deliberately covering up after his crimes, so that no one knows who he really is. That's why he blew up the ark.' Giosa snorted disgustedly. 'That's not the handiwork of one of the old-time *ramos*. This is a guy who's terrifying people so that they're all running away to hide, leaving him to do whatever it is he wants to. He is trying to frighten people. I don't even think he particularly wants to kill anyone. He just wants to stir up a lot of fuss on Malaita for some reason.'

'But why?' Kella demanded.

The tree shouter shrugged. 'You're the detective,' he said.

Put like that, it made some sense, Kella admitted to himself. Could the dead men all have been selected at random for some reason, or even for no reason at all, perhaps by a deranged person? What would have been the point of that? Was he wrong to be looking for reasons? Of course not, he told himself. Nothing happened without a reason, and there were no coincidences.

'Aha!' said Giosa suddenly, quivering with triumph, a craftsman vindicated in his work.

The old man was staring across the clearing. The axemen, working in relays, were beginning to make progress. Their hatchets, which previously had rebounded harmlessly from the unyielding glossy bark of the *akwa* tree, were now finding a purchase. Wooden chips were flying wildly into the air like hyperactive brown butterflies. Such encouragement gave the fellers renewed strength, and now they were working harder than ever.

'Like I've always said,' Giosa murmured happily, 'bringing a tree down is very much like dealing with an opponent in a fight. You've got to soften both of them up first and then move in for the kill.' He looked surreptitiously at the policeman. 'I'm just giving you the theory of course, Sergeant Kella, and telling you what I've heard.'

'You underestimate yourself. I would call it more of an informed opinion,' Kella said.

'In fact,' said a perfectly straight-faced Giosa, 'strange as it may seem, I have also heard that it is the custom of whitey to treat his women in much the same way, by paying considerable attention to them at first. What a waste of time and energy! Of course, you would know much more about that than I would. I shall defer to your opinion on the matter.'

Kella ignored the barbed remark, which was just as well, because the old tree shouter seemed to be rambling on at a tangent.

'You can never tell with the expatriates,' Giosa said. 'It is a problem that has often occupied my thoughts over the years. They have no customs of their own, so we cannot judge them by ours. It is good when we get a chance to see them at first hand and can work out what they are trying to do, no matter how stupid or dangerous what they are attempting may appear.'

'But so few of them come to this part of Malaita to take part in your no doubt valuable survey,' said Kella, wondering where this was taking them.

Giosa seemed to agree. 'True, *aofia*. The climate is not good for their delicate pale skins, and the crashing of the great waves can be so daunting to their sensitive ears.' The tree shouter stood up. 'Well, much as I'd like to, Sergeant, I can't stay here chatting all day. I must go and find the headman and collect my fee. Is there anything else I can do for you?'

'You haven't done anything for me yet,' Kella pointed out. 'In fact, however, there is something you can help me with. I'd like you to look for someone.'

'Who might that be?' asked the tree shouter.

'His name is Abalolo. He's a Tikopian. I believe he's been on Malaita for a few months now. I think he may have been hiding in the bush somewhere near Papa Noah's ark for most of that time.'

'How – disguised as a tree?' asked Giosa sceptically. 'These Tikopia are big, awkward fellows and hard to conceal. Besides which, they know nothing about living in the jungle, and they usually start to go mad unless they're herded with at least a dozen of their own kind, like dolphins.'

'That should make him all the easier for you to find,' said Kella.

'Is he the one you think has been doing the killing?'

'We're hoping that he might be able to help us with our enquiries,' said Kella. It was another phrase that he had always wanted to use in the bush and could now at last tick off his list.

Giosa pretended to consider the request. Although he owed Kella for looking after his son, he still retained enough basic bloody-mindedness to make the sergeant wait each time the latter requested a favour.

'Do you think you can find him for me?' Kella asked.

Giosa flashed his two verdant teeth in his dentally challenged response. 'Do skinks copulate in the treetops?' he asked.

25

FINISH NOW!

Sister Conchita stood in the clearing on the plateau by the waterfall and looked at what remained of the ark. She could hardly recognize Papa Noah's former labour of love. The building had been flattened into a pile of kindling, the remaining planks and spars twisted out of shape by fire. A few feathers of flame still fluttered defiantly through the shattered wood on the ruined site.

On her dogged eight-mile trek up from the coast she had passed several almost deserted villages, but she had been conscious all the time of frightened islanders hiding in ditches and behind trees, witnessing her progress. There must have been hundreds of men and women on this small section of Malaita alone still reluctant to return home. On her way Sister Conchita felt increasingly angry that so many decent, harmless people should be affected like this. Soon she was simmering with indignation at the injustice of it all.

The track was rough and little used. Part of it consisted of a dried-out riverbed, caked with thick red mud. This gave way to a swamp bridged by a succession of gigantic tree trunks with no handholds except for guiding creepers slotted into long canes along the way. The path was steep. At one point Sister Conchita emerged from the trees to find herself on the edge of a cliff. Far below she could see the tops of trees wreathed in clouds. She drove herself on because ever since she had awoken that morning she had felt convinced that there was to be a special purpose to this day. Enough things had fallen into place, or the Lord had so designed them, that it would be possible to make a special decision. From this would follow an action, she was sure.

By the time she reached the plateau, the weather had cleared up. The air smelt clean and fresh. Sister Conchita recalled the black aroma of sin and malevolence she had encountered the first time she had entered the ark. It seemed to have been washed away entirely by the fire and then the cleansing rains. She could have sworn that the evil had slunk away back to its hole.

So much had happened in such a short time, she thought. Briefly the ark had been the focal point of intense activity. Because of its existence both Papa Noah and Shem had lost their lives. Now that their sacrifices had been made, the evil spirits had departed from the hollowed out, blackened shell, she was convinced for ever.

Sister Conchita's sense of outraged decency deepened still further. It was wrong that basically good-hearted and well-meaning men like Papa Noah and Shem should have been used and then discarded by the shades inhabiting the ark. If, as she was convinced, the evil spirits had gone back to their festering pits, it was her duty to see that they did not return. She could not allow the area to remain a vacuum when with a little effort it could be filled with God's benevolent presence again.

Cautiously the nun patrolled the clearing, examining the scorched ruins of the ark from every angle. She was conscious still of being watched by many pairs of eyes from among the trees. A growing sense of conviction was beginning to strengthen within her. She went back to the debris and continued to study the blackened remains. She was no longer aware of any sense of wickedness in the clearing. In the background, the purifying force of the waterfall pounded down to the frothing river below. Soon the blackened grass would be green again and the singed branches of the trees would be renewed. The nun fell to her knees and started to pray for guidance

When she had finished, she rose and looked around the clearing. In one corner she saw the store of wood and metal accumulated by Papa Noah ready to be used for the construction of his ark. Some of the contents had been scattered over the plateau by trampling feet during the storm, but the fire had not reached this part of the glade with any great ferocity. She selected two thin pieces of wood, each about two feet long. She searched for nails and found a cache of used but serviceable ones in the lid of an old cocoa tin. Using a flat stone to pound away at the nails, she joined the two sections of wood together to form a rough but recognizable cross. Then she took a deep breath, and with trembling hands held the cross high above her head and walked to the centre of the clearing.

'Finish now!' she cried. 'It is over! The ghosts have gone! Mefella talk true! Tambarin himi go finish! You can go home! It is safe!'

Using a combination of English, pidgin and the few Lau phrases that she had taught herself, Sister Conchita beseeched her listeners to emerge from the jungle and return to their homes in the village below. At first there was no response, but slowly a few women and children came out of the trees. They were followed by half a dozen men, clutching their spears aggressively. As she continued to beg, more and more islanders began to congregate. They looked weary and emaciated and regarded the nun with wary, scarcely flickering hope. Sister Conchita pointed down the hill to their huts.

'Go!' she cried. 'God is here! He will guide us!'

Several of the older men exchanged uncertain glances. Then, shoulder to shoulder, they walked with obvious trepidation down the hill. Halfway down, they linked hands. Other men fell in behind them. The women took their place at the rear of the now surging crowd. Children joined in everywhere, darting in and out and getting under the feet of the adults. Sister Conchita watched the villagers approach their huts and stand in the village square, casting watchful glances over their shoulders. Then one or two, greatly daring, entered their huts. Others followed. Soon most of the homes were occupied again as the village gradually came back to life. Cooking fires were lit and smoke curled up to the sky. Neighbours started gossiping. Children needed little urging to begin to play together. Even so, the circumspect headman placed half a dozen of the younger men as temporary guards on the fringes of the settlement.

Sister Conchita looked on from the plateau on the top of the hill. Only when she was satisfied that all was well did she turn aside and enter the jungle, holding her cross before her.

Later, when the events of that day had entered Malaitan legend and were being recounted regularly over cooking fires all around the island, the diviners, whose task it was to discover the truth behind events, started to embellish the tale by declaring that they had it on the best authority that in the course of one afternoon the Praying Mary from Ruvabi had traversed the length and breadth of the northern part of the island with giant strides, from Farasi in the south to Fouia in the north, and that in the process she had even approached several villages among the foothills of the central mountain range. All the time, said the story-tellers, this time with truth, the nun called upon everyone she met to return to their villages, promising them that the killing time was over, that enough blood had been shed and that her God would protect everyone. By the time darkness fell, averred the tale-bearers, hundreds, perhaps thousands, of men, women and children had emerged from their hiding places in the bush and at the missions and were returning home in great streams, the latter stages of their journeys illuminated by blazing torches, following the passionate sister all over the island.

In fact, in the course of that day, Sister Conchita progressed in an uncertain and unplanned zigzag line along a number of different bush tracks from the plateau of the ark to Ruvabi Mission far below along the coast. Some time afterwards, when variously exaggerated versions of the story were even being recounted amid much condescending laughter at expatriate dinner parties in Honiara, Auki and Gizo, an inquisitive government geologist took the trouble to measure the actual route of the young nun's pilgrimage, as endorsed by reliable eyewitnesses. The official confirmed that over half a morning and a long afternoon in temperatures averaging ninety degrees Fahrenheit, Sister Conchita had covered sixteen miles of rocky, undulating terrain on foot. In the course of her journey she had climbed four sheer hills, forded six rivers in spate and thrown half a dozen stones, most of which had missed, at a young crocodile with the temerity to threaten to impede her path. In the whole of that time no one ever noticed her lower her cross for more than a few minutes.

No researcher ever managed to detail the number of islanders she rescued from their primitive hiding places and sent on their way home. Later, on the very few occasions that she could be persuaded to give the most fleeting account of her hot-headed actions during what became known in pidgin as 'plentyman', the day of the crowds, Sister Conchita would declare that by the time she set out to gather them in, the majority of the refugees were heartily tired of their current self-enforced nomadic lives and were easily persuaded to return to their abandoned villages. Senior members of the church in conclave in the capital agreed privately that this may have been true, but that the islanders had needed a catalyst to start them moving, and that this impetus had undoubtedly been supplied by Sister Conchita, undisciplined, unpredictable and indisputably courageous.

It was a fact, ascertained by patrolling government officers as well as village headmen and occasional missionaries, that word of the mass return in the nun's wake spread amazingly quickly all over northern Malaita, and that within three days most islanders were settling back with relief into their villages and taking up their normal lives again.

Back on the coastal strip on the first day of plentyman, dusk was beginning to fall as the bedraggled and exhausted nun finally reached Ruvabi mission station. She was still cradling her wooden cross in her arms. Word of her clarion cries across the valleys that everyone should return home had already reached the station ahead of her, and many of the refugees had drifted away to take advantage of the remaining hours of daylight for their journey. Several hundred still remained, however, to claim that they had seen with their own eyes the Praying Mary on this her day of days. They looked on in silent wonder as the sister dragged herself to the centre of the compound and thrust one end of the quivering cross into the muddy ground.

'No more killim,' she croaked. 'Him true now. Go long place bilong youfella.' She gave up the effort of struggling with pidgin, deciding that she was almost too weary to compose a coherent sentence in English. 'Go home,' she implored her listeners. 'Please, all of you, go home. Everything's going to be all right.'

It was enough. Over the months Sister Conchita had built up a store of moral credit with the islanders of the district that would have surprised the young nun had she been aware of it. The refugees scattered to collect their belongings and started to straggle out of the gates of the mission. Within thirty minutes all that remained in the compound were dozens of makeshift hovels and the solitary, tiny figure of Sister Conchita. When Father Kuyper came out of the mission house, he found the nun slumped on her knees beside the now lopsided cross.

'Sister, what is going on?' he asked with surprising gentleness.

Sister Conchita looked up at him vaguely, panting, her face smeared with an amalgam of sweat, dirt and mud. She must have looked like this the first time she had met the priest at the mission, she thought. Wistfully she wondered how nice it might be never to have to get up again.

'You wanted me to get rid of them,' she heard herself say to the mighty bishop's inspector. 'Well, I've got rid of them.' She paused and considered. 'Father,' she added politely.

26

SOMETHING SOMETHING ALLSAME

Kella stood on the hill overlooking the bay and wondered why the six dolphins had been penned up in the makeshift pool below, and how anyone could be so cruel and misguided as to place them in captivity in this region of all places. As far as he could see, they were bottlenoses, snub of snout, tractable and sociable. What were these ones doing so many yards from the open sea? It looked as if they had been trapped and imprisoned. Who would want to do that? Their meat was reputed to be tough and unappetizing. Besides, they were protected on earth and in the spirit world; everyone knew that.

Kella started walking down the hill. Behind him in the trees he could hear the reverberation of the hollowed-out logs used by the coastal dwellers as talking drums. Messages, almost certainly about the dolphins, were being passed on for many miles. Kella wondered if their high priest was within earshot yet, and if so what plans he was making. Whatever they were, they would not prove beneficial for the men who had captured the dolphins.

The great mammals were being held in a small, clouded stream running down to the open sea. The water had been dammed with a series of logs piled on top of one another to form a small lake six feet deep in which the creatures were lying inert. The top pole was about fifteen feet high, too tall for even the most agile dolphin to surmount.

Kella was incensed. Who could make such beautiful creatures suffer in this way? He increased his pace.

Two men were waiting for him at the foot of the hill in front of half a dozen tents pitched on a level patch of land on the coastal strip. They looked uncertain but determined not to budge. Kella recognized one of them.

'Hello, Schuman,' he said.

'Kella,' nodded the other man.

Ralph Schuman was a light brown half-caste in his late thirties, tall and broad-shouldered. He was a good-looking, arrogant man, with high cheekbones and a discontented expression. His father had been German, a veteran of the First World War who had married a local girl and bought a plantation on Choiseul in the western islands when land had still been cheap. Although the Japanese had overrun the area in 1942, Schuman senior had been allowed to continue to run his plantation, partly, it had been rumoured, because he had secretly declared his allegiance to the Axis cause. When the conflict ended, the occupying Americans had tried him for treason but the case had been dismissed due to insufficient evidence. The older Schuman had died soon afterwards. Eventually Ralph had returned from Australia, where he had been educated at a series of private schools, being expelled from most of them. After several years as a professional gambler on Australian racecourses, he had started to work his inheritance.

The plantation had not done well in the post-war years, due to the worldwide slump in copra prices. Ralph Schuman had been unable to find alternative employment in the colonial government's service because of the general antipathy towards his family's reputation, and had drifted from one ill-fated project to another. As a half-breed his mother's clan distrusted him, especially those who had risked their lives scouting and fighting for the Allies. Kella knew him to be both tough and clever, a bad combination for an unsuccessful but ambitious man, and one tending to result in considerable bitterness and self-pity. Lately Schuman had been suspected of hiring himself out as an intelligent and resourceful strong-arm man and enforcer for a number of Chinese businessmen in Honiara, but so far he had been too wily to establish a criminal record.

The sergeant turned his attention to Schuman's companion. He was a slight, erect white man in his fifties who looked as if he was accustomed to issuing orders and expecting them to be carried out. There was an undeniable power to the man, but he seemed oddly unfinished in appearance His arms hung loosely from his hard frame and his head was cocked interrogatively to one side at an angle. His face was a strange shade of grey. He reminded Kella of roughly finished carvings he had seen in Papua New Guinea, which revealed the original stone rather than resembling the humans they were supposed to portray.

'This is Sergeant Kella, the local policeman,' said Schuman. 'Kella, this is my employer, Herr Boehrs.'

Boehrs extended a hand with watchful affability. 'How do you do, Sergeant,' he said. 'I hope there's nothing wrong.'

'I was interested in the dolphins you seem to have trapped,' said Kella.

'Ah, the project is still in its infancy,' said the German. 'All the same, we're rather proud of our set-up here. Allow me to display it to you.'

The three men started walking towards the pool. Boehrs, who seemed to have well-developed antennae, had already detected the atmosphere of constraint between Kella and Schuman. 'I take it you two have met before,' he said.

'We used to be in the Solomons rugby team together some years ago,' Schuman said. 'Kella went on to greater things and played professional rugby league in Australia. Maybe I should have followed his example.'

'You were good enough,' said Kella, 'but you had one fault. You could never control your temper.'

'For that matter I've seen you clear a Honiara bar on your own once or twice when you were sufficiently aroused,' said Schuman. 'Perhaps we have something in common – something something allsame.'

'Perhaps,' said Kella. 'I hope not.'

'Rapid action is not always a bad characteristic under certain supervised circumstances,' said Boehrs placatingly. 'I find docile people rather boring and lacking in character. They are also predictable.' He changed the subject adroitly. 'Actually I spent a few years in Australia myself. I found it a most interesting country.'

'Which part – Loveday or Katarapko?' Kella asked.

A brief smile of acknowledgement alighted on Boehrs' chipped granite face like a passing insect, to be brushed aside automatically. 'Dhurringile, actually,' he murmured, 'but still perceptive of you, Sergeant.'

Of all the Australian prisoner-of-war camps occupied by captured German officers during the war, Dhurringile Mansion, north of Melbourne in Victoria, had been reserved for the highest-ranking, the most dangerous and those considered highly likely to try to escape. After the war, a number of those now rootless German nationals with little inclination or incentive to return to their shattered country had opted to remain in the South Pacific. There was one small colony of former servicemen in Honiara and another in Auki. They were hard-working, reserved and as clannish as a group of high-bush *kanakas*.

The three men stopped by the dolphin pen. Kella hoped that he was not displaying his feelings of utter revulsion. The dolphins were floating listlessly on top of the water. They looked like poorly modelled facsimiles of the lively, energetic and affable mammals he was accustomed to seeing sporting in the waters of the islands.

'May I ask the point of imprisoning them?' he asked.

'I note an expression of disapproval in your voice, Sergeant. You surprise me. I wouldn't have taken you for a sentimentalist. This could be a breakthrough in the economy of Malaita.' The hitherto sedate Boehrs could not keep the enthusiasm from his voice.

'And presumably for your bank balance,' said Kella.

'The labourer is worthy of his hire,' Boehrs said, the friendliness expunged from his tone at once. Here was a man who did not like to be contradicted, thought Kella, presumably because he was not accustomed to it. He seemed the sort who preferred to conduct his affairs from the bridge of a U-boat.

'Actually, this is something completely new,' Boehrs continued. 'I am starting to export bottlenose dolphins to the USA, specifically to hotels in Florida.'

'Hotels?' asked Kella. 'Do they get a special rate for their rooms there? I hadn't thought of that, a tourist company for dolphins. They probably make much more considerate and entertaining guests than rich American tourists.'

'Very funny,' said Boehrs without interest. 'Actually, it's the latest craze in the States, so I'm not surprised that you are sceptical. In fact, in my opinion it's going to be the next big market for South Pacific exports. Most big tourist hotels in the area of Miami are installing special pools, called dolphinariums. There the creatures are taught to perform tricks – leaping through hoops, jumping for food, that sort of thing. Believe me, such displays are attracting huge crowds. The hotel people can't get enough dolphins of the right sort. I'm hoping to rectify that. Bottlenoses are in particular demand.'

Once again Kella felt physically sick. To think of the graceful, soaring creatures languishing so pitifully in the water before him being forced to perform circus tricks was enough to offend even the meanest of the bad spirits that abounded in the dark places of the islands.

'You see,' Boehrs went on, 'it is an established fact that bottlenose dolphins are the most intelligent of all non-human species, cleverer among the animal kingdom even than gorillas and chimpanzees. A good trainer who stands no nonsense from them can whip them into shape in no time at all.'

'*Whip* being the operative verb, I suppose,' said Kella.

Boehrs shrugged. 'I have no idea,' he said indifferently. 'I take no interest in that side of the affair. My main concern lies in getting the wretched creatures to the USA in one piece; well, a reasonable percentage of them, anyway. Naturally there is an acceptable amount of wastage.'

'What do you consider acceptable, Mr Boehrs?'

'At the moment, about fifty per cent,' said the German.

'And just how do you export them?' asked Kella, trying not to dwell on the German's chilling answer.

'Once a month a Chinese vessel picks up the ones we have caught and transports them on wet rubber mattresses to Honiara, with Mr Schuman supervising their inter-island transit by sea. In fact, the ones you see in the pen in front of us now will be collected tomorrow. From there my American contacts have them flown in hammocks on cargo aircraft to the west coast of the USA. I can assure you, it's a growth industry. What do you think of it? I truly believe that in a few years' time, a tractable dolphin will be fetching ten thousand dollars in the open market.'

'I think it's obscene!' said Kella, stung out of his usual good manners. 'Your whole tawdry money-making racket is immoral!' He forced himself to lower his voice. 'To many islanders the dolphin is a sacred animal.'

'And other clans hunt them down and kill them just for their teeth, to make necklaces,' Schuman pointed out. 'The bride-price for a virgin in some villages on Malaita is twenty thousand teeth. That represents a lot of dead dolphins.'

'There are only three dolphin-calling villages on the island: Fanalai, Walande and Fourau,' said Kella. 'That is their custom, and has been for centuries.'

'And mine is making money,' said Boehrs. 'More to the point, my company is operating a perfectly legal enterprise. If you don't believe me, check with your superiors in the capital. I even have an export licence.'

Kella was sure that the man was right. Some glorified expatriate clerk in the Secretariat who had never left the capital would not have the remotest idea of the harm he was doing by giving Boehrs' wicked project the go-ahead.

'Please, Mr Boehrs,' he said. 'I beg you to reconsider. Your operation would be distasteful anywhere in the islands. Here in the Kwaio district it is positively dangerous. Some of the islanders on this part of the coastal strip worship dolphins and regard them as holy. There is even some affinity in their faith between the blood of Jesus and the blood of the dolphins they sacrifice from time to time. That's why you've found it so easy to trap them. They're half-tame. They come into certain lagoons regularly to be fed by the priests. Word will have got out about what you are doing. I'm sure that the locals will already be making plans to retrieve the animals.'

'I would regret it exceedingly if that were to occur,' Boehrs said. 'But naturally I have taken precautions against such an eventuality.' He indicated a group of islanders lounging on the beach. 'They're hardly storm troopers, I agree, but Mr Schuman here assures me that they are eminently fit for purpose should they be required.'

Kella had already noticed the men. Their tribal markings denoted that they were from the Weather Coast of Guadalcanal, a notoriously violent area. The ones watching him from the shore seemed typical of their kind: dispossessed villagers tired of trying to extract a living from thin soil, who had drifted over to Honiara in a quest for a better life. They had soon found conditions in the capital to be even less attractive than their previous rural subsistence existence. Forced to hire themselves out as casual labourers at one Australian dollar a day, when they could get it, increasing numbers of them were resorting to petty crime or working as bodyguards for dubious petty would-be entrepreneurs like Boehrs.

'I am convinced that my men over there will be able to withstand any local pressure,' went on the German. 'And should opposition come from other sources, such as your good self, Sergeant, well in that case I shall just have to rely on Mr Schuman, my head of security, to deal with any such eventuality, within the law, of course; always within the law. Do you think you are up to the task, Schuman?' he asked with forced joviality.

'If that is what you wish, Herr Boehrs,' said Schuman stolidly, looking at Kella for the first time. 'It might take some time and cause a little damage to your property, but it could certainly be done.'

Kella edged round so that he was facing Schuman head-on. The half-caste regarded him impassively. Professional brawlers to a man and quick to recognize trouble when they saw it, the Guadalcanal men began drifting over towards the group by the pen. Boehrs swivelled his head from side to side, looking on with evident gratification. After a moment, with excellent timing, he broke the tension with a casual wave of his hand.

'But of course there would be no question of such unpleasantness,' he said. 'We're all friends here. Sergeant Kella, I am sorry that you object to my venture, but I have assured you that I am operating within the law. I have taken out a lease on this land. I am breaking no regulations. On the other hand, technically, I'm afraid that you are trespassing. I must ask you to leave now. I'm sure that you will appreciate that we are very busy.'

At the top of the slope leading away from the camp, Kella paused and looked back. Boehrs and Schuman were still watching him. Schuman raised a hand in mock salute. Kella did not respond. He walked on until the camp was out of sight and he was in an outer ring of trees on a track running parallel to the coast far below. Out at sea he could see the cluster of grey rocks known as the Ten Crocodiles. These were what Giosa, the tree shouter, had been referring to so cryptically the previous day.

The whole conversation at the tree felling had been a triumph of the Melanesian delight in wrapping a few salient points inside a mess of verbiage. Giosa had given the sergeant a precise geographical location when he had made his pointed reference to expatriates finding waves daunting. A few years ago a Seventh-Day Adventist missionary approaching in his canoe had been drowned while misjudging the currents swirling around the Ten Crocodiles, leaving the rocks with the irreverent and terse sobriquet of Whitey's Folly. Giosa had thus been informing Kella, although not in so many words, that an expatriate was up to something in this area.

The old man had also made a pointed reference to the fact that it was impossible to judge a race without customs against traditional Melanesian standards, by his yardstick almost a direct accusation of chicanery on the part of some white man. When Giosa had given the policeman his opinion that it would be worthwhile examining the expatriate in question at work immediately, the remark had been tantamount to a hurry-up call. The old man had even mentioned dolphins when he had compared the mammals vaguely with Tikopians.

Giosa had been right, thought Kella as he started walking again. Boehrs and Schuman may not have been breaking the white man's laws by attempting to export live dolphins from the island, but they were offending against local customs, an equally heinous and potentially much more dangerous crime. All around him he could sense bloody payback.

27

THE SINGING COP

Sister Conchita was studying a map of North America in the mission lounge and realizing how little she knew about the geography of her own country when Sergeant Ha'a called in at Ruvabi Mission shortly before noon. He was rotund and jet black, his uniform shorts and shirt straining threateningly over his haunches and stomach.

The globular, sweating police sergeant was too exhausted to say anything until he had collapsed like a small avalanche into a chair and drunk two glasses of lemonade, hardly pausing for breath. Ha'a came from the laid-back western islands. His main ambition in life was to be sent on as many overseas attachments as possible. He had once spent three months in the north of England, where he had moonlighted at the local working men's clubs as the lead singer of a group of other Pacific Island sergeants and inspectors, ignoring geographic and ethnic niceties, under the title of Curly Ha'a and His South Sea Island Serenaders. It was an experience that the sergeant was desperate to repeat.

'Going on your holidays?' he asked indifferently, indicating the map, when he had recovered his breath.

'Improving my knowledge of my native land,' said the nun. 'Take it easy; it's a long walk from Auki.'

'Don't remind me,' said the sergeant miserably. 'There should be a map with *Here be dragons* printed on it. Three days of purgatory:

187

mosquitoes, leeches and scorpions everywhere; and then the constant screams of agony echoing through the bush at all hours of the night and day, and that was just me! I'm not built for bush walking, I can tell you. I'm more an ideas man, and my idea at this moment is to get back to Honiara just as fast as I can.' He paused and frowned. 'How did you know that I've just walked across from Auki?'

'Your fame precedes you, Sergeant.'

'You mean those jungle drums have been announcing my arrival for days.'

'I thought you were a bit off your usual beat,' said Sister Conchita calmly. 'What are you doing here on Malaita anyway?' She folded up her map and put it away in a drawer. You learn something new every day, she thought.

'Looking for Kella, what else,' Ha'a said. 'The untold grief that man has caused me since I've known him! You don't know where he is, do you? Nobody else on Malaita seems to. Or if they do, they're not telling me. My boss wants him back in Honiara.'

'I'm afraid not. The last time I saw him was a couple of days ago. He said he was going on patrol.'

'We all know what that means,' said Ha'a with a shudder. 'The man's a masochist. For another month now he'll be going out of his way to climb the highest mountains he can find and ford rivers that frighten even butch crocodiles. Well, I've done all I can. I'll go back to Chief Superintendent Grice and admit failure. He's used to me doing that. It will reinforce his colonial-native serf mentality. Anyway, I'm not on my own. Fifty Vella Lavella constables and three expatriate inspectors are climbing the central mountain range as we speak. Since the ark was destroyed, Chief Superintendent Grice has been convinced that a Japanese survivor is still fighting a one-man war up in Kwaio country.'

'Will they find him?' asked Sister Conchita.

'I doubt it. They've got battery-operated loudspeakers to hail him with and leaflets written in Japanese explaining that the war ended fifteen years ago. I hear they're thinking of offering a reward of a hundred dollars to any islander who gives the Japani up. Waste of time! It will be the Exhausted Army all over again.'

'What's the Exhausted Army?'

'Haven't you heard of it? Back in the 1920s, when a district officer was murdered in Kwaio country, the local expatriates founded their own vigilante force, armed themselves and went looking for his killers. It was a real ragtag and bobtail lot; traders, prospectors, labour recruiters, beachcombers, you name it, they were there.'

'What happened?'

Ha'a laughed. 'You could write the script! They climbed one small hill and found they were so knackered they gave up and went back to their homes. The whole expedition lasted a couple of hours. They had to wait for an Australian warship to be sent for to blast the hell out of the Kwaio. Anyway, if you don't know where Kella is, I'd better be moving on.'

'Hang on a minute, Mr Ha'a. While you are here, there's something you might be able to do for me.'

'Oh yes?' said Sergeant Ha'a, who had showed no perceptible sign of moving anyway. 'And what could that possibly be?'

'What do you know about pidgin songs about the war in the Solomons?'

Ha'a shook his head and sucked his teeth reflectively. 'They're not very commercial,' he said. 'They're all about fighting. If you're thinking of hiring me for a mission concert, and incidentally my rates are very reasonable, my version of "Big Rock Candy Mountain" goes over much better.'

'I'm sure,' said Sister Conchita. 'But you do know any pidgin World War Two songs?'

Ha'a tried to concentrate. 'Oh, sure, there's "Knife Bilong Me", "Japani No More", "Bushman Kill-kill"—'

'That's great!' said the nun, already heading for the door. 'Come along, Sergeant Ha'a. We're going to pay someone a visit. I have to go to a couple of bush schools later in the day, but I want you to meet a friend of mine first. I can drop you off on the way.'

'But I've only just sat down,' complained Ha'a.

'Regard this as being in the nature of an audition,' said Sister Conchita.

The sergeant reacted manfully to the spur of ambition. 'Really?' he asked hopefully, lumbering after her. 'In that case, if your contacts, may they be blessed eternally for their taste and discrimination, are thinking of letting me cut a disc, tell them that I want to be billed as Johnny Ha'a, the Singing Cop.'

'Sergeant Ha'a, I think you are going to be the answer to my prayers,' said Sister Conchita.

28

SERGEANT HA'A FINDS AN ADMIRER

When they landed on the small artificial island, Florence Maddy was sitting at a trestle table outside her hut going through a pile of books in a desultory manner. Each of the volumes was wrapped in transparent cellophane. The musicologist looked bored and forlorn and, as usual, sunk in apathy. She was wearing a drab pink dress.

'I don't have a great deal to do,' she said wanly, indicating the books. 'Mr Wainoni let me borrow these to while away the time.'

'Dr Maddy, this is Sergeant Ha'a,' said Sister Conchita. She resisted the temptation to shake the other woman and order her to snap out of her obvious depression. Florence Maddy did not initiate events; she reacted to them, usually adversely.

The musicologist nodded, but her habitually downcast expression showed no sign of thawing. Silently she went into her hut and returned with a pitcher of lemonade and several glasses. She poured each of the visitors a drink.

'What are you reading?' asked Sister Conchita, searching for something to say.

'They're books by some of the academics that Mr Wainoni has guided over the islands.' A tincture of self-pity entered Florence's voice. 'I must say, they all seem to have been eminently more successful with their research than I have so far.'

'I'm sure it's just a matter of being patient,' said the nun soothingly. 'Your time will come.' She hefted some of the volumes in her hands. Their contents seemed as uniformly dull and dispiriting as their covers. The very titles growled with ennui at her.

'*The Stone Structures of Small Mala, A Treatise on Molluscs of the Lau Lagoon, Friendship Patterns of Maquata,*' she read aloud. '*Custom Beliefs of the Kwaio People, Folk Tales of the Western Solomons . . .*'

'Wainoni never guided him,' yawned a bored Ha'a, speaking for the first time since he had landed on the island.

'I beg your pardon?' asked Sister Conchita.

'That last title you read out was about my island in the western Solomons. My father and some of my uncles helped the writer gather his stories before the war. I remember them talking about it. Wainoni would only have been a baby then; he wouldn't have had anything to do with it. What was the American's name?' Ha'a closed his eyes as an aid to concentration. Reluctantly he opened them again. 'Cardigan, that's it. Professor Cardigan.'

Sister Conchita glanced at the front cover. 'James Cardigan,' she said. 'Snap!'

'He was a real pioneer of Pacific anthropology,' said Florence. 'Such a determined man, to overcome so much prejudice and continue with his work.'

'I've brought Sergeant Ha'a along because he might be able to help you,' said Sister Conchita.

'I might?' blinked Ha'a.

'Look, this is very kind of you both,' said Florence, 'but I've made my bed and I must lie in it. I should not have chosen this subject for my study. I'll never be able to collect enough songs for my purposes. I'm going to book a passage back to the States next week.'

'Suppose', said Sister Conchita, spacing out her words with a flourish, like a gambler laying down a royal flush, 'I was able to provide you with a living compendium of what you are searching for? Would that help?'

She looked almost proudly at Sergeant Ha'a. Florence followed her gaze without enchantment. 'I don't understand,' said the musicologist.

'Sergeant Ha'a is a man of many parts,' said the nun. 'Police officer, intrepid bush walker and troubadour.'

'Well, two out of three isn't so bad,' said Ha'a, shifting from one foot to the other and wincing.

'Hardly a concert goes by in Honiara without Sergeant Ha'a giving his versions of songs from the shows, or a tribute to Ray Charles, to great acclaim. I haven't been privileged to see it myself yet, but I'm told that his cover version of "Whispering Grass" puts even the Ink Spots to shame.'

'Not their fault; it's not an ensemble song,' said Ha'a.

'I'm not sure . . .' Florence said.

'What's more, the sergeant also has a collection of pidgin songs about the war,' concluded Sister Conchita, like an artist unveiling her latest portrait.

'Not one of my better ideas,' Ha'a said. 'Lately we've started getting ex-GIs who fought here in the war coming back with their families. I thought they might be interested in hearing some of the old war songs I'd collected. I should have stayed in bed! If it wasn't Johnny Ray or Frankie Laine they didn't want to hear it.'

Florence was looking at Ha'a in a way that no woman had ever looked at him before. 'Have . . . have you written these songs down?' she asked with trepidation.

'No need,' Ha'a said. He tapped his forehead complacently. 'They're all up here.'

'How many of them have you got?' pressed Florence, almost before he had finished speaking.

'Oh, I don't know, maybe thirty or forty. I could find more if you want them. In 1942, at night, when they stopped killing Japs for the day, there wasn't a lot for the local scouts to do except sit around campfires swapping lies and making up pidgin songs about how brave they'd been. Would you like me to sing you one?'

'Yes please,' breathed Florence.

Ha'a looked surprised but did not ask twice. He placed one hand beneath his ear and hummed speculatively to find the right pitch.

'Well, there's always "Japani Ha Ha!" for starters,' he said. He took a deep breath, expanding his chest to a spectacular degree, and started singing rather well:

Me fulae olobauti, longo isti, longo westi.
Me sendere olo rouni keepim Solomoni.
Me worka luka luka longo landi long sea.
Ha ha! Ha ha! Japani ha ha!

'And you know more of these?' asked Florence, sounding as if Christmas had come almost too early for her.

'Try me,' said Ha'a confidently.

As Sister Conchita tiptoed away, the sergeant was singing to the enraptured musicologist "Knife Bilong Me", about two brothers who had scouted for the coast-watcher Martin Clemens on Guadalcanal. The nun was confident that she would not be missed. She untethered the canoe, started the engine and headed contentedly for the mainland of Malaita.

It took her ten minutes to reach the shore. She felt in her pocket to make sure that she had her miniature version of the Bible with her. She was about to drag the canoe up above the high-water line on the beach when someone splashed out through the shallow water to meet her. It was Brother John. He grasped the prow of the canoe and dragged it effortlessly up on to the sand.

'This is quite a coincidence,' said Sister Conchita suspiciously.

'No coincidence,' admitted the missionary. 'I asked around and I was told that you would be teaching at Bethezda today. There's someone up there I'd like you to meet. I want to get something off my conscience. I haven't actually told you all I know about the Church of the Blessed Ark.'

They had met on one of the more depressing sections of the coast. Great forests of mango trees swept down to the narrow strip of black sand. The mangled roots of the trees festooned with oysters jutted out from acres of stinking mud. They walked into the trees and began the climb up the track into the forbidding dark interior of the island. Brother John offered no further explanation as to his sudden arrival and Sister Conchita asked him no questions. When he was ready he would tell her. She devoted her time to thinking about what she would teach that morning. Now that she had persuaded the people to return to their villages, most of the small one-teacher schools up in the bush had opened again. Sister Conchita was doing her best to resettle the teachers and make sure that some sort of basic curriculum was once more being followed, so that at least the young pupils were beginning to learn English.

Several hours passed before they reached the first village on her itinerary. By this time, as usual on the outskirts of the bush country, it was raining hard. She guessed that at least an inch of water had fallen in the last hour. She and Brother John were both soaked to the skin and beginning to get cold as they toiled up the incline. Bethezda was a small village, just a collection of a dozen huts, but the last time she had visited the area there had been an encouraging total of six children between the ages of four and seven regularly attending its single class.

Sister Conchita peered ahead through the stinging rain. At first she was not quite sure what she could see on the far side of the clearing. Brother John stopped, equally disturbed. A large brown-skinned man was sitting upright under a tree, his arms secured behind his broad back. The nun stepped forward uncertainly. Wiping the rain from her eyes, she saw that the man was bound to the tree by lengths of vine.

As she drew closer, Sister Conchita could also see that the prisoner was the Tikopian she had twice encountered briefly in the ark. She looked at Brother John in alarm. At the same time, half a dozen islanders holding spears at shoulder height stepped out menacingly from behind the huts.

29

DROWNING WITH DOLPHINS

Kella had decided to take the high coastal road along the clifftop, where the trees crowded impatiently towards the edge. This proved to be a mistake, because the sea lay only a hundred feet or so below him and he was still within range of the keening voices of the dolphins and the soft entreaties of their gods as they were carried on the breeze and over the softly lapping waves. He tried to tell himself that he could only hear the sobbing of the wind among the branches and the grunting of rooting wild pigs deep in the bush, but he knew that in reality the alien spirits were laying siege to him with considerable determination, reminding him of his obligations to them and the helpless dolphins.

Other people better qualified than he was and with more local knowledge would respond to the entreaties in time, he told himself. Plans would have been laid already. As the *aofia*, when he had been in trouble far from home he had sometimes enlisted the support of the gods of other Melanesian religions, but he had never felt comfortable in doing so. Now some of these ghosts were asking for payback, demanding that in turn he should support their cause. This had never happened to him before. To make matters worse, he did not understand the language of the dolphin gods. Only a little of what they were trying to say to him was filtering through. Perhaps his own shark gods were becoming jealous and reminding him of his true allegiance to them. It was very confusing, like most encounters with the spirit world.

Kella stopped walking when he had judged that he had put sufficient distance between himself and the bad *mana* of Boehrs, the German, and the mistreated dolphins. Slipping his pack off his shoulders he sat with his back to a banyan tree. As he sipped from his water bottle he tried to consider the situation. He thought about the spirits generally, and the important part they had played so far in the case upon which he was supposed to be concentrating. He had to admit that the humans involved had suffered a considerable buffeting at the hands of the heedless immortals. How often, he wondered, did the gods interfere just to see how humans reacted?

Poor, simple Papa Noah had been approached by some of them in a dream and encouraged to form his own faith, a mixture of Christianity and any number of pagan beliefs. The old man had based his cult upon what he knew of the ark of the Christian Bible. At the same time Atanga, one of the chiefs of the Tikopia, had finished planning to restore the pagan faith to his area of the island. His gods would have insisted that he establish his revival around their great icon, the big canoe. Somehow they would have pointed out the connection between the big canoe and the ark of the new Malaitan sect, and directed Atanga to liaise with Papa Noah by sending his son, who even took the new name of Shem. The young man had been a most reluctant adherent to the faction, wanting only to continue to enjoy the freedom that had become his during his voluntary and much-enjoyed exile from his constricted home island.

Nevertheless, as his father had ordered, the obedient Shem had made the Church of the Blessed Ark a haven for Tikopians on Malaita, further swelling its numbers. With so many conflicting loyalties rending the new church apart, the evil spirits of the rocks and trees in the area had been able to make their homes in the ark, joining the animals being assembled there by its now bewildered founders. These malevolent ghosts had wielded power far beyond their numbers and had instigated many of the wicked things that had started to occur in the ark, through the actions of some of the humans involved, culminating in the death of Papa Noah and the other two followers of his faith.

Some time during this period, Kella was convinced, Brother Abalolo, the Christian pastor on Tikopia, had become aware of the threat to Christianity on his island. Convinced that the assault on his church was emanating from the Church of the Blessed Ark, he had abandoned his home and travelled to Malaita to try to stem the problem at its roots.

Kella wondered what could have happened next. Did Abalolo murder Papa Noah in an attempt to destroy the power of his cult? Could he then have gone on to kill the other two members of the new church, hoping that this ruthless action would frighten away many of its recent recruits? If this was the case, what awful danger could the pastor have envisaged that would turn a follower of the Christian God, sworn to the path of peace, into such a merciless killer? Did he receive any help on his killing spree?

Kella decided to give his brain a rest. He folded his hands in his lap and tried to go to sleep. Perhaps during his repose the various gods would stop squabbling and obscuring the issue and allow him to get on with his work.

He had conditioned himself to wake up as night fell. The night invaders were beginning to stir as he stood up in the cool air and took out a torch before burying his pack beneath a pile of debris secured by a rock. Giant skinks were swinging by their muscular tails from branch to branch above his head. Horned frogs were calling from a mangrove swamp close to the beach. Bats, humming insects and anopheles mosquitoes darted between the trees. At his feet he saw for a slithering moment a five-minute snake, so-called because its bite was said to be lethal in that amount of time.

Shielding his torch with his free hand, Kella made the steady descent back to the dolphins' camp on the coast. All the time he was aware of other forms accompanying him through the bush. They were stealthy and light-footed but still too substantial to be the spirits or their representatives. These were humans, and they were waiting for something, probably a signal. It had started to rain, the preferred time for islanders to launch attacks on their enemies.

When he reached the collection of tents and huts on the coast, there were no lights on at the foot of the hill. Even the lanterns swinging in the tents seemed to have been extinguished. As far as he could see, no guards had been posted. Boehrs must be supremely confident that there would be no nocturnal intruders. Perhaps he was relying on the reputation of his hard-nosed Guadalcanal mercenaries. Certainly when Kella had seen them earlier in the day they had seemed to be spoiling for a fight.

The dolphins were still languishing dolefully in the pool. The water was less than six feet deep. The only access lay through the dam of logs piled on top of one another at the sea end of the pen. The stream on the far side of the dam leading to the ocean had dwindled to a trickle. If he could break the dam, the released water would gush through, taking the dolphins with it by sheer force out into the bay, or so Kella hoped.

He walked to the far side of the pool. He had studied the construction of the simple log barrier surreptitiously while he had been talking to Boehrs and Schuman earlier in the day. Several poles about fifteen feet high had been hammered into the ground on either side, with flat sides jutting out upon which the logs were resting. It should be simple enough to dismantle the structure by the simple method of sweeping the logs from their ledges one at a time, starting at the top. He would not be able to help making a noise in the process, but he was not particularly worried about being apprehended by the German. Almost certainly Boehrs was about to face many more serious problems than Kella could offer him.

It took the sergeant a quarter of an hour to demolish the crude and hastily designed rampart, by the simple process of swimming across the clouded pool and scaling the shifting logs until he reached the top one. Clinging on to the long vertical pole, Kella eased his side of the top log free of its horizontal supporting ledge, swung it away from him and let it drop on to the ground on the far side of the dam, where the seeping stream crawled down lethargically to the water's edge.

He repeated the process with most of the other logs, until he was standing waist-deep in the pool with the released water pouring past him down the beach in a great burst of energy, taking with it the still dazed but soon rejuvenated dolphins. Only one did not move. Kella guessed that the creature was too dazed or unwell to be able to make the effort. If it did not follow the others soon, it would be stranded on the dry bed of the rapidly emptying dam.

Kella plunged into the water and began banging on the surface with both hands in an effort to get the last dolphin to move. At first he thought he had left it too late, but slowly the great creature began to stir. With a squeal it thrashed its tail into the water, catching Kella across the shoulder and sending him to the bottom of the pool. He inhaled water but forced himself to use his hands and arms to reach the surface again. He came up, spluttering and gasping, in time to see the dolphin forcing its way across the remains of the dam and down to the open sea in what was left of the water in the stream. A minute later, with a final great thrust of its glistening body, the rejuvenated mammal had joined its companions in the open sea.

Kella's shoulder ached from the force of the blow it had just received. He stood watching the dolphins gambolling in the moonlight before they headed for deeper water and were lost to sight against the white-tipped waves. Then he looked round for Boehrs and Schuman.

They were waiting for him as he waded back to the side of what was left of the pool. The Guadalcanal men were formed up in a truculent line just behind their employers.

'Kella! Schuman said that you would be back, but I thought you had more sense. What the hell are you doing?' demanded the German, shaking his head at the policeman's stupidity.

'Isn't it obvious?' asked the soaked Kella. 'I'm afraid your dolphins have gone walkabout. They'll be long gone by now, as you can see.'

'You fool! Do you think I could possibly let you get away with this?' asked Boehrs. 'If the natives heard that I'd let you go unpunished, I'd have no credibility left in the district.'

Kella saw that the German was carrying a French steel Mle. 1950 automatic pistol, while Schuman had a Yugo Mauser rifle cradled in his arms. The German was not stinting on armaments, thought Kella. Perhaps that was why he had been lax about posting a guard on the dolphin pen. With the calibre of artillery he seemed to possess, he could be fairly confident of tracking down anyone who offended against him and then exacting retribution.

'I suppose you could report me to my superiors,' Kella said. After all, he thought, why should Boehrs be different to everyone else?

'It's not a matter of reporting you, Sergeant Kella,' Boehrs said softly, walking forward until he was standing in front of the sergeant. 'You attacked and destroyed my property at night. I would be perfectly within my rights to assume that you were a thief and fire a shot to warn you off. It would be most unfortunate if that shot were to kill some hapless intruder – you in this case.'

'I don't think so,' said Kella.

'Why not?' asked Boehrs.

'Because this is my island, not yours, and I'm afraid you have very little say in what goes on here, Mr Boehrs. In fact the only major decision you're going to be able to make over the next few minutes is whether you're going to be a living visitor to our shores or a dead one.'

At the German's side Schuman cleared his throat politely. 'Excuse me, Herr Boehrs,' he said, 'but unfortunately Kella really does have a point. It wouldn't be a good idea to dispose of the sergeant. He has certain traditional affinities in this area and indeed all over Malaita. If anyone were to handle him the way he undoubtedly deserves to be treated, then I'm afraid that once word got around, his killer and any of his associates would be cut down before they had a chance to leave this camp.'

'What are you talking about, man? Are you suggesting that I let him go?' asked the German.

'Certainly not,' said the half-caste. 'Sergeant Kella has broken the law by entering our camp, destroying the dam and releasing the dolphins. I suggest you make a citizen's arrest and that we take Kella back to Honiara on the Chinese boat when it arrives, and hand him over to the authorities there. From what I hear, some of his senior officers will be only too pleased to make an example of him. The islanders around here won't know what's going on. They're used to seeing Kella associating with white visitors.'

Boehrs thought for a moment and then nodded. 'All right,' he said unwillingly. 'I hope to make a good living in this area, despite tonight's little setback. I wouldn't want to antagonize the natives unnecessarily. Lock Kella in the supplies shed. He can wait there until tomorrow when we ship out.'

'Nice try,' Kella told Schuman. 'But I'm afraid you won't be locking me up tonight.'

'Are you serious, Sergeant?' asked Boehrs. He gestured at the Guadalcanal men waiting impatiently behind him. 'I suggest you make your way to the store shed immediately. For some reason my colleague Mr Schuman seems averse to seeing you get hurt. I have no such reservations.'

'I should save your breath,' Kella said. 'I'm afraid you've both got rather a long walk ahead of you.'

He nodded towards the shadows under the trees leading up the cliff path. They were materializing into dozens of semi-naked crouched forms moving out of the bush area. The latest arrivals spread out into a deep, threatening semicircle. They were small and slim, wearing loincloths and armed with spears or bows and arrows. Kella wondered if the tips had been coated with the customary poison made of ivy paste. The Guadalcanal men looked around in alarm. Another flotilla of islanders was swimming ashore, and more men were advancing up the beach, shaking the water vigorously from their bodies like savage dogs, to complete the encirclement of Boehrs and his men. Taking in the situation, the Guadalcanal mercenaries stood very still, clustering together for comfort and reassurance. Boehrs half raised his pistol. Kella shook his head.

'Not a good idea,' he said. 'At best you'd get off two or three shots before they turned you into a human pincushion.'

'You would be the first one I'd kill, I promise you that,' Boehrs said vindictively.

'That's why it's not a good idea, for either of us,' Kella said.

Without waiting for his employer, impassively Schuman lowered his rifle to the ground and placed his hands on his head. Boehrs hesitated and then reluctantly followed suit. A plump islander with an amiable face, wearing shell bracelets on his wrists, pushed his way through the crowd. People made way for him respectfully. The plump man issued a few orders to the crowd. The men around him scattered in silence. Some of them started putting the finishing touches to the destruction of the dolphin pens. Others entered the tents and huts distributed about the camp and started carrying out their contents and piling them on the ground. Boehrs uttered a grunt of protest and moved forward involuntarily. Schuman placed a restraining hand on his arm. Boehrs subsided, chewing his lip and looking on as his possessions were ransacked. The plump man indicated that Kella should walk down to the beach with him.

'Thank you, Kella,' said Solodia, the high priest of the dolphin people. 'We could have done it without you, but it was brave of you to risk your life for our dolphins.'

Solodia was in his forties. Like his forebears he had been selected for his position by acclaim, because of all men of his clan still alive, not only was he the finest navigator but he also had the greatest affinity with the sea beasts. Already he was being allowed to swim with the dolphins out at sea. It was accepted among his followers that when he died, he would become a dolphin and sport out in the great ocean with the others for ever.

'Not so brave,' said Kella. 'I knew that the men from your villages were watching everything that was happening from the bush. They must have been there for days, ever since the German white man started trapping the dolphins.'

'But you also knew that they would not attack until I gave the word,' said Solodia. 'You couldn't be sure that I was near enough to take control, so you freed the dolphins on your own.'

'The last time I saw you, by the reef shark shrine before I left for Tikopia, you were heading south,' Kella said. 'That probably meant that you were walking to the dolphin villages on Small Mala, which, as you say, are a long way from Kwaio country. However, the German told me that he was shipping the dolphins out of the country tomorrow. That meant I couldn't wait until I was sure that you'd got here, which was what I wanted to do. I had to destroy the dam on my own and hope that you were on your way.'

'You made the German very angry. We could all see that. He could have shot you.'

'He might have,' said Kella. 'But the half-caste who works for him is a clever man. He knew that if I died there would be a blood feud between the Lau people and him. Under those circumstances it would serve his interests for him to do his best to persuade his boss to let me live.'

'And the dolphin people would have been after him as well,' promised Solodia. 'The half-blood and the German would have been dead before the next full moon, that is certain. But that wouldn't have done you any good if you had two or three bullet holes in you by then. It was a courageous action and the dolphin people are in your debt.'

Call it a professional courtesy, thought Kella self-deprecatingly, but he could not think of a phrase in either of their languages or in pidgin that would cover the expression. Instead he extended a hand to the high priest of the dolphins.

'I must be on my way,' he said. 'May the dolphins and the sharks live together in peace under the protection of Agalimae, the high god of the universe.'

Kella walked over to Schuman, who was standing quietly under the shelter of a palm tree. 'I'll remember that you persuaded Boehrs not to kill me,' he said. 'I had no idea you were so kind-hearted.'

'Don't flatter yourself,' said the half-caste. 'I know you, Kella. You would never have come back and released the dolphins and made so much noise about it in the process unless you were pretty sure that help was on its way. You knew that Mr Boehrs and the rest of us were about to be overwhelmed by an invasion from the dolphin worshippers. If they had found your dead body by the pool, our throats would have been cut by now.'

'Probably,' agreed Kella. 'So you made sure that I stayed alive. Well, if you weren't soft-hearted, at least you showed a bit of common sense. You'd better start taking your boss back to Auki. I'm going to ask you to walk all the way, I'm afraid. That will give you time to reflect upon the error of your ways and give everyone the opportunity to cool down. I take it you know the way over the mountains? You should reach Auki on foot in three or four days.'

Schuman nodded. 'Very well,' he said quietly. 'I'm sure we'll be meeting again, Kella.'

'If I were a gambling man, and I am, I'd put money on it.'

'I'll look forward to that,' said the half-caste. He looked over at the stunned Boehrs, who was watching in disbelief the systematic looting of his goods by the islanders. He beckoned to the German to join them. 'We'd better be on our way, Mr Boehrs,' he said.

'Are you going to let them treat me like this?' asked Boehrs dazedly. He seemed too overwhelmed by what was happening to remain outraged. 'I'm paying you to deal with these situations.'

'You pay me to keep you alive, Mr Boehrs, and so far I've managed to do that. Take my word for it, not everyone who comes up against Kella is that fortunate.'

'But he's a policeman!' said the German. 'Does that mean nothing to him?'

'He's a lot of things, Mr Boehrs, and at this moment upholding the British rule of law among the dolphin worshippers is very low on his order of priorities. Kella has just sorted out a very difficult custom dispute in rather a clever manner. You may have lost a little money on the deal, but at least you're still alive. I don't think we should impose upon the sergeant's good nature any longer. In short, my urgent recommendation is that we stop pushing our luck and start walking. Shall we go?'

'But what about all my equipment?' asked Boehrs, gesturing wildly at the piles of loot.

'That stays here,' said Kella. 'The islanders will divide it up among themselves after you've gone. If it's any consolation to you, you will have contributed significantly to the local economy and general standard of life for the next few months.'

'But this is theft!' screamed the German.

'I prefer to think of it as reparation for all the damage you have caused to the dolphins and their gods. As Schuman says, you're a businessman; I suggest that you enter it in your ledger in the losses column.'

'Are you serious? What's the matter with you, man? You're supposed to be one of the civilized natives! Whose side are you on, for God's sake?'

'Nobody's,' said Kella. 'That's part of the problem.'

With an effort Boehrs brought himself under control. 'As soon as I get back to Honiara I shall be making an official complaint about your part in this matter,' he promised.

'That is your privilege, sir. However, my role in the affair has been relatively trivial. You interfered with local traditions and trespassed on custom land. I was fortunate enough to come along in time to save you from the consequences of your impulsiveness and general ignorance.' Boehrs started to speak, but Kella raised his voice. 'Oh, I know you have a temporary lease on the land on this section of the coast, but through hundreds of years of usage, the dolphin men happen to own all the sea. By taking the dolphins from their waters, you broke both the local and the national law.' He paused. 'The expatriate official who granted you your lease probably didn't know that, but that's a matter you can discuss with your legal representatives when you get back to Honiara.'

'Don't worry, I shall! We'll see what the courts have to say about this!'

Kella studied the islanders surrounding them, checking them off and identifying some of them. 'As you wish, Mr Boehrs, but I wouldn't raise your hopes too much if you're thinking of seeking compensation. Among the witnesses I could call from this assembly before us, in defence of any legal action, I can see four government-appointed headmen, two former scouts decorated for bravery during the war and a young man soon to embark upon a degree course at the University of the South Pacific. You, of course, will be free to summon Mr Schuman and your Guadalcanal toughs to give evidence on your behalf, should you require it.' Kella paused. 'Now, I don't wish to speed the parting guest, but you really ought to be on your way, Mr Boehrs. If you start now, you'll get a few hours of walking in before the sun rises.'

'Is that your last word?' asked Boehrs stiffly.

'No, my last word is this: stay away from the dolphins!'

'We're going,' said Schuman, starting to trudge up the track towards the cliff. Boehrs hesitated, and then hurried after the other man, stumbling over the great roots growing out of the ground in his haste. Neither man made any effort to pick up their weapons. At the top of the track Schuman stopped and looked back at Kella, while the German brushed past him heedlessly, his head lowered, lost in his bitter thoughts. The sergeant wondered under what circumstances he and Schuman would meet again. He was sure they would.

He walked over to the Guadalcanal men, who were sitting in an apprehensive circle on the ground, their hands on their heads. They were being taunted sadistically by a guard detail of Malaitan warriors. Every now and then one of the dolphin worshippers would drive the blunt end of a spear into the side of one of his prisoners with a loud smack, just to make sure that he had the captive's undivided attention. Kella frowned disapprovingly. The last dolphin man to strike a prisoner grinned and took an exaggerated step back, lifting his free hand to show that he had only been playing. Kella cleared his throat and addressed the bowed heads of the utterly dispirited and resigned Guadalcanal mercenaries.

'You have two choices,' he said abruptly. 'You can stay here in Kwaio territory and take your chances. Personally, after all that has happened, I would not recommend that option.' The expressions on the faces of the Weather Coast men attested to their complete agreement with his remark.

'Or', he went on, 'you can make your way down to Aio harbour and wait there. It should take you about two days' hard walking. I guarantee your safe passage through the tribes on the way. You must not touch any gardens nor hunt any animals, but you may pick fruit from trees in the bush and drink from streams. In less than a week a ship called *The Spirit of the Islands* will put in at Aio. You will be offered a free deck passage on board back to Guadalcanal. After that you're on your own.'

Kella need not have bothered with the last sentence. The Guadalcanal prisoners, hardly able to believe their luck, were already on their feet and jostling one another on their way across to the beach. Kella watched the relieved men shuffling away along the sand before he walked over to Solodia. The villagers were still industriously carrying goods out of the tents and huts and apportioning them among themselves with a minimum of squabbling. Not for the first time Kella marvelled at the sheer volume of items regarded as essential by expatriates on tour. There were piles of cooking utensils, sacks of tinned goods, bags of rice, several portable beds, sheets, blankets and pillows, fold-up chairs and tables, a shotgun and cartons of ammunition, a camera, a radio, clothes and even a pile of spare clothes hangers.

Solodia nodded. 'I have decided,' he said. 'I shall spread the word. White men will no longer be welcome on my coast.'

'There is a Catholic sister from the mission,' Kella said. 'Her name is Conchita.'

'The one they call the Praying Mary? I have heard of her.'

'I would regard it as a personal favour if you allowed her to come and go freely among your villages when she wants to do so.'

'So be it,' said Solodia, taking the sergeant's proffered hand. 'She will be welcome, as will you, *aofia*.'

'Tell me,' Kella said. 'Those two dolphins who pushed my canoe around when I was talking to the reef god, were they trying to tell me about Boehrs and his trap?'

'I don't know,' said Solodia. 'Maybe. One day I'll ask them for you.' The high priest paused. 'I have heard certain things as I walked up the coast to destroy the foreign hunters.'

'What have you heard?' asked Kella.

'They tell me that Kella the peacemaker is looking for a Japanese warrior who is still in the bush.'

'There is some truth in that. It is certainly true that I am looking into such a matter,' said Kella, not wanting to go into the whole story.

'In that case, I can help you,' said Solodia. 'I know where this Japani is. I can send a boy with you to show you the way. You won't be the first to get there, but that doesn't matter. The Japani doesn't get many visitors.'

30

BUSH WALK

'I take it that this is the famous Mr Abalolo that you have been at such great pains to conceal from us,' said Sister Conchita, looking down at the tethered, abject Tikopian. The dejected figure did not look up.

'This is Abalolo,' said Brother John cautiously. 'What makes you think that I've been hiding him?'

They were standing in the centre of the village. Scrawny dogs and pigs snuffled hopefully among heaps of rubbish. The men who had brought them up the track were standing a hundred yards away, watching them expressionlessly. Tendrils of smoke from a dozen cooking fires drifted out through the open doorways of the huts. Five minutes earlier, some old women had brought them coconut husks filled with brackish water. It was not much, but it was probably all they had, thought the nun.

'It was pretty obvious that you were concealing something,' she told him. 'I've never known you late for a meal before, yet you only just got to Papa Noah's last feast in time. You were obviously worried about something, so I suppose you had hidden Mr Abalolo in the ark for some reason. Then, when the storm started, you disappeared. Again this was out of character. Normally you would have been in the thick of the action, taking control. I can only assume that you were hurrying Mr Abalolo away from the ark to safety somewhere.

Later, when Shem had a dispute with someone on the track outside
the mission, it seemed likely that his assailant was Mr Abalolo.'

'How so?' asked Brother John

'Shem was badly marked up in the fight. Apart from Sergeant
Kella, very few Solomon Islanders would be big enough to hurt a
Tikopian. I'm guessing that you were having one of your secret
consultations with Mr Abalolo when Shem happened along. The two
men fought over which of them should be taking over the Church
of the Blessed Ark, or something of that nature, and you persuaded
Abalolo to run away before anyone else came along. At the time it
seemed to be too much of a coincidence that you should just happen
be in the vicinity to break up the fight and allow Mr Abalolo to
escape into the bush while you brought Shem to the mission, instead
of pursuing his attacker, which would have been more in character.'

'Anything else?' asked Brother John.

'I was interested in your actions when we reached Tikopia. You
didn't seem very worried about Mr Abalolo's disappearance from his
church on the island. This led me to surmise that you already knew
where he was. Unluckily for you, Dr Maddy told us that Abalolo was
supposed to be on Malaita.'

'You don't miss much, do you?' asked Brother John.

'Am I right?' asked Sister Conchita.

'More or less,' said the missionary. 'For some time it had been
obvious that the Church of the Blessed Ark was attracting a lot of
Tikopians into its ranks on Malaita. At the same time Abalolo was
worried because the revival of the pagan faith on Tikopia was
affecting his church numbers adversely. It was obvious that the
Church of the Blessed Ark was being infiltrated by Tikopians on
Malaita, who associated the ark with the big canoe icon of their pagan
beliefs. Against my advice he came up to Malaita to persuade the new
adherents of Papa Noah's church to return to Christianity. To that
end, he insisted on attending the feast before the storm. I managed
to hide him in the ark, as that was a *tabu* place and I didn't think

anyone except Papa Noah would dare enter it.' He sighed. 'That was before you decided to gatecrash.'

'That was why you asked me to attend Papa Noah's funeral on your behalf, wasn't it?' she asked. 'You had to get back into the bush to look after Abalolo.'

'He wasn't doing too well on his own,' said Brother John. 'There isn't much bush country on Tikopia. He needed all the help he could get on Malaita.'

'Why did you meet me on the beach today?'

'I heard that you were coming up to teach at Bethezda this morning. I felt that I owed it to you to explain as much as I knew, so I left Abalolo here while I came down to meet you. As you saw, when we got back, he was a prisoner.'

Before he could say any more, six of the islanders who had escorted them up to Bethezda came over. One of them slashed Abalolo's bonds with a knife and hauled the still silent Tikopian to his feet. The men gestured to their captives to follow the track leading up the mountain on the far side of the village. Obediently Sister Conchita and her two companions started walking. The islanders, armed with spears, fell in silently behind them.

'Anything else you want to know?' asked Brother John, looking over his shoulder as they left the huts behind them.

'Yes: who is the killman?' asked Sister Conchita.

'I have no idea,' said Brother John.

They walked for three hours before stopping at another small village, where they were given more water and some yams as they rested. When they set off again, Sister Conchita noticed that they had a fresh set of guards. It was almost as if they were being handed on from one group of escorts to another. This reinforced her conviction that she and the two men were being conducted somewhere specific, and that each set of captors would be glad when their part in the journey was over.

All the time they were climbing into the mountains. Occasionally they passed groups of women returning from their gardens down the path, carrying huge loads of bananas and firewood on their backs. Whenever they passed, the local women hurried off the track out of sight into the trees. Sister Conchita was reminded of the story of one of the last great inter-tribe battles that had taken place in this part of the high bush, as told to her once by Father Pierre. One village had invaded another and killed thirty of the men there, severing their heads with machetes. The weeping women had been forced to carry the heads of their husbands, fathers and brothers in their arms up to the village of the victorious clan, where they had been decapitated in turn.

By mid-afternoon it was raining steadily. The smell of decay was overpowering, as if the whole forest was in the process of rotting around them. Mist rose from the ground, obscuring the vegetation to knee height. They passed hovering hornets, wasps and bees all humming in different keys. Lizards lurked camouflaged on leaves, their long tongues flickering out to trap unwary butterflies and moths. Once they crossed a wide river with much deliberate splashing and shouting to deter predators. Downstream Sister Conchita could hear the steady *pukpuk* grunt of a crocodile, the sound from which the creature got its local name.

They passed another set of gardens enclosed by low fences consisting of tottering bamboo poles linked by jungle vines. The tilled soil within the enclosure was mainly devoted to the cultivation of yams. Each root had been buried in a separate hole scooped in the ground and marked by a short pole around which the vegetable's wispy creeper could curl and grow.

They spent their first night in another small bush village. Just before it grew dark, Sister Conchita caught a glimpse of mountain peaks some distance ahead of them. They were encased in clouds and seemed as far away as ever.

Brother John and Abalolo were taken off under guard to the men's house on the far side of the clearing. Sister Conchita was installed in a recently vacated hut. Judging by its size and the presence of a number of pig tusks tied to a wall with creepers, she guessed it to be the residence of the village headman. A fresh bed of leaves had been spread for her on the beaten earth of the floor, and she was fed with fresh coconut milk and bananas. Later, in the dusk, she was taken by a group of women to a stream to wash. She tried to engage them in conversation, but no one would respond. She noticed that unlike the wiry saltwater dwellers, these denizens of the high bush were small, stunted people, bearing on their almost naked bodies the unmistakable scars of yaws and ringworm.

She was taken back to the hut through the trees, utterly exhausted from her day's climbing in the stifling heat. She fell asleep at once, despite the scurrying sound of rats on the ground near her bed.

31

JOURNEY'S END

The next morning, soon after dawn and a meal of pineapples, the three of them were walking again. Six new guards from the latest village were now in charge of them, as slight, silent and expressionless as the previous ones had been. As they moved out, Sister Conchita caught a glimpse of the escorts from the afternoon of the previous day hurrying back home with obvious relief down the track.

They walked for another six hours. The track was steeper than ever, and even the lithe and fit Sister Conchita found the going hard as they headed up the mountain path in the baking oven-like heat. It was soon raining steadily again. The nun had heard that 150 inches could fall in a year this high in the bush on Malaita. When at last the rain ceased reluctantly for an hour or so, dozens of birds used the respite to swoop down through the glistening golden foliage of the sodden trees and settle on the ground, pecking avariciously at the helpless caterpillars and worms that had been washed from the branches during the recent downpour.

Sister Conchita could tell from occasional glimpses of the sun through the crowded trees that it was almost noon when they stopped for the last time. The bushmen who had been guiding them stood in a straight line across the track behind them. For a heart-stopping moment Sister Conchita wondered if her surmise had been wrong all along and that the three of them had been brought to this remote area merely to be slaughtered and their bodies left to decompose. If that should be the case, it could be years before their remains were discovered.

To her relief, the nun saw that the islanders were making no attempt to fall on them. Instead they were pointing urgently with their spears up the track as a sign that their three captives should continue on their own. A foolhardy Brother John decided to ignore their implicit instructions and in a fit of bravado tried to shoulder his way back down the path in the direction from which they had come. Deftly two of the bushmen adjusted their grips on the thin, pliable spears and used them as whiplash rods, smashing them vigorously in concert against the big missionary's body. The Guadalcanal man howled with pain and hurried ignominiously back to rejoin the other two. Again the bush warriors indicated with short jabbing movements of their spears that their prisoners should continue up the path alone.

'I really think we should continue walking,' said Sister Conchita.

Brother John ran his hands over his body with rueful tenderness. 'Good idea!' he said, taking the lead with a will up the track.

The path bent through the trees and undergrowth at the top of the current incline. As they turned, Sister Conchita glanced back over her shoulder. The bushmen were still regarding them intently from below.

The trees were beginning to thin out ahead of the three tired travellers. Sister Conchita was aware of an unexpected cool breeze coming from before them. By now they must be several thousand feet above sea level, she thought. After another hundred yards of hard walking they emerged from the trees and stopped in surprise. They were looking upon what could only be described as a freak of nature. Although the forested mountain peaks could still be seen looming in the distance, immediately before them was more than an acre of flat land surrounded by dozens of blossoming banana plants. On the other side of the field of tough cropped grass, the steaming jungle started to flourish again on the way up to the cloud-obscured peaks. The sight they were witnessing with stupefaction was almost like an oasis in a desert.

A hundred yards away Sergeant Kella was sitting on a mound of grass in the clearing. A fire of small sticks smouldered beside him. He was eating a chunk of baked taro and the remains of a river slug. He greeted them with a nod as they crossed the grass in his direction. He removed some of the charred skin of the vegetable with his fingers and dropped it fastidiously to the ground.

'I expect you're wondering why I sent for you,' he said.

32

THE MAE

'I think you just got rounded up in the net almost by accident,' said Kella. 'I thought it was about time that I questioned this mysterious Abalolo, so I called in some favours, found out where he was and arranged for him to be brought up here to me. It just so happened that Brother John had already linked up with him.'

'Are you actually apologizing to me, Sergeant Kella?' asked Sister Conchita. 'That's a first!'

'Not at all,' said the sergeant. 'I was just explaining the situation to you. The people who were helping me out didn't know whether I just wanted the Tikopian or all three of you.'

'Like we all look the same,' said Sister Conchita. 'A Tikopian, a Guadalcanal man and a Boston nun are practically indistinguishable. It was an understandable mistake. Anyone could have made it.'

'I didn't say that either,' said Kella unhappily.

But Sister Conchita was only getting into her stride. 'So you got us in a package deal. Good housekeeping! Did we come cheaper than way, Sergeant Kella? Is that why I've been climbing a mountain under duress for a day and a half?'

Sister Conchita was beginning to achieve a modified sense of enjoyment out of the obvious discomfiture of the police sergeant, but her heart was not really in it. After all, it was only sensible that Kella should want to interrogate the Tikopian who kept flitting in and out of his investigation in such a maddening manner. It was fairly obvious too that Abalolo would have needed a trustworthy fellow Anglican missionary as a source of contact on Malaita, and Brother John filled the bill there, which accounted for the Guadalcanal man's inclusion in the party. As for her own role up here in the high bush, well, Ben Kella had not yet articulated it, but it was becoming fairly obvious to Sister Conchita why he needed her on this occasion, as he had at least once before.

'Are you enjoying giving me a hard time?' asked Kella.

'Not as much as I'd hoped,' Sister Conchita said.

They were standing on the field of rough *batiki* grass. At Kella's request Brother John and Abalolo had gone back to the bush to collect branches with which to make lean-to huts for the night. Cool winds rolled across the unexpected haven provided by the smooth green plain, channelled refreshingly through the narrow fissures and valleys in the forested mountains above them. Behind them lay the jungle. The three sides of the flat field ahead of them were bounded by hundreds of green-leaved banana plants, each growing to a height of over twenty feet. It was an incongruous sight, a few hundred yards of rare open beauty somehow carved by nature out of the sweltering enclosed bush and dropped pristine and intact from the skies before the tangled wooded ground started rising steeply again.

'Come with me,' said Kella. 'I want to show you something. I'd heard about this place, but I've never seen it before.'

They reached the plantation of banana bushes fringing the field. With their sturdy bases enfolded tightly in huge paddle-shaped green leaves and large clusters of fruit, they looked to Sister Conchita as much like trees as bushes. Kella skirted the bright walls of leaves, stopping occasionally to part the large fronds and peer into the hidden interior of the plantation. The nun began to grow impatient.

'Father Kuyper will be worrying about me at the mission,' she said.

'I don't think so,' said Kella. 'I sent a messenger down telling him that you had been delayed treating an outbreak of yaws at a bush village.'

They walked up an incline. The top of the slope had been flattened out.

'There,' said Kella, pointing. 'I found it yesterday.'

Someone had dug a grave on the hillock and covered it with grass. Although there were no obvious sources of water, the mound had been well tended; the grass on it was a shining green in colour. It had been trimmed recently. Across the top of the grave were a number of military accoutrements. Sister Conchita saw a rifle, several bandoliers of ammunition and a hand grenade. At the head of the grave a couple of identity tags had been attached to a length of cord and placed on top of a closed biscuit tin. The nun could see that the characters hammered on to the discs were Japanese.

'How did you find this?' she asked.

At first she thought the sergeant was going to ignore her, but then he began to speak.

'There are a number of drawbacks to being a Melanesian,' said Kella, apparently following his own line of thought. 'There's the climate for a start, and the mountains and the mosquitoes. Worst of all, there's the language, or rather the languages. We've got over eighty different dialects, you know. And most of them have dozens of words for the same thing. In my own tongue alone there are six different names for rock.'

'I don't—'

'Also', said Kella, ignoring the interruption, 'we're a devious lot. Even with the parcel of words and phrases at our disposal, we seldom say what we mean. That would be too easy.' He picked up the rifle, examined it and put it down again. 'That doesn't make it easy for a detective. It doesn't even make it easy for a man who simply wants to be told how to get from one end of a straight trail to the other. I can only put facts and rumours together and try to make deductions from them. I try to understand what I've been told, even when I haven't been told anything.'

Kella regarded the tidy grave in silence. When he had been recounting his litany of disadvantages of living in the Solomons to Sister Conchita he had not mentioned the obverse side. It was the only place he had seen in his ever-increasing round of travels in which the spirits of every possible faith and belief could dwell together. It was true that sometimes they squabbled like vicious siblings, but every now and again they could put aside their differences and combine in the aid of a righteous cause. He had seen this happen a number of times since he had become the *aofia*, and he was convinced that on least one occasion on the top of Mount Austen on Guadalcanal, the sensitive and receptive Sister Conchita had experienced the same amazing coming together of spiritual forces to add to her own unshakeable faith.

'For example,' he said, 'someone told me that I would find a Japanese soldier up here. He didn't happen to mention that he was dead.'

'Who told you that?'

'Another witch doctor,' said Kella, almost smiling. 'An unimpeachable source, naturally. Right now I'm asking you to go and fetch Brother John and Abalolo. They deserve to see this and make what they can from it. Hurry, please! Make sure that you go back exactly the same way that we came. I've been here for twenty-four hours and not a single islander has come near this field, so I think we can assume that there's a very powerful *tabu* on this place.'

By this time the sister was halfway across the field, heading for the bush where Brother John and Abalolo were selecting dead branches. Kella walked down the hill and studied the gently waving barricade of plantains. There was the faintest of indentations between two of the adjacent bushes. He summoned up his resolve and stepped into the plantation. It was not as impenetrable as he had at first feared. After a few yards he even encountered a track leading through the banana bushes. He heard a noise behind him and turned. A woman was standing glaring at him. She was small and unkempt, extremely dirty and clad only in a skimpy loincloth. Instinctively Kella moved towards her. The woman hissed at him like a malevolent wild animal.

'Plenty too much, plenty too much! No more come!' she shrieked, and turned and ran off among the bushes.

Instinctively Kella went after her. 'Come back!' he called. 'I can help you!'

33

THE PLANTATION

The dishevelled woman was running deeper and deeper into the banana plantation. Kella did his best to keep up with her, but soon she was out of sight. He could hear her bare feet pattering along the ground as she went. The shape of the plantation was beginning to change. What had seemed a lush green Elysium was altering its character even as he ran through it. The path was growing narrower and the plant fronds were darkening in colour and entwining in a squirming clasp only a few feet above his head. He was stumbling along a dark, narrow tunnel that seemed to lead nowhere. What had previously seemed idyllic was now dismal and threatening. Kella had heard of beautiful tropical flowers that lured insects and then devoured them. Could he be entering the same sort of grotesque, indescribably hazardous trap?

Although he had been convinced that there was at least an hour of daylight left this high up in the mountains, already he could hardly see more than a foot or so ahead of him as the track started taking abrupt and unexpected turns through the intimidating foliage. The knotted fronds of the bushes whipped at his sweating face. The proliferating drooping bunches of bananas lunged back at him as he disturbed them, as potent as the war clubs of a raiding party thudding against his bruised body.

Kella stopped to rest and collect his thoughts, his shirt and shorts permeated with sweat, his feet and legs wet with slime. He leant for support against a tall bush, but found himself sinking into its languorous, soft embrace, welcoming him to rest there for ever if need be. He pulled himself upright and forced himself to move onwards. Ahead of him he could still hear the woman, stopping when he did and then moving forward again like an unseen shadow. With the brutish disregard to pain that had anaesthetized so much of his rugby football career, Kella would not stop. Either the woman was in need of his help or she possessed the answer to questions he wanted to ask. She would stand still eventually, he was sure of that, even if only to show him that she had won by leading him successfully away from his own gods into the lair of the spiteful mountain spirits. Briefly he wondered if the woman had transported herself into one of the Mae, the bush gods able to take the form of man or woman in order to prey upon travellers and conduct them on the agonizing journey to the pit of doom.

He blundered relentlessly on for at least half an hour, although he suspected that it was longer. Time seemed to be losing its shape, just as the bushes and insects around him no longer held set positions. The tiny insects that fed upon the banana plants were growing and changing shape before his eyes as they buzzed around him. Eelworms slithered over his squelching boots in huge clusters, like teeming mobile anthills, weighing them down. Aphids and spider mites stung his eyes. An amorphous square of almost transparent stick insects hovered in the air.

Kella followed the stick insects around a corner in the path. The trail seemed to end in a wall of fronds waving in a tentative breeze. The woman was waiting for him, her back to a bush. For a moment her face was obscured by the cloud of hovering insects.

He felt his strength dwindling. He fell to his knees, his senses dulled. He struggled to get up, but all his energy had gone. The woman glided forward smoothly, as if she had no legs. She thrust her malicious face into Kella's. He tried to meet her gaze, but her red-rimmed eyes bored into his. Kella felt himself falling helplessly on to his side. So this was how it was going to end, he thought. He had carried his own magic once too often into the bush and it had been nullified by the power of the resident gods. Soon there would be nothing left but blankness, the dry, arid desert of oblivion. Even if his own gods were good to him and forgave him for his shortcomings on this last unsuccessful climb up into the mountains, there was nothing they could do for him here. Some of the more forgiving among them might feel that the actions of his life so far justified their transferring his spirit to the body of a hunting shark, but he was dying, defeated, too far from his saltwater home for that to be possible. Kella consigned his spirit to the waves and the reefs he had loved so much and waited for the Mae to strike. Through all the fatigue and desperation he found that his mind was concentrating on one thing. What had the woman said to him back at the grave? It was important! Considering his situation, it might also turn out to be irrelevant, he thought wryly as the energy seeped from him.

'*I exorcize thee, most vile spirit, the very embodiment of our enemy . . .*'

The cool, calm voice came from behind him. Kella squirmed round. Sister Conchita, holding a miniature Bible in one hand, was pointing at the Mae with the other. The nun looked completely self-possessed. Kella gazed up at her, hope beginning to surge within him.

'*He commands thee, who commanded the sea, the winds . . .*' went on the young nun steadily.

A fragment of the litany of his own religion entered Kella's mind. Still unable to stand, he looked up at the old woman standing before him.

'*Alu mwela,*' he croaked, condemning the woman to burn in her own hell.

'*Hear therefore and fear,*' said Sister Conchita, raising her voice.

'*Bouruuru, dalafa,*' whispered Kella, demanding that the woman fall down and strike the ground hard.

'*Why dost thou stand and resist?*' asked the nun.

Kella felt the strength returning to his legs. Clutching at a plant, he pulled himself to his feet.

'*Duge, fakalfi!*' he snarled, expressing his intention of seeing the old woman sink even lower and burst open her entrails.

He advanced on the woman, feeling the strength returning to his legs. He could hear Sister Conchita following him, still chanting determinedly. The old woman stood her ground stubbornly. Kella made himself keep moving. Suddenly the old woman was no longer there. Only a slight quivering of the wall of fronds stood testament to the fact that she had ever existed.

But had she?

34

THE BONE PICKER

The fire had burnt for four days and then the ashes of the skeleton had been allowed to cool for another three, assisted by a number of squalls of rain, before Mayotishi started to gather them and wrap them in a series of white silks. He then placed them in a box he had brought up from *The Spirit of the Islands* along with two members of the crew, who had dug up the remains of the Japanese soldier reverently and carried them to the deep pit prepared by the official in the open field.

He was being watched by Sister Conchita, Kella, Brother John and Abalolo. Earlier, Brother John had volunteered to walk back down to the coast and guide Mayotishi and the seamen back up to the *tabu* banana plantation. After one bad night Kella had slept well for the remainder of the week and was feeling better. He had insisted on witnessing the cremation ceremony with the others.

Mayotishi was wearing a blue kimono. He had chanted prayers, struck a small portable gong, burnt a vase filled with incense and scattered Japanese rice and salt over the pit.

'Is he a priest?' Sister Conchita whispered to Kella.

'I'm not sure,' said the sergeant. 'During the war some Japanese warriors were allowed to become priests for special occasions. Perhaps this is one of them.'

He remembered the aftermath of the Battle of Ilu, erroneously called Tenaru by the Americans on Guadalcanal. On 23 August 1942, he had been scouting with Sergeant Major Vouza just before the Japanese, underestimating the strength of the Marine forces, had launched a full-frontal assault through the bush. Only a hundred out of almost a thousand troops from the Ichiki regiment had survived. Afterwards the Japanese prisoners had buried their own dead in a series of ceremonies like the one that Kella and the others were now witnessing. The ritual was called *shokut*, and it was supposed to bring a final peace to warriors who had died in battle.

Mayotishi issued orders to the seamen. Sister Conchita and Kella turned and walked away from the pit.

'Thank you for coming in so far after me,' Kella said. It was the first time he had referred to the matter. 'I'm surprised that you managed to find me. I must have been running through the plantation for the best part of an hour.'

The nun looked at him curiously. 'No, Ben,' she said quietly. 'You hadn't moved more than a hundred yards from the spot where I left you to fetch the others.'

Kella nodded. He could remember little of the encounter. All he knew was that the young nun had shown great courage and resolve to come looking for him on her own. One day, when the time was right, he would tell her that.

Brother John and Abalolo joined them. 'So that's it then,' said Brother John, shaking his head in wonderment. 'You came up against one of the Mae and she almost devoured you, but when Sister Conchita joined you, your combined magic was stronger than the Mae's and saved you.'

'Something like that,' said Kella, in a tone that discouraged further comment from the others.

Across the field Mayotishi finished supervising the loading of the silken parcels into the wooden box. The two seamen started carrying it carefully back down the bush track to the coast. The Japanese walked over to the others. He was holding the soldier's helmet, dogtags, rifle and the tin box that had been placed on top of his grave.

'He kept a diary in this box,' said Mayotishi. 'I've had time to go through it now. His name was Shimadu and he was a lieutenant. He fought at the Battle of Bloody Ridge on Guadalcanal, and after we withdrew from the island in 1943 he was taken on board a destroyer heading for Rabaul. Unfortunately it was intercepted at night by a US submarine and torpedoed off Malaita. Shimadu managed to get ashore but lost touch with the other survivors. Over a period of weeks he came inland through the bush up to the plantation here, where he made his home.'

'Did the bush people attack him?' asked Brother John.

'There were one or two skirmishes at first, but Shimadu was a trained infantryman. He still had his Arisaka and a good supply of ammunition, not to mention a few grenades. After he had shown the bush people that he could protect himself, they pretty much left him alone over the succeeding years. They let him have the plantation for his home. It was supposed to be a *tabu* area dedicated to the gods anyway. He built himself a garden, shot a few wild pigs and lived off bananas, and fish from the rivers and lakes.'

'And all the time he thought the war was still going on,' said Sister Conchita.

'What about the woman?' asked Kella.

'That's the interesting part,' said Mayotishi. 'According to the diary, her name was Toiliu and she was a slave of the local bush people, captured by them on a raid on one of the saltwater villages. By this time Shimadu had started trading with the village. He bought Toiliu from them for two bandoliers of ammunition and she went to live with him on the *tabu* plantation. According to the diary they were very happy together. The last entry was made in June 1952, eight years ago. Presumably Shimadu died soon after that, and Toiliu buried him and went on living on her own on the plantation, looking after his grave.'

'So she's been up here on her own for years,' said Sister Conchita. 'The poor woman!'

'She had no choice,' Kella said. 'The bush people wouldn't take her back. She'd been living in a *tabu* place for too long. Even if she had tried to return to her old village they would have driven her away and made her an outcast.'

'I don't understand,' said Brother John. 'Do you mean that after this woman Toiliu was forced to live on her own on the plantation she turned into one of the Mae?'

'Or perhaps the Mae adopted her as a forsaken one and shared their secrets with her,' suggested Abalolo seriously. 'The evil spirits can take on great power when events are thrown out of balance. I saw that for myself on Tikopia.'

'I still don't get it,' said Brother John. 'Are you trying to tell me that after her husband died, his widow took the form of an evil spirit and continued fighting on his behalf? She killed Papa Noah and the two islanders?'

Kella shook his head. His eyes were fixed on the backs of the two seamen, who were struggling with their precious load as they carried the long and heavy box through the trees. He hoped that Mayotishi was paying them well for their work.

'No,' he said, 'it wasn't like that at all. Even if she had been possessed of magical powers, Toiliu would not have had the strength to overpower men. Because she was an outcast living in a *tabu* area, no one would have helped her with such attacks. Anyway, after the death of her husband, her quarrel would not have been with the islanders. Shimadu's enemies were the Americans and the British. Believe me, there is no way that Toiliu could be the killman.'

While he was tidying matters up in his mind, there was one more box that he needed to tick. He took Mayotishi to one side and lowered his voice. 'You were the guest expected by Papa Noah at his last feast, weren't you?' he asked.

The Japanese nodded, showing no surprise. 'How do you know that?' he asked. 'Have you been conferring with your spirits again?'

'Not for something as simple as that. There were a couple of indications. Why would the choir sing "Japani Ha Ha!" unless it was to remind a Japanese visitor of the war? I'm afraid that Papa Noah had rather a warped sense of humour. After all, who else would greet a visiting nun with a chorus of naked dancing girls? To the best of my knowledge you were the only Japanese on Malaita at that time. And according to eyewitnesses, Papa Noah announced at the feast that he was about to become rich. Hardly anyone's got any money in that region. As an expatriate, you would be considered truly wealthy. What did you do, offer to make a contribution to his church funds if he set his adherents to look for a Japanese soldier in the bush?' Mayotishi nodded without speaking. 'So what happens next?'

'I shall inform the authorities and make arrangements to transport Lieutenant Shimadu's ashes back to Japan, where they will be buried with full honours.'

And as sure as fate, you will keep the contents of the lieutenant's diary a matter between yourself and your superiors in Tokyo, thought Kella. The book had been a thick one and the Japanese official had given them only a perfunctory summary of what had befallen Shimadu and the woman in their years on the banana plantation. How thorough an account might the dead officer have given of the withdrawal from Guadalcanal seventeen years ago, and the subsequent sinking of the vessel upon which he and the others had been embarked? Almost certainly the contents of the diary were destined to remain for a long time in the secret archives of the Japanese intelligence service. That still left the problem of Mayotishi. If the Japanese had been lurking in the area of the ark when Papa Noah had been killed, could he have been the killman?

'We'll start back in an hour,' Kella said. 'I have something to do first.'

Sister Conchita walked across the field to fetch Kella. She found him sitting a few feet into the banana plantation. He was holding a bush knife and was surrounded by the decapitated sodden stubble of half a dozen bushes. It looked as if he had run amok.

'Letting off steam?' suggested the nun.

'I was wondering how the grass on top of the grave was kept so green,' said Kella. 'Also, I've been thinking about the killman.'

'What's to think about?' said Sister Conchita. 'We don't know anything.'

'It's not quite as bad as that,' Kella said. 'We know that he's big and strong. All right, so Papa Noah was an old man, but the two islanders who were killed were young and tough. Even if they were attacked from behind, the killman would have to be prepared for a struggle. He was confident enough to go for them. He is a strong man.'

'What else?' asked Sister Conchita.

'He seems to know his way about Malaita. The two islanders he killed lived a long way apart. The killman got from one district to another without trouble.'

'Perhaps he had a guide.'

Kella shook his head. 'No,' he said. 'This killer delights in setting puzzles and making people guess what he's going to do next. He's a solitary *ramo*. He wouldn't risk an accomplice giving him away.'

'You've forgotten something,' said Sister Conchita.

'What's that?'

'He also has magical properties. He can drown people where there isn't any water.'

'There's nothing magical about that,' said Kella, standing up.

'How does he do it, then?'

'Think about it,' Kella said. If he made things too easy for the nun she might stop working things out for herself, and she had a great natural talent for that. 'I just have.'

They followed the bush track back down to the coast for about a quarter of an hour. The trees around them were still as scrawny as witches and spaced irregularly, allowing plenty of light to percolate. Then they heard the crackling of flames. They turned and looked back in the direction from which they had just come. Smoke was drifting into the sky.

'The plantation is on fire,' said Brother John.

Without a word Kella got the others moving again, pushing them roughly down the sloping track. Only Sister Conchita tried to resist, but Brother John and Mayotishi took their cue from the sergeant and closed in on the nun, urging her forward. Kella stood looking back, and then hurried to catch up with the rest. There was nothing left among the banana bushes for the lieutenant's wife now that even her husband's bones had been taken from her. As the group hurried in subdued silence along the track, Kella, whose hearing was keener than that of the others, could just distinguish a woman's screams being carried over the smoke-filled air.

35

STAYING ON

Kella left the Honiara police headquarters building on Guadalcanal early in the morning and started walking in the direction of the Roman Catholic mission at Visale,

He was lucky and picked up a lift on an empty truck returning from the town market. He sat in the back with a few other villagers as the vehicle jolted along the coastal road on the ten-mile trip on one of the few made-up thoroughfares on the island. As the sun rose in the sky, they passed the villages of Kakanbona and Tanavasa and then skirted Bonegi Creek, where two Japanese troop carriers had sunk at the beginning of 1943. It was said that both vessels, partially submerged beneath the surface only twenty metres from the shore, provided ample opportunities for tourists wishing to dive and snorkel, but in common with most veterans of the war, Kella had never attempted to visit either ship.

He thought about the interview he had conducted the previous day at police headquarters with Abalolo, the Tikopian pastor. The man had been of little help. Yes, he had been driven to despair by the revival of the pagan faith on his island, reinforced by a stream of Tikopians who had joined the Church of the Blessed Ark on Malaita. Yes, he had travelled to Malaita in an effort to stop this, but had been unable to do anything about it. He had been reduced to lurking in the bush, relying on supplies of food from Brother John. One night, almost demented with loneliness, he had accosted Shem and fought him, to no good purpose. Kella did not think that the shy, inarticulate Tikopian was a killer, but he was still not sure where Brother John fitted into the equation.

The truck dropped the sergeant off at the village of Tambea, with its distinctive beaches of black and gold sand, before carrying on to its destination at Lambi Bay at the very end of the road. Kella walked along the beach, avoiding the village, which was a little way inland. From this makeshift natural harbour the Japanese had secretly evacuated ten thousand sick and wounded men under cover of darkness when finally they had abandoned their campaign on Guadalcanal at the beginning of 1943. He wondered whether Lieutenant Shimadu had been one of them. Perhaps he had hoped that his war was almost over and that he would be returned home. Instead he had spent the rest of his life as an exile on a *tabu* site in the high bush of Malaita, with only a former slave girl for company. The pair of them had tried to form some sort of life together, thought Kella; according to the lieutenant's diary entries they had even achieved a modicum of happiness. He hoped that had been true.

A hundred yards past the village he turned inland and walked along a track through a copse of palm trees. At the end of the path a small house had been erected on stilts. It was more substantial than a typical village house but in a bad state of repair. It had a galvanized-iron tin roof and large windows across which shutters could be folded at night. A lopsided veranda with holes gaping dangerously in the floor leaned precariously at an angle in front of the house. It was the sort of dwelling once found all over the islands when expatriates defied the climate and disease to scrape a living as planters and traders. Kella climbed a couple of steps on to the veranda and tapped on the open front door of the house. There was no answer. He entered the main room.

The shutters on the window had been closed, leaving the room in semi-darkness. One door led to a bedroom and another to a small kitchen. The room was cluttered with heavy, old-fashioned chairs and settees that looked as if they had been in place for a long time. There were framed sepia photographs on the walls. The floor was covered with empty whisky bottles and half-eaten tins of food. A man lay asleep on a settee in the gloom, breathing stertorously. Kella tiptoed over to him and saw that it was Ebury, the retired government officer. He was unshaven and reeked of alcohol and cigar smoke.

Ebury stirred in his sleep and opened his eyes unwillingly. He saw Kella and scrabbled for a shotgun lying amid the debris by the settee. He swung his feet to the floor and sat up unsteadily, the shotgun cradled on his lap.

'Who the hell are you, and what do you want?' he demanded in a husky but cultured voice. 'How dare you enter my house uninvited!'

'I'm Sergeant Kella of the Solomon Islands Police Force,' said Kella.

'I don't care who you are. You're still a *kanaka* and you're trespassing on my property. Get the hell off it!'

Kella recalled an episode on a government boat taking him back to Malaita immediately after the war. The vessel had been crowded. Ebury had been the only white man on board. As of right he had occupied the solitary cabin, below decks. After a few hours he had complained petulantly about the noise being made by the feet of the women and children deck passengers above his head. Acting on the expatriate's instructions the bosun had crowded the passengers uncomfortably together at the rear of the ship, so that the district officer's sleep had not been further impeded.

'I need your help,' Kella persisted.

'Well you're not going to get it. Clear off now!'

'It's like this,' said Kella. 'Most of the government records were destroyed when Tulagi was evacuated in 1942. There are no colonial officers still serving who were in office before the war. That's why I've come to you.'

'You've come to the wrong place, Sergeant. In case you don't know, I was dismissed from my job for incompetent and drunken behaviour. I don't remember a bloody thing, and I don't want to. Now will you go?'

Ebury bent forward and felt on the floor for a bottle. He unscrewed the top and drank deeply. 'Are you still here?' he asked.

'I don't know if you've heard about them,' Kella said, 'but there have been a series of murders on Malaita.'

'So what? You guys have been killing one another since God was a little boy.'

'That may be true,' said Kella, 'but I don't think this is a case of internecine tribal warfare. The killings have been planned carefully and approached with subtlety. I think that either an expatriate is involved or that the reason for the killings is something much more important than a bush quarrel. That's why I've come to you. You were an administrator before the war. Can you think of any court case or local appeal anywhere in the islands at that time that might cause someone to bear such a grudge that he would want to achieve payback on a really large scale? Something that would be enough to make a man or woman want to kill and, if necessary, be prepared to spend years planning revenge against the administration?'

For a moment Ebury almost looked interested. Then he shook his head abruptly and drank from the bottle again.

'Don't know what you're talking about,' he said.

'For a time we thought that perhaps a surviving Japanese soldier was conducting a one-man private war in the bush,' said Kella, almost talking to himself. 'That would be motive enough for the killings, if someone thought he was still fighting for his country.'

'He knew how to fight, Johnny Jap.' The cue sparked Ebury into life for a moment. 'Got to give him that. Never knew when he was defeated. I had a lot of time for the bloody sons of Nippon. I had a good war, as a matter of fact. It was the peace that buggered me up.'

The expatriate's head rolled back and his eyes closed. Kella gave up. 'I'll be at Police Headquarters in Honiara until Thursday,' he said, without much hope. 'I'm staying on for the farewell ceremony at Henderson Field for a Japanese soldier whose body we found on Malaita. If you do think of anything, try to get a message through to me.'

Heedless, Ebury started snoring. Kella walked to the door.

36

DEPARTURE

There was a brief lull in the ceremony on the airstrip at Henderson Field outside Honiara. The police band had played a selection from Gilbert and Sullivan and the students' choir from the British Solomons Training College had sung 'Abide with Me'. Now, just outside the small one-storey departure lounge that doubled as a customs reception area, the senior members of the administration were getting into arthritic position for the farewell ceremony to mark the departure of the ashes of Lieutenant Shimadu from the Solomon Islands to Tokyo.

The High Commissioner, resplendent in his white uniform, referred to by his wife in one of her more disenchanted moods as his ice-cream seller's suit, topped precariously by a plumed hat, was standing with the Chief Justice in his more subdued but equally sweat-inducing robes of office. A little to one side of them, the expatriate heads of the various government departments were lining up in three ranks with the practised ease of permanent and pensionable officers who had been jostling for position in the cruel heat of the sun for most of their careers. They were uniformly middle-aged, most of them wearing rather shabby suits that were a little too tight for them. Their hand-stitched artificial sharkskin jackets and trousers had originally been purchased in happier times during overnight stops in Hong Kong on their way home on leave, from the celebrated twenty-four-hour tailors of the crown colony. Unfortunately, with no one quite certain when the cold hand of localization might start sending them on a more permanent departure, few had invested lately in new suits, which at best might be worn only several times a year at official receptions at Government House.

Perspiring in the early afternoon heat, the Accountant General squeezed in between the Director of Agriculture and the Registrar of Co-operative Societies. Next to them the Comptroller of Customs and Excise stood gloomily with the Conservator of Forests, the Commissioner of Income Tax, the Superintendent of Marine and the Director of Medical Services. Behind them the Commissioner of Police and the Government Statistician fell into line with the Financial Secretary, several district commissioners and a dozen chief executive officers.

Behind them on hard-backed chairs under a slanting awning affixed to the roof of the airport building sat the wives of the officials, upright, uncomfortable and rigidly resigned to whatever boredom the afternoon might bring, in print dresses, stockings, long gloves and large hats. They resembled a slightly ageing but carefully preserved chorus line from an amateur production of *Floradora*. At the back stood several hundred islanders, headmen and government office workers bussed out to the airstrip for the occasion. There was even a press section, a roped-off square next to the wives. The Chief Information Officer had hoped for an influx of newsreel companies for the occasion, perhaps even several cameramen from television stations, but he had had to be content with half a dozen reporters from Australasian newspapers and the wife of a Chinese merchant who worked part-time as a stringer for an American press agency.

A small fence separated the crowd from the landing strip upon which waited a thirty-nine-seater turboprop Fokker F-27 Friendship aircaft in the orange livery of Trans-Australia Airlines, waiting to take its passengers to Papua New Guinea and connections on to Hong

Kong and Tokyo. Crates of cargo had already been loaded into the hatches and the pilot was awaiting the signal to take off as soon as the guest of honour arrived and the other passengers were released from the airport waiting room.

The only relics remaining of the war years lay a couple of hundred yards to the west of the airstrip. These were a few crumbling sheds and an abandoned open-air steel control tower consisting of a winding staircase leading to a platform forty feet high surrounded by a knee-high rail.

Sister Conchita stood at the back of the crowd on tiptoe, in an effort to see what was going on on the tarmac. She had been invited to the ceremony at the insistence of Mayotishi but had been too shy to claim the reserved seat she knew awaited her up front among the great and the good. She could not see any of her companions on the last trek up to the banana plantation of the Kwaio bush, though as she scanned the crowd she noticed Florence Maddy talking vivaciously to Sergeant Ha'a. The musicologist was wearing a white suit and carrying a bag. Presumably she was travelling on the Fokker Friendship and was saying a temporary goodbye to the sergeant. She was looking almost animated, her hand on Ha'a's sleeve as she stared into his rolling, rather embarrassed eyes, reinforcing Sister Conchita's opinion that Florence Maddy, although a perfectly pleasant and inoffensive woman, was a throwback to a previous age in which some females preferred to defer to a man, any man. The thought gave her an idea. She waited a few minutes for them to complete their farewells and then walked towards the couple.

Ha'a nodded to the nun and sketched a salute before scuttling off with relief to resume his perfunctory attempts at crowd control. Sister Conchita smiled at Florence.

'How's the music collection going?' she asked.

'Wonderfully,' said Florence, uncharacteristically enthusiastic. 'Johnny's got such a collection of songs. It will take me weeks to sort them out when I get home.'

'That's good,' said Sister Conchita. She decided to chance her luck. If Florence had transferred her allegiance to Sergeant Ha'a and was about to leave the Solomons, she might consider herself less securely bound to previous loyalties.

'You know, there's one thing I've been trying to work out,' she said as casually as she could. 'It wasn't Shem who persuaded you to go to Tikopia, was it? There wouldn't have been any point in it. He already had enough problems of his own.'

Florence hesitated, and then nodded. 'You're right,' she said. 'It was Mr Wainoni. He practically insisted on it. He was sure that I'd find plenty of material on Tikopia. He was quite wrong, of course. I don't know where he could have got that idea from! I didn't tell anyone about it because I didn't want to get him into trouble. I know that Sergeant Kella was cross because I'd gone to Tikopia. I really shouldn't be telling you this now, but you've been very good to me.' She looked at her watch. 'In fact I must find Mr Wainoni to say goodbye. The plane leaves in an hour. Thank you for all your help, Sister.'

Florence eased her way through the crowd. Sister Conchita decided that she had better look for Sergeant Kella. Perhaps the information she had just garnered from the musicologist might be of use to the policeman.

Kella stood beside the outside-broadcasts van being used by the Solomon Islands Broadcasting Service and surveyed the crowd. A Melanesian commentator was standing on a box outside the van, describing the scene excitedly in pidgin. The fledgling local radio station seldom dipped a toe into the fraught technical waters of on-the-spot commentaries, because too much could and usually did go wrong, but this afternoon those outer islands in possession of radio sets that actually worked and had batteries would be tuning in to the great event.

The preoccupied and depressed Kella hardly noticed what was

going on. For the great occasion he had been relegated to keeping a place free for the car bringing Mayotishi and his precious cargo from the Mendana hotel to the airport.

He had shared a farewell drink with the Japanese in the latter's room at the hotel the previous evening. Both of them had ignored the baleful glares of the manager in the lounge. Mayotishi had produced a bottle of whisky and two glasses from a drawer.

'Scotch, not Japanese,' he had commented.

They had drunk mainly in silence, but just before Kella left, Mayotishi had shaken his hand.

'Regard the next couple of years as an interim period,' he had said. 'The next time we meet, I suspect that we shall both be doing different jobs.'

Sergeant Ha'a gave up trying to marshal his section of the crowd and strolled over. 'It's all right for some,' he said. 'How come you get all the cushy jobs?'

'Don't kid yourself,' said Kella, ushering a crowd of excited small boys out of the way. 'This is the equivalent of being exiled to Elba.'

'Whitey's an ungrateful bastard all right; he expects a lot from poor sergeants for his thousand dollars a year,' sighed Ha'a. He looked sideways at Kella. 'Although it must help if you and your brothers own a copra plantation on Malaita that's so big it takes a pigeon three days to fly across it.'

'Could I have a word, Sergeant Kella?' asked an incisive voice from behind them.

Ha'a faded into the crowd again at the first hint of a salvo from authority. Kella turned. For a moment he did not recognize the white man addressing him. Then he saw that it was Ebury, but an Ebury transformed almost beyond recognition. The former government officer had showered and shaved. He had plastered his hair close to his head with some sort of gel. He was wearing sharply pressed drill trousers and a spotless white shirt. On his shirt front was pinned a row of medals, among them the ornamental silver Military Cross. For the first time that Kella had seen him in the last decade he was erect and sober. Aware of the sergeant's surprised scrutiny, the expatriate looked self-conscious.

'After you left the other day, I started thinking about what you said about the Japanese officer's remains being taken out of the Solomons,' he said awkwardly. 'Didn't seem right that the Johnny should go out unrecognized, as it were, so I thought I'd better come and see him off.' He looked around almost shyly. 'I didn't realize that it was going to be a scrum like this. Maybe I'm not needed after all. Best be getting back home perhaps.'

'No!' Kella heard his voice crackling with authority. He paused and went on apologetically. 'I'm sure that Lieutenant Shimadu would have wanted you here today. You've more right than most.' He beckoned to the lurking Sergeant Ha'a, who moved back over, crab-like with apprehension at his sudden proximity to a white man who might have the power to exert a deleterious influence on his future comfort and well-being.

'Sergeant,' Kella said, 'I want you to take Major Ebury to the VIP stand and find him a space there. Is that clear?'

'It's clear enough,' objected Ha'a, 'but it's not going to be easy. All the places there are reserved.'

Ebury's broad shoulders went back an inch further. Thirty years seemed to have dropped off him since his recent encounter with Kella. 'Just get me to the stand, Sergeant,' he told Ha'a confidently. 'I'll find my own place in the sun when I reach it.' He reached into his trouser pocket and produced a crumpled sheaf of handwritten papers. 'By the way, you got me on something of a run down memory lane after we met. Sorry if I was a bit brusque at the time. I started thinking about what you said concerning civil cases brought by locals before the war. Actually there was something that might be relevant to your investigation. I had a personal link with it, actually. I must have been half asleep not to make the connection when you first brought it up at my place. Good day to you.'

Ebury nodded in response to Kella's salute and followed Ha'a through the crowd into the airport building. Kella watched them go. You weren't half asleep, he thought; you were stoned out of your mind. But you've come good when it matters. He started reading the papers. After the first few lines he stopped and started again. He walked away, totally absorbed, from the airport buildings across the uncultivated fields surrounding them. The grass grew longer here, covering the concrete foundations of the old hangars and huts of the wartime days. The mouths of the disused communications bunkers in the rows of hillocks were overgrown with creepers, like the dirty green webs of huge spiders.

Kella heard a car jolting across the field in his direction but did not look up at first. When he did, it was too late. A dusty 1949 Australian Holden sedan jolted to a halt and two young men leapt out. They were young Chinese in cheap suits. Kella clenched his fists, but forced himself to relax when he saw that both youths were carrying knives. One of them indicated the waiting car. Its engine was still running.

'Inside!' he shouted.

37

AN IDEA FROM THE DOLPHIN PRIEST

The two men hustled Kella into the back of the car and sat watchfully on either side of him. A third Chinaman, a cigarette drooping from his mouth, was sitting behind the wheel. He bounced the car back into life, the tyres shrieking across the field towards the main road to Honiara.

They rejoined the road a few hundred yards away from the airport and drove erratically in the direction of the capital. Kella could see that all three of the young men were strung out. For their day jobs they were probably hired by Chinese merchants as debt collectors and minders at floating games of *pai gao* and *sic bo* in Chinatown. Kidnapping a police officer would be a little above and beyond their normal call of duty, and it was showing. He tried to engage the nervous youths in reassuring conversation, but the three men ignored his tentative overtures. He wondered, if he got out of this alive, whether he could suggest a new police manual to his superiors: *100 Ways to Conciliate Your Abductors*.

A quarter of a mile down the road, the car turned off and bumped its way up a wooded track leading to the foothills of the central mountain range. The track narrowed to a trail and then petered out into a well-trodden patch of bare ground outside a sagging wooden hut overlooking Honiara and the sea through the trees. Kella recognized the construction as a cheap Chinese restaurant serving basic meals of curry, rice and beer on paydays to workers from the labour lines, impoverished Voluntary Service Overseas cadets and itinerant visiting seamen who could not afford to eat in the town. A covered Bedford truck was parked outside the hut.

The three men pushed Kella into the restaurant and stood over him until he had sat down on a hard chair against one wall. It was a square room containing a dozen wooden tables with a long bar running the length of one side. Through an open door behind the bar Kella could see the kitchen. The proprietor, an elderly Chinaman, and his wife were standing disconsolately amid the pots and pans. When they saw the sergeant, the old man winced and shuffled over and shut the door, shrugging his narrow shoulders helplessly.

The three young men sat on a bench against one undecorated wooden wall, regarding Kella balefully. A few silent minutes later the outer door opened and Wainoni the Gammon Man came in. He sat at a table facing Kella, safely out of the sergeant's reach.

'Why?' Kella asked at once. 'It was all going so well for you. Why did you have to carry me off like this? You've probably got a boat stashed away somewhere to take you to Papua New Guinea as soon as night falls. Nobody would find you there.'

'I had no option,' said the Gammon Man. He was breathless. 'Dr Maddy sought me out at the airport to say goodbye. Her conscience was troubling her. She confessed that she had told Sister Conchita that it was I who had sent her to Tikopia. Well, I ask you! Wherever Sister Conchita is during the investigation of a crime, Sergeant Kella is not far away. I had to remove you before she informed you and you started putting two and two together and came looking for me.' He glanced disparagingly at his spartan surroundings. 'It called for some rapid improvisation, I can tell you. Still, you'll be safe enough here. I've done similar business with old Mr Ho and his lads before.'

'Not kidnapping a police officer,' said Kella. 'This is serious. It's all over. You don't stand a chance.' He realized to his annoyance that he was beginning to quote from low-budget movies without even thinking about it.

'I like to think that I've planned it pretty well so far,' said Wainoni. 'I don't believe my gods will desert me at this late stage. I suppose you're wondering what all this has been about.'

'I know what it's about,' Kella said. 'Most of it, anyway. You've been carrying out payback.'

'Ah,' said Wainoni. 'Now how did you know that? Are you going to surprise me yet again, Sergeant Kella?'

'Ebury told me, just a few minutes ago.'

'Ah,' sighed Wainoni. 'I thought he was too much of a piss-artist to remember anything these days. I should have dealt with him, but he was good to me once and I owed him.'

'I suspected you before that, but I had no proof,' Kella said. 'It's not as if revenge is so uncommon in the Solomons. We can be a vindictive lot when we're roused. And you covered your tracks well.' He thought of the eagle bearing the released soul of the old woman over Savo. 'In fact, yours is the second case of mistaken identity I've dealt with this month. The first one was meant to alert me, but I was slow. Your mother comes from the western islands. Forty years ago she became the mistress of an American researcher called James Cardigan. After you were born, he returned home without making any provision for you or your mother. Not unnaturally, your mother resented this. As you grew up, she constantly dinned into you the perfidy of your father in abandoning you without making restitution to either of you.'

'It wasn't so much to ask,' said the Gammon Man. 'Other wealthy expatriates who had their fun with local girls gave them money afterwards. It was custom.'

'But Cardigan ignored any letters that you sent him. He was too busy establishing his own career back in the USA. So you grew up with this festering sense of grievance that the expats owed you big time.'

'One of them brought me into the world.'

'True enough,' said Kella. He tried to recall the details in the papers stuffed into his hand by Ebury at the airfield earlier that afternoon. 'What I don't understand is why you made an official demand for restitution to the British authorities in Tulagi. With respect, that was an unusual step for an islander back in 1940.'

'My mother took the matter to Mr Ebury, who was the district officer at the time. He helped us make out our complaint and submit it officially.'

That explained a great deal, Kella thought. Ebury must have been an interesting man before the drink took hold of him. He wished that he had known him better. The young, idealistic and in those days sober official must have felt impelled to take up the abandoned Wainoni's case. It would not have stood much chance in an old colonial court of law, even if it had got that far. Ebury probably would have had his knuckles rapped even for forwarding such a document, let alone helping to prepare it. Probably he would have had a black mark entered on his record at the same time.

'What happened?' Kella asked.

'This was the early 1940s, just before Japani attacked the Solomons. Most of the expats ran away and didn't come back after the war. Tulagi was bombed and shelled and all the government records were destroyed. My appeal would have been among them.'

'So you stopped looking for payback through official channels. What about Ebury? He stayed on. Couldn't you have taken your case up with him again?'

'He was spoiled by then,' said Wainoni simply, using the pidgin word for a man ruined beyond redemption. 'Too much whisky.'

'So the poor sod was already out of the running, and there was nobody else to remember the case. How old were you by then?'

'Maybe twenty-five,' said Wainoni.

'And you spent the next fifteen years planning your revenge. You married a Lau girl after the war and moved to the artificial islands.

There was a lot of movement around then. As long as you kept your head down and didn't cause trouble, no one would pay much attention, or bother where you came from.' Kella thought of the old Tolo woman who had lived anonymously in the Lau fishing village for so long. 'Ironically you made a good living by guiding some of the very people you hated, the visiting whiteys from colleges. And all the time you were plotting to get your own back. You could move anywhere you liked on Malaita and no one would be surprised. What made you decide to start this killman stuff this year?'

'Time,' said Wainoni. 'By then my quarrel was with the white authorities who wouldn't give me justice, not with my so-called father. We'll be kicking them out before long. It was time I did what I could to stir up trouble for them on Malaita before they left. One final boot up the backside for all their indifference and indolence.'

'So you started a one-man reign of terror on the island to get everyone agitated. You pretended to be the killman, used the Church of the Blessed Ark as your base and killed Papa Noah and two of his members, to terrify people and make them believe that a religious war was about to start. You caused a panic all over Malaita. You even dressed up as a Japanese soldier to destroy the ark and confuse people more. All this just to make the government worried.'

'And drowning people where there was no water, don't forget that.'

'I'd worked that one out,' Kella told him. 'I ran through a banana plantation in Kwaio country and found that I was soaked as a result. Bananas store water in their stems. Cut the top off one and within an hour or so the decapitated stem fills almost to the brim with pints of water. Then I remembered: you always carried at least one of those books you were so proud of on tour, to show would-be employers. You wrapped them up in plastic bags. When the right time came, you poured the water into a bag, knocked out the poor islanders, stuffed their faces in the bag and drowned them. Very clever! No wonder people started fleeing from their villages in panic.'

'I wish I could have done the same with Papa Noah, but there wasn't time. Still, I couldn't pass up on a chance like that in all the confusion. I stayed on in the bush after I had dropped Dr Maddy off and walked up to the feast at the ark. I had to use the good old-fashioned method of drowning a man by sticking his head in a puddle. All the same, it was well enough thought out, until you started interfering. What put you on to me?'

'I couldn't understand how Florence Maddy came to be involved,' Kella said. 'She wasn't an interfering sort. She wouldn't have stirred up trouble on her own. Yet suddenly she goes off to Tikopia, an inoffensive woman like her. I guessed that she must have got in someone's way. You were the only islander who had much to do with her, so I began thinking about you.'

'I never did get all of that woman's research grant money off her,' said Wainoni regretfully.

'You really needed a bit of peace and quiet to build on killing the two islanders and Papa Noah,' said Kella. 'You were planning to cause more trouble by raiding the ark dressed as a Japanese soldier and panic the islanders even further. You couldn't risk her stumbling across anything, so you bribed Shem to persuade some of his Tikopian friends to take her home with them on the *Commissioner* and get her out of the way.'

'Let's say I made an anonymous donation to Shem's church funds,' Wainoni said. 'He had no idea what I was going to do.'

'There were too many other people blundering about in this case as well,' Kella said. 'That obscured the issue for me. Abalolo had come up from Tikopia to attempt to sort Shem out. Brother John was trying to look after him. You might have got away with it, but then Sister Conchita took a hand. She persuaded the Lau people to go back to their homes. That meant that the panic on Malaita was almost over. All your plans came to nothing.'

'Who would have thought it?' said Wainoni. 'All that preparation, yet Praying Mary rounded them all like sheep and took them back to their pens.' He looked at his watch and stood up. 'I must be leaving,' he said. 'The aircraft is due to take off in half an hour. I shouldn't have come here, but I had to make certain that Mr Ho's boys had done their job properly.'

For some time Kella had been aware of the comforting sound of voices coming from outside the restaurant. The three Chinese stood up with their leader. There was a hammering on the front door.

'Open up! We want beer!' came a shout.

'Closed!' snapped back one of the Chinese.

The shouts solidified into a chant: 'Beer! Beer! Beer!' One of the young Chinese men went to the front door and unlocked it, inching it open and hissing: 'No beer! This place closed!' He gave a startled yelp as the door crashed open in his face, sending him staggering back. Twenty or thirty islanders stampeded into the room, trampling on the man who had opened the door and hurtling into the main restaurant. One of the two remaining Chinamen managed to produce his knife but was overwhelmed and borne to the floor in the rush of whooping islanders. At the same time the back door was kicked in and more islanders hurtled into the kitchen.

Wainoni backed against a wall but made no further movement when he saw how many islanders were occupying the room already. His face was expressionless. The headman of the Lau fishing village outside the capital emerged from the main pack and stood by Kella, beaming.

'I was worried when I saw you being taken away in a car,' he chuckled. 'But luckily, that meant that they had to stay on the road, and I'd placed men every two hundred yards along it into Honiara just in case. We were able to regroup at the bottom of the turn-off and come up on foot and break in, as you ordered.' He looked at his prisoners. 'What do you want done with these? It would be no trouble to slit their throats; they're only Chinese. No one would miss them.'

'Leave the old man and his wife alone,' Kella ordered. 'Take the other three to the village and keep them there until I come for them tonight.' He had already decided that he would give the three younger men a choice. They could embark upon a new career path and work for him as informers in Chinatown, or face kidnapping charges.

The headman nodded. 'What about the big man?' he asked.

'Send him with six of your strongest men to the police station in Honiara. Tell the sergeant on duty that he is to put the Gammon Man in a cell and keep him there until I arrive to prefer charges of murder. Before you go, search him and the others and bring me the car keys.'

The headman issued rapid instructions. Islanders escorted Wainoni and the three young Chinamen roughly outside. At the door, Wainoni looked back. Then he shook his head and allowed himself to be manhandled out of the restaurant. Kella was puzzled. He would have expected more emotion even from such a notoriously bland character as the Gammon Man. He and the headman followed the others out.

'What made you ask us to watch your back the entire time you were at the airport?' the headman asked.

'I felt that something might happen,' said Kella vaguely. In fact he had seldom had a stronger premonition. On the night before he had sailed from Malaita to Honiara, he had seen a cloud of fireflies and had later fallen asleep to the persistent clicking of cicadas, a sure omen of trouble to come and a warning to be on his guard.

'I thought I'd ask you and your men to mingle in the crowd and keep an eye on me to be on the safe side,' he said. 'Actually, a dolphin priest gave me the idea. As a rule, you can never find the right people when you want to lay on a good ambush.'

The headman shook his head uncomprehendingly. One of his men handed Kella several rings of keys taken from the prisoners. Kella stood thinking. So far things had gone well but not perfectly. There were pieces of the jigsaw that had not yet fitted completely into place. The sergeant liked completion in all that he did. Wainoni's plan had been well prepared, but it lacked a suitable climax. Surely the Gammon Man would not have been content merely with causing minor civic uprest on Malaita. His sense of drama would have demanded a much more effective resolution to all his efforts.

Unbidden passages of conversation were passing through the sergeant's mind in a continuous loop. He knew that somewhere in his memory lay stored the words that would explain most things, or at least lead to their explanation. A recollection of the woman among the bushes in the Kwaio country banana plantation clamoured to be attended to. What had she spat out when she had come across him after he had been looking at the grave of her former husband on top of the incline? Slowly the sentence reassembled itself in his mind: *Plenty too much, plenty too much! No more come!*

Musing on the phrase, Kella walked in the direction of the parked Bedford truck. What had it been about the Gammon Man's reaction in the restaurant that had set off a tiny alarm bell in his mind? Suddenly Kella thought he knew.

He pulled aside the tarpaulin cover and climbed into the back of the truck. Inside the dark, enclosed space the stench of bananas greeted him like a nest of snakes. Then, utterly and completely, Kella knew what the Gammon Man's dreadful climax was intended to be. He jumped out of the truck and hurried over to the sedan. In a minute he was accelerating down the track towards the main road.

One question reverberated in his mind. Why had Wainoni been so concerned about the time the Fokker Friendship took off? Had he wanted to watch it, perhaps from the vantage point of the old control tower next to the airport?

Why would anyone want to watch an aeroplane leaving the ground? Or perhaps it was never meant to take off.

38

AN ORDERLY WITHDRAWAL

Kella brought the sedan to a halt outside the airport with a squeal of brakes. The clock on the wall told him that there still remained another twenty minutes before the Fokker Friendship was due to take off. He forced himself to remain behind the wheel of the car, making sure that he had gone through everything in his mind at least twice.

Of course someone as malevolent as Wainoni would not have been satisfied with initiating a vague sequence of events merely to inconvenience the colonial authorities. He would have wanted to end his planning almost literally with a spectacular display of fireworks, and that would take place at the airport before one of the few major assemblages of the top brass to take place in the Solomons for years.

Where Kella had got it wrong was in thinking that Wainoni's reinvention of a Japanese soldier in action had been just a ploy to add to the general confusion. Instead it had been central to the Gammon Man's plans. By attracting the attention of the colonial administrators to the possible presence of a Japanese survivor on Malaita, he had ensured that a large-scale manhunt would be launched, allied to the promise of a reward for any islander finding a soldier still alive in the bush. It had also brought the wealth-distributing Mayotishi to the islands, with the full backing of the Japanese government.

Sometime in his travels though the high bush, Wainoni had come across the grave of Lieutenant Shimadu. The woman had as good as told Kella that when she had screamed 'Plenty too much, plenty too much! No more come!' at him. The phrase was open to several interpretations. Kella had assumed that it had meant that his arrival was proving too much for the woman and that he should leave and not return. In fact she was saying that someone else, presumably the Gammon Man, had visited the site before him and that she wanted no more strangers to come.

Wainoni had known that sooner or later the search would lead to someone else coming across the remains of the officer, especially with Mayotishi willing to spend so much money on returning the ashes to Japan. Back at the restaurant the Gammon Man had evinced a desire to leave before the aircraft took off for Papua New Guinea. He probably wanted to watch its departure. And then there had been the reek of bananas in the back of the Bedford truck.

It was time to take action. Still Kella hesitated. If he should be wrong, his next actions would condemn him irretrievably in the eyes of his superiors. 'So what else is new?' he muttered, opening the door of the car and entering the airport, where the High Commissioner was in the act of shaking hands with Mayotishi before a beaming assemblage.

Aware of the murmurs of consternation coming from the august assembly behind him, Kella ran across the empty runway to the waiting aeroplane. The mobile rack of steps was in place and the door had been left open to admit air. Kella took the steps two at a time into the aircraft. A white-coated male flight attendant shouted at him angrily, but the policeman ignored him. He ran down the aisle to the cockpit and threw the door open. The captain and first officer were in their seats reading newspapers. They looked up as Kella burst in.

'You're not allowed in here, mate,' said the captain mildly. The irate attendant appeared at the sergeant's shoulder.

'I tried to tell him,' he said.

Kella ignored both men. 'Excuse me,' he said, gasping for breath, 'you must deal with this information as you see fit, of course, but I thought you'd like to know that there's an explosive device on board, probably timed to detonate when the aircraft takes off. Now, if you'll excuse me, I must share this information with the proper authorities.'

'Bloody hell!' said the flight attendant.

Kella ran back down the aisle, aware of the clattering feet of the crew members gaining on him with every stride. As he emerged from the aircraft, the heat greeted him like a blast from a furnace. He hurried back down the steps, aware of the startled, indignant and in some cases scandalized gazes of hundreds of the Protectorate's leading citizens in their serried ranks. Fortunately Kella was seldom shy. He ran towards them, waving his arms like a windmill.

'Bomb!' he shouted. 'There's a bomb on board! Get away from the airport at once, before it goes off!'

Silence fell over the crowd. There was no panic and at first very little movement. All eyes went to the High Commissioner, whose face, as sharp as a honed hatchet, betrayed no emotion. His aide-de-camp, a young flight lieutenant on secondment from the Royal Air Force, whispered into his ear. The High Commissioner nodded.

'I agree,' he said. 'Just in case there's something in it, see to the women first.'

The young officer ran to the seated section and started ushering the unruffled wives out of the airport. Within a few moments the government officials were streaming in their wake with well-drilled nonchalance.

Sergeant Ha'a walked out of the crowd and stood at Kella's shoulder. He watched the dignified, straight-backed mass retreat of the old colonials with something between wonder and admiration. Soon the spectators' area had emptied as the expatriates reassembled in restrained decorous groups according to rank in an adjacent car park. Ha'a turned his attention to the deserted airstrip. A few discarded paper cartons blew across the tarmac in the light breeze. It was a peaceful scene. The fat sergeant sucked his teeth judiciously and placed an arm like a flipper around his fellow policeman's shoulder.

'For your sake, I hope you've got this one right, old son,' he said.

39

REPORT OF THE BISHOP'S VISITOR

The farewell ceremony for the bishop's visitor at Ruvabi was over. As such events went, it had been an oddly restrained affair. The local sisters had sung a Malaitan lullaby and a slightly overambitious version of 'Ave Maria' that had foundered bravely on several of the high notes. As Sister Conchita watched the rows of demure young sisters in their long blue robes, she thought of the cheerfully naked choristers of the Church of the Blessed Ark singing 'Japani Ha Ha!' a few weeks ago. The matter of Papa Noah's death could be said to have started with one anthem and finished with another, but under very different circumstances. In a way, that seemed to sum up the cheerful dichotomy of her life in the Solomons.

After the farewell, there had been a simple feast of taro and pineapples. An unemotional Father Kuyper had made a brief anodyne speech about nothing in particular and had then left Ruvabi amid a flurry of cursory handshakes to walk to the roadhead, where a truck should be waiting to take him to Auki and passage on a vessel back to Guadalcanal.

Before he had made his departure, Father Kuyper had walked round the mission compound saying his individual farewells. Sister Conchita had been disappointed with their fleeting final encounter, which consisted of several half-heard sentences. The man had even avoided eye contact with her, she thought. Did that mean that his official report to the bishop was going to be even worse than she had feared?

She looked around the compound before starting to help the local sisters clear up. There had been a surprisingly good turnout for the feast. Father Pierre was sitting in a basket chair on the veranda talking to an attentive Sergeant Kella towering over him. There was an old shawl around the priest's shoulders and he looked pale and drawn, but he was definitely on the mend. Thanks be to God, thought the nun.

Brother John and Abalolo walked over to her. Both men were in the uniforms of the Melanesian Mission and carrying packs on their backs. They were smiling.

'Going already?' asked Sister Conchita.

'We thought it might be only sensible to slip away before Sergeant Kella has time to catch up with us,' said Brother John. 'He might be a little annoyed because I wasn't always frank with him about all aspects of the Church of the Blessed Ark, and the fact that I knew that Brother Abalolo had left Tikopia and was in hiding on Malaita waiting for a chance to reclaim Papa Noah's sect for Christianity.'

'That might not be such a bad idea,' agreed the nun. She shook the hands of both men. 'Where are you going now?'

'I'm going back home to reopen my church,' said Abalolo in one of his rare incursions into speech. 'Brother John has offered to come with me for the first few months.'

'Won't that be dangerous?' asked Sister Conchita.

'No more than usual,' shrugged Brother John. 'There are four kingdoms on Tikopia. Three of them are still Christian. That only leaves Chief Atanga's province as a pagan one, and the old man won't live eternally. Without an heir, the old beliefs will die out when Atanga goes. If we've re-established the faith in the other three areas by then, we can move back into his.'

'Don't forget how the remaining Christians helped Dr Maddy when she arrived,' said Abalolo proudly. 'That took courage and faith.' The shy pastor seemed determined to set a new record for loquacity, thought Conchita.

'Well, good luck to both of you,' she said, but the two missionaries had espied Sergeant Kella walking across the compound towards them and had made their departures, moving remarkably quickly for men carrying heavy packs.

'I wanted a word with those two,' said Kella, arriving too late.

'Somehow I don't think it was mutual,' said Sister Conchita. She changed the subject quickly. '*Was* there a bomb on the plane at Henderson Field? There's been no more news about it on the radio.'

'Oh yes,' said Kella. 'It was inside one of Wainoni's banana crates. He used half a dozen sticks of dynamite he'd had stolen to order from one of the logging camps. There were also a couple of primer caps, a timer and a six-volt battery, all held together by binding cord. Apparently it was a rough-and-ready job but effective enough. It was timed to go off before the aircraft left the ground. The device would have been powerful enough to destroy the aeroplane and most of the spectators in the stands. Luckily Makepiece, the army warrant officer who's defusing bombs in the bush, was in the crowd. He managed to render the bomb harmless. They say he may get a medal.'

'And this was all for revenge,' said Sister Conchita.

'It seems so,' said Kella. His eyes went round the compound, measuring and assessing as usual. 'What still puzzles me is line,' he said.

'Line? Oh, you mean relationships?'

Kella nodded. 'I thought that Wainoni couldn't have been descended from an expatriate,' he said. 'That would make him a half-caste, but he's darker than I am.'

Sister Conchita's mind went back to the day on the artificial island when she had introduced Ha'a to Florence Maddy. 'I think I can help you there,' she said. 'Dr Maddy happened to mention that Professor Cardigan was a pioneer who had to overcome a great deal of prejudice in his time.'

'So?' asked Kella.

'Prejudice – that usually only refers to one thing. If we look him up in the appropriate record books, I believe we'll find that Professor Cardigan was black,' said Sister Conchita. 'That would explain why Wainoni passed as an ordinary Solomon Islander.'

'Like the Tolo woman who was accepted as a Lau for most of her life,' said Kella. Everything seemed to keep coming back to the exorcism of the old eagle-worshipper. Had that been designated by the gods as his entry into the solving of the case?

'Come again?'

'That's another story,' said the sergeant. 'Remind me on a particularly long sea voyage to tell you of the time that I carried out the *manatai burina* ceremony at the Guadalcanal fishing village.'

'I can hardly wait,' said Sister Conchita. 'But there is something you can tell me now. What made Wainoni suspect that you were on to him, so that he had you abducted?'

Because you got it out of Florence Maddy and in turn she told the Gammon Man, thought Kella. He shrugged. 'I've no idea,' he said. 'I don't suppose we'll ever know.' Before the nun could say anything, he went on: 'There was something else I wanted to see you about. Did you arrange for my posting to Alaska to be cancelled?'

'I think you overestimate my influence among the ranks of the great and the good,' said Sister Conchita innocently. 'Why, what's happened?'

'It's all very strange,' said the sergeant. 'One minute I was being told to pack my bags again, and then suddenly I was informed that my secondment had been changed and that Johnny Ha'a was taking my place in Alaska.'

'Why on earth was that?' asked the nun, trying to maintain a straight face.

'Well, it seems that Florence Maddy is based at an Alaskan university. Did you know that?'

'Juneau,' said Sister Conchita truthfully. 'She did tell me, but I didn't know where it was until I looked it up on a map.'

'Well, it seems that Johnny Ha'a has, or claims that he has, a supply of pidgin songs about the war in the Solomons. Dr Maddy urgently needs these songs to complete her thesis, so Johnny is taking my place with the Alaskan state police for six months, where he can help Dr Maddy as well. They tell me he's even got a regular singing slot on the university television station. Ha'a thinks that he's died and gone to heaven.' He looked at her suspiciously. 'Are you sure you didn't fix this for me?'

'I can assure you, Sergeant Kella, that I haven't spoken to any administrative officers in Honiara for many months. Anyway, you didn't want to go on another course, did you?'

'No, no, I'm delighted. I can get on with some real work now. It's funny how things work out. I believe that Dr Maddy is very happy with developments on a personal level as well.'

'In what way?' Sister Conchita remembered how close Sergeant Ha'a and Dr Maddy had seemed in the crowd at Henderson Field. 'Remember before you answer that you are addressing a sister in holy orders.'

'Quite so, Sister Conchita. In that case, let's just say that I've heard over the grapevine that in the cold Arctic climes Dr Maddy will shortly be helping Ha'a with his enquiries in more ways than one. It's all right for some.'

Kella sketched a salute and wandered off to talk to a group of the headmen who had charged him with hunting down the killman at the *kibung* meeting on Sulufou what now seemed a long time ago. They greeted his arrival with approving gap-toothed smiles.

Sister Conchita picked up a stack of dirty plates and carried them through to the kitchen. She did her best not to think about the liaison between Dr Maddy and Sergeant Ha'a described by Ben Kella. The musicologist would always want someone to lean on, although she doubted if the happy-go-lucky police sergeant would prove to be much in the way of a long-term prop. Still, business bilong her.

On her way back along the corridor, she glanced through the open door of the mission lounge. The room had been restored to its former shabby comfort. On the table was a small pile of notepaper covered in writing. Intrigued, Sister Conchita walked into the lounge. She recognized the handwriting as belonging to Father Kuyper. The nun hesitated. She should not read private correspondence. Then she dismissed the idea. Father Kuyper had never done anything inadvertently in his concise and exact life. If he had left something on the lounge table, he had intended it to be read. She picked up the sheets of paper. The first one was headed: *Ruvabi Mission: Draft Outline of Report.* She sat at the table and started to read.

Ruvabi is definitely not a run-of-the-mill mission station, began the spidery scrawl. *It is staffed by Father Pierre Meurth, the priest in charge, who has been working in the region since 1916. He is assisted by Sister Conchita, a young nun who is relatively new to the Solomons. It might be expected that, on the face of it, such a well-established institution might be run strictly on traditional lines. Such is far from the case.*

Both Father Pierre and Sister Conchita are fully aware of the problems inherent in a mission operating in what is still traditionally a pagan area. They accept that the faith even of the local converts is held in conjunction with many of the old-established custom beliefs of these islanders. While remaining steadfastly true to the Catholic doctrine in all its particulars, they take the existing situation into account in their dealings with the indigenous population. They treat the old ways with respect and expect their own beliefs to be regarded with the same consideration.

Sister Conchita put down the sheet of paper and wiped away a tear with the back of her hand. After a moment or two of earnest contemplation she resumed her reading.

As a result, the mission has become a pillar of the Catholic religion in the area, but at the same time is regarded by all who come into contact with it, adherents and non-adherents alike, as a vigorous, useful and living entity ministering to the spiritual and practical lives of all in the district. Above all, Ruvabi Mission is relevant.

Father Pierre is a wise and compassionate leader of his flock, with a wealth of practical experience. He is extremely vigorous in mind and body. It is devoutly to be hoped that he is allowed and encouraged to continue to perform his pastoral duties in the same exemplary manner as he has always done in the past, for as long as he wishes.

Sister Conchita is inexperienced and inclined to be headstrong. She does not always pause for thought before taking action. It has to be wondered if she could more effectively curb the extent of some of her activities. Even with her undoubted energy and pronounced sense of justice she cannot expect to investigate every problem and right every wrong that swims within her line of vision. Nevertheless, she has a faith that shines like a beacon, a courage that recognizes no obstacles and a selfless sense of purpose that sometimes can, almost literally, seem to move mountains.

Sister Conchita started sobbing a little again. When she had recovered, she blew her nose resolutely and resumed her reading.

To sum up: the team responsible for the running of Ruvabi Mission may on the face of it appear unusual, even eccentric. Neither member, it is suggested, could always work easily within the confines and discipline of a large urban church organization. However, in their present situation, at a momentous time of change for the faith and for the islands, they are probably both exactly what this unusual but highly effective mission needs. To sum up, I am minded of the saying, 'If it ain't broke, don't fix it!'

(signed) Albert Kuyper

Kella put his head round the corner of the door. His scarred and battered face seemed unusually content. 'I'm off,' he told her. 'I just came in to say goodbye. I should be passing the mission on my next patrol in about six weeks' time. Will you be here?'

Carefully Sister Conchita folded the draft report and put it away in a drawer of the table. There was a tinge of colour on her tear-stained cheeks.

'Do you know,' she said, 'I rather think I might be!'